A WOLF IN WOLF'S CLOTHING...

A dark shape on the ground. Kincaid drew closer, slowly. The shape gained definition. A man lying on his face. But still just a dark shape, with a touch of light around the shoulders—a *kerchief*. Goddamnit, it was a *soldier*. That fool guard had come out after him. But what . . . ?

The shape suddenly twisted, rising up toward him. He caught a glimpse of high Asiatic cheekbones and the glint of a knife headed toward his belly.

The night seemed to explode with sound. There were battle cries all around as he felt the knife hit and begin to thrust into him . . .

EASY COMPANY

EASY COMPANY

AND THE MEDICINE GUN

JOHN WESLEY HOWARD

A JOVE BOOK

First Jove edition published April 1981

First printing

Printed in the United States of America

Jove books are published by Jove Publications, Inc., 200 Madison Avenue, New York, NY 10016

*Also in the EASY COMPANY series
from Jove*

EASY COMPANY AND THE SUICIDE BOYS
EASY COMPANY AND THE GREEN ARROWS

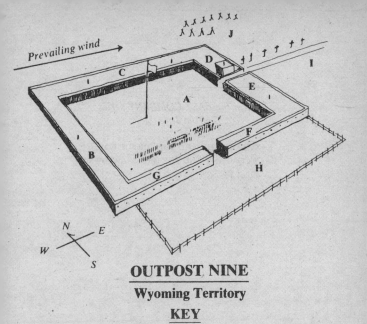

OUTPOST NINE

Wyoming Territory

KEY

A. Parade and flagstaff

B. Officers' quarters ("officers' country")

C. Enlisted men's quarters: barracks, day room, and mess

D. Kitchen, quartermaster supplies, ordnance shop, guardhouse

E. Suttler's store and other shops, tack room, and smithy

F. Stables

G. Quarters for dependents and guests; communal kitchen

H. Paddock

I. Road and telegraph line to regimental headquarters

J. Indian camp occupied by transient "friendlies"

INTERIOR   OUTSIDE

OUTPOST NUMBER NINE
(DETAIL)

Outpost Number Nine is a typical High Plains military outpost of the days following the Battle of the Little Big Horn, and is the home of Easy Company. It is not a "fort"; an official fort is the headquarters of a regiment. However, it resembles a fort in its construction.

The birdseye view shows the general layout and orientation of Outpost Number Nine; features are explained in the Key.

The detail shows a cross-section through the outpost's double walls, which ingeniously combine the functions of fortification and shelter.

The walls are constructed of sod, dug from the prairie on which Outpost Number Nine stands, and are sturdy enough to withstand an assault by anything less than artillery. The roof is of log beams covered by planking, tarpaper, and a top layer of sod. It also provides a parapet from which the outpost's defenders can fire down on an attacking force.

one _____

The sun was sure crossing Nebraska faster than they were, thought Elmer "Trash" Jimson, a private recently assigned to the U. S. Army of the West. He turned to his companions and said as much.

"Apollo and his fiery chariot," brayed Private Edward Mulberry III, also a recent addition to that same army.

Jimson waited to hear what Apollo was up to. "So? What does *that* mean?"

Mulberry shrugged, mopping his brow, too whipped to continue. He hadn't expected summer in Nebraska to be so hot. Where were those damned snow-capped mountains he'd heard about?

Roscoe, Ogllala, Brule, Big Spring, one prairie town after another crept by. Slowly.

"Excuse me, but where are you boys headed?" A chubby man with a fringe of whiskers and a bowler hat had leaned across the aisle to address their little group.

James Evinrude, the remaining member of the group, studied the orders. But it was Trash who spoke up:

"Somewhere smack-dab in the middle of the Territory of Wy-*ohm*ing," he declared.

"I think that's about it," confirmed Evinrude. "An Easy Company at a place called Outpost Number Nine."

1

"What regiment's that?" asked the chubby man. "Sounds like the Foreign Legion." He giggled.

Evinrude frowned, studied once more the crumpled and stained paper containing the orders, then told him.

"Aha," said the chubby man. He'd never heard of the regiment, but supposed it was in fact there. "A fine outfit. Er, are you the only ones? An awful lot of Indians out here."

"Naw," said Trash, "but we're the best, an' the only ones headed for Easy. There're about forty more toward the back."

The chubby man leaned back in his seat, reassured for the moment.

"Jesus," cried Trash, bringing Chubby bolt upright again, "how much longer we got?"

"No hurry," said Evinrude. "Easy ain't going nowhere, and you're still young."

"I won't be by the time we get there," said Trash. "But hell, why should you care? You're *already* old."

True. Hardly ancient but an unlikely recruit, Evinrude had seen action in the Civil War, gone home to Maine in one piece (surely a good omen), and then watched helplessly as, over the next ten years, his entire family fell victim to age, disease, and violence. His son had been the last, skull split by a drunken young logger. Evinrude had killed the logger with his bare hands.

No one wished to prosecute, seeing all the grief he'd already come by, but they had to do something, so they simply told him to leave that part of the country.

He'd heard the army needed men out West, so he'd reenlisted. And since he'd never been more than a private, he didn't mind being that again. He didn't think anyone was after him—that had been an unspoken part of the deal—but now, after five days clackety-clacking two-thirds of the way across the entire continent, he almost wished somebody was. Maybe he should have stuck around, even if it meant hanging. What the hell did he have to live for?

"That town we just passed, Ogllala . . ." Trash's nasal twang pierced Evinrude's thoughts. "Don't that sound familiar?" Who was he talking to? Evinrude wondered.

"That's an Indian tribe," said Mulberry. "A noble tribe. And they spelled it wrong. It should be O-G-L-A-L-A. That's Crazy Horse's tribe, I—"

"Crazy Horse!" squawked Trash, turning a few heads in the coach. "That bloodthirsty maniac?"

2

"A victim as much as anything," disagreed Mulberry.

"Tell that to them what ain't got their scalps no more."

"I've heard Crazy Horse himself rarely scalps."

"Who you been talking to, his *mother*?"

Evinrude stared at Mulberry earnestly. "I have yet to understand what a peace-loving man such as you—"

"*Indian*-loving," Trash interjected grinning.

"What you are planning to do out here," persisted Evinrude. "The main pastime hereabouts seems to be killing Indians."

Mulberry gazed at Evinrude for a moment, and finally shrugged.

"Christ," said Jimson, "I'm ridin' with an old man and a saint. Hope there's no trouble ahead."

Mulberry eyed him, smiled, sighed, and then took out his notebook.

"You gonna *write* them to death?" sneered Trash. "Always writin'."

"Recording impressions."

"Yeah? Record *this* impression." He grabbed his own crotch. "Just see you spell my name right."

"Trash is trash," muttered Mulberry.

"No it ain't. You know how I got—"

"You told us," said Evinrude.

"'Cause there ain't *nobody* I can't trash."

"He's trying to say *thrash*," Mulberry informed anyone who might be listening.

"Damn right," sputtered Jimson. "'Specially some of them ee-feminate cavalry. You seen any yella-stripers around?"

"Just those Blue Legs in the back."

"I said *Cav*, not infantry. . . . They got infantry up front too, the baggage car. Saw 'em loadin' on. Got a big ol' gun."

Mulberry looked up. "Really? Artillery?"

"Infantry, I said. Damn, don't you never listen? Heavy weapons prob'ly, got a whole baggage car— Hey! Maybe *they* got somethin' t' drink, all by their lonely. I'm 'bout to dry up and blow away."

"You know they don't want us drinking right out in public."

"It's the baggage car. That ain't public."

At the next stop the three recruits hopped off the train, toting their duffels, and ran up to the baggage car. Along the way Jimson started squawking, "Hey, that sign said Julesburg, *Colorado*. I thought we was in Nebraska."

"We was—er, *were*," said Mulberry. "The train takes this

3

little loop into Colorado. Next stop we're back in Nebraska."

They pounded on the baggage car door. "Hey, open up, we're army."

The door slid open to reveal a second lieutenant.

"Whoops," said Jimson. "Guess I didn't see you . . . sir."

The train started to move.

"Oh, for God's sake," said the lieutenant. He had a tenor voice.

Jimson grinned, then he and the others started to trot alongside the moving train.

"Get them in here," said the lieutenant to a couple of burly teamsters, one black and one white, who yanked the recruits airborne as easily as if they were feathers, and dumped them in the car.

Jimson, unruffled, leaped to his feet, which he cautiously spread to combat the sway, yelled, "Private Jimson reporting, *sir*," and then threw up a wizard salute.

The lieutenant, eyes dulling, returned the salute desultorily and then threw up his hands as he saw Evinrude and Mulberry preparing to match Jimson. "Christ!" he swore. A trio of parade-ground nitwits. "I'm Lieutenant Clark," he went on, "and I don't know what you think you're doing up here, but—"

Clark told them the proper way to and from the rear of the train while Jimson looked around for booze. He thought he spied a bottle, half hidden, but how could he explain about his sudden thirst? Easy. Mulberry would do it.

"Jimson came because he thought there might be something to drink up here, sir—"

The lieutenant's eyes got even duller. "There is. What'd he do, smell it? Too damn much, in fact, but I don't know anything about it. It's unmilitary, General Grant notwithstanding."

"But I," continued Mulberry, "Private Mulberry, sir—I came up to look at that gun you're hauling. A Gatling, sir, unless I'm mistaken."

The lieutenant brightened. "Indeed it is, and you men keep that booze hidden for a while." He strolled toward the rear of the car, thin shoulders squared, head erect on a slender neck, pride of ownership manifest. Gunner Foreman and Gunner's Mate Willoughby winked at each other. Mulberry followed the lieutenant, trailed by Jimson and Evinrude.

"This is the newest model," Clark said. "The 1877 Gatling. It's similar to the '74, but each year has brought a number of improvements. This is the standard musket-length model, ten 32-inch barrels, 49 inches overall."

"What kind of ammo does it take?" asked Evinrude, eyeing the piece.

"Standard," answered Mulberry.

"Yes, standard," repeated Lieutenant Clark, glaring at Mulberry, "the .45-70 issue cartridge."

"Fires pretty fast, huh?" offered Jimson.

"In the latest tests, at Annapolis," Clark said, "the guns were fitted with ammo drums containing four hundred cartridges. In slightly more than ten minutes, ten of those drums were emptied. That's about four hundred a minute. Theoretically, its rate of fire is a good deal faster than that, but—" a smile—"it's physically impossible to push it to its limits. Cranking it, changing magazines, all that sort of thing wastes time."

"Sure wish we had those things in the War," said Evinrude wistfully.

"Actually you did—that is, *we* did. Toward the end, there were some. Butler—*Beast* Butler—he had some. And Lincoln was always ready for a new invention, a new weapon. But they'd already tried some revolving guns, revolving-chamber rifles, but they'd proved impractical, and that kind of soured everybody. Also, they used an *awful* lot of ammo. This Gatling's much improved. The early models couldn't change elevation, couldn't traverse, but this one can. And the early ones were also apt to be used like artillery. Quite ineffective. Then there were, and are, the logistics. You have to plan a whole new way of fighting. You don't just pick it up and run to the next place, it weighs too much. The gun alone weighs two hundred pounds. Its carriage weighs 326, and the limber—" he pointed to the other two-wheeler— "that carries the ammo caisson weighs 287, *without* the ammo."

"What do you haul it with, elephants?" Jimson seemed to be trying for Clark's shitlist.

"Some privates like yourself, most often," said the lieutenant dryly. "We chain them to the gun and whip them along the trail."

"Are there many of these guns out here?" asked Evinrude.

"Quite a few, actually. The army bought eight of the '74 model, forty-four of the '75 model, eighteen '76ers, and eleven of this model. A large number, I should imagine, are out West

5

here. I know they had some up around Little Big Horn. General Terry had three, General Gibbon two. Custer had a chance to take the three from the Twentieth Infantry—Terry's outfit—but he left them behind. He was probably right. They were these big kind, hard to haul over difficult ground, and they probably couldn't have kept up with the cav. Later, when Terry tried to haul them over some rough ground, they went so slowly they finally got lost. But Terry's still got them. And General Howard's got them. He's up there somewhere, chasing the Nez Perce I think. *This* one, this one's headed for Fort Keogh and General Miles. . . ."

Mulberry was scratching his head. "Begging your pardon, sir, but one might conjecture that they'd be better off with camel guns."

Clark gave Mulberry a long stare. Finally he said, "*Or a bulldog.*"

Mulberry frowned. Score one for Clark.

"What in the world's a camel gun?" asked Jimson.

"It's a short Gatling," said Mulberry, with permission. "An eighteen-inch barrel, ten of them, weighs a lot less, can be fitted on a lightweight cavalry cart, or a tripod. But never a camel, as far as I know. There was a picture of one mounted on a camel, but that was just for advertising. But the bulldog? . . ." He looked to Clark.

"Lighter yet," said Clark. "Just five barrels. Weighed about ninety pounds. The camel gun weighs in at 135. This gun here is the full-size model. But it'll go on a tripod, too."

"Oh, yeah?" sneered Jimson. "With who liftin' . . . sir?"

The lieutenant smiled unpleasantly. "I don't think you're long for this army, trooper."

"*Trooper?*" yelped Jimson. Didn't this looie know *cav* were called troopers? "Well, sir, now that I know what you're luggin' around, I kin see why your squad looks like a bunch of wrasslers."

"Don't mind him, sir," said Evinrude. "He's just ignorant."

Trash seemed to take no offense at this, and smiled widely.

"And now," said Lieutenant Clark, "I think I'll go join a few of my fellow officers. Don't overdo the drinking."

"You can depend on us, sir," said Corporal Foreman, the gunner.

Clark's eyes narrowed. But without any further word, he left.

Jimson whistled. "You been with him long?"

"Hardly," grinned Foreman. "We're still alive, ain't we? Naw, he's never seen any combat. What he knows he's gotten from books." Hearing that, Jimson eyed Mulberry. The gunner went on, "He's really just along to learn how to fight and to sign papers, and get us where we're going."

"What are you writin' *now*?" cried Jimson.

"Notes on the gun," explained Mulberry.

"*Always* writin'. Readin' and writin'," complained Trash. "How come you're so interested in this gun, and such a peace-lovin' person?"

Mulberry didn't bother answering.

And the group fell to drinking from bottles plucked out of various hiding places.

Gunner Foreman and Gunner's Mate Willoughby were both squat, brawny men. They weren't old, but the way they patiently tolerated Jimson made them seem older. Perhaps the fact that either could have broken Jimson in two accounted for it.

They tried not to drink much, just enough to loosen them up. The two teamsters—white, raw-boned Cummings and black, musclebound Jefferson—drank more. Mulberry and Evinrude hardly drank at all. Jimson drank as much as all the rest combined.

The gun crew talked about the fighting they'd seen, filling the recruits in on the finer points of Indian warfare. Of course, they hadn't seen that much action themselves, but they waxed eloquent nonetheless.

"This'll be Cheyenne country we'll soon be coming into," said Willoughby. He was sandy-haired, with a slow grin. "Hang onto your scalps."

Jimson grinned, stared at Jefferson, and said, "Injuns would have a hard time gittin' hold of *your* scalp."

Jefferson ran a hand over his stubbly, close-cropped scalp. "Sure as hell would. That's if he even got close enough."

"Fast on your feet, huh? Wonder if there's anything special 'bout a nigger scalp—"

Jefferson's ebony features clouded. He began to rise.

"To an Injun, I mean," Jimson added hastily.

"What's yo' name, *boy*?" drawled Jefferson ominously.

"Jimson. I already *told* the looie."

"Trash Jimson," elaborated Evinrude helpfully, earning himself a glare from Trash.

"Trash?" said Jefferson. "*Trash*."

"Yeah, 'cause of how I got the rep of trashin' anybody that stands in my way."

Not true, thought Mulberry, who was tired of hearing that explanation. Trash, in a drunken moment, had told him the truth. His family, poor to start with, had headed South after the War and, with apparently hereditary stupidity, had ended up even poorer. Had ended up white trash. And the name had stuck. But Mulberry didn't offer this revelation to the immediate gathering, despite his irritation.

Mulberry distracted himself by staring down the car at the Gatling, the magnificent gun. He muttered, "Medicine gun."

The talk had abated at just that moment, and all heard him. "What's that?" asked Foreman. "Medicine gun? What's a medicine gun?"

"The Gatling. That's what the Indians call it."

"How do *you* know?"

"'Cause he read it," said Jimson. "That's how he knows everything. You oughta hear him talk about 'loose women,' 'soiled ladies.'"

"Why 'medicine'?" pursued Foreman.

"Because medicine doesn't mean the same thing to an Indian as it does to us. Medicine, to an Indian, is somewhere between magic and luck—"

"So?" interjected Jimson, laughing. "That's what it means to white men too, don't it?"

"Anyone with a killing machine like this," Mulberry went on, "an Indian has to think he's got powerful medicine. They'd probably make it sacred if it wasn't busy killing them. As a matter of fact, I'm surprised they don't call it an owl gun, or something like that. Owl, to them, means death and destruction."

"Jeez," said Jimson. "Does General Sheridan know about you? Indians wouldn't have a chance with you giving him advice."

"Medicine gun, huh?" murmured Foreman. "Guess they'd probably like to get hold of one."

"Probably," agreed Mulberry. "And as for *you*," he said, looking up at Jefferson and deciding to impress them all, "there's a story about a hostile who was going to scalp a colored man, and the colored man's short, kinky hair puzzled him so much he decided the colored man must have some special medicine, so he hauled him off and nursed him back to health."

8

"You hear *that*, boy?" Jefferson roared at Jimson. He bent over, showing Trash his head. "This here burr-head is powerful medicine." And he roared with laughter.

Jimson didn't care for coloreds. "Let's get this here door open," he said. "It's *hot* in here. And I wanta see some of this Cheyenne country."

They exchanged looks. Why not? The door was slid open. Flat, rolling prairie, not an Indian in sight.

The men spent a few minutes looking out at nothing, swaying as the train rocked. Finally Jimson said, "Well, bust my britches if this ain't the boringest trip I ever took. Not even one of Mulberry's noble Cheyenne."

They all eyed Mulberry, who replied defensively, "I never said the Cheyenne were noble."

"Who *did* you say, then?"

Mulberry was trying to think of an inoffensive Eastern tribe, and Foremen was muttering, "Troublemaker, ain't he?" when Jimson went galloping off in still another direction. "Hey! Gunner!"

Foreman groaned. "*Corporal* to you, *private*."

"Yeah, you. Show us how the gun works. Fire off some rounds."

"In here?"

"Out the door, dummy."

"In about two seconds, *you're* going out that door."

"Gee, I'm sorry," oozed Trash. "So c'mon, Corporal, do it."

Foreman was about to refuse adamantly when he saw Mulberry come alive. And the corporal might have had a bit too much to drink. "The lieutenant—"

"He's getting sloshed with them officers, you know that."

"All right," he agreed reluctantly. "We'll give it a try." He grinned foolishly. "Prob'ly scare the bejesus outta them soldiers in back."

"Good. They're likely as bored as us. Come on."

The seven of them wrestled the Gatling forward and around until it was pointing out over the passing plains.

Willoughby opened a box and loaded several twenty-round magazines and shoved one into the gun's hopper. It was top-loading, the rounds fed by gravity.

"Take a look out the door, Will," Foreman said.

Willoughby looked out and then yelled, "Let 'er rip!"

9

Foreman took a deep breath and started cranking.

An earsplitting roar filled the car as twenty .45-caliber slugs shot off across the prairie.

Then there was silence, save for some muffled noise from farther back along the train, and a few peremptory squawks, also from farther back.

Jimson's mouth was open, Mulberry was writing, Evinrude croaked, "Jesus wept," and the gun crew were all grinning.

Jimson grabbed another magazine and replaced the empty. "Let me try it," he said, "'fore the lieutenant gets here screamin'."

"Naw."

"C'mon. What could happen?"

"What could happen?" asked Mulberry with a faraway look. "I remember reading about the early models. After firing a while they got real hot and expanded and were impossible to crank. But they had a screw that adjusted the space between the barrels and the breech. The only thing was, to turn this screw you had to stand out in front of the gun." He grinned. "They had a few casualties before they put a crank-lock on it."

Jimson stared at Mulberry, then demanded of the gun crew, "You got a lock on this?"

"Yeah, we got one," Foreman said, though he wished they hadn't. "But you ain't plannin' to stand in front of it, are you?" And he wondered what was keeping Lieutenant Clark.

"Hell, no," said Jimson, taking that as an invitation, and Foreman had to scramble to get out of his way. Foreman sort of staggered to the side. What the hell, he thought boozily, my ass is already in a sling.

"Wait'll I take a look—" began Willoughby, but before he could do it, Jimson started cranking. And the deafening roar started up again.

Just then, some cattle came into sight. They'd been grazing by the track and were now stumbling away as the train passed. They began to stumble even more, going to their knees. Blood spurted from the neck wound of one. Then, suddenly, there was a mounted cowboy, a puzzled look on his face. And he went down. And the gun went silent, even though Jimson kept cranking away.

"You killed him!" screamed Willoughby.

"Killed who?"

"That cowboy. Didn't you see him? And all those *cows* you shot?"

"Cows? *Cowboy*? No, I didn't see. Who the hell can see when this thing's going off? An' what the hell was he doing out there anyway? This is *Cheyenne* country. You said so yourself."

"Maybe I was wrong."

They looked back. Cattle were running, but there was no sign of cowboy or horse, except, way off in the distance, someone was riding hell-bent after the train.

"Lemme have them magazines!" Trash shouted. "Either those are Cheyenne out there, or we're in big trouble."

They all caught on fast, and soon the Gatling was spraying more death out onto the plains, assuming there was anything out there to die.

The door at the rear end of the car slammed open and Lieutenant Clark entered with gun drawn and, as predicted, screaming. "What the hell's going on?!"

"Cheyenne," said Jimson.

"Road agents," said Mulberry.

"Cheyenne?" repeated Clark, flabbergasted. "Road agents?"

"Train robbers. Sorry. Got confused."

"Yeah," said Jimson. "First we thought they was Cheyenne, since this is Cheyenne country, an' they kinda rose up outta the grass after the engine passed. But then we saw they was owlhoots. Probably wanted the Gatling. We got the gun going and left them in the grass."

Clark was still pop-eyed. But now his eyes began to narrow. "Now just a minute. What are *you* doing behind that gun?"

"I was closest, they was right there, I started cranking..."

Clark was staring down the baggage car at where the Gatling used to be. "Why was the—"

"One of the robbers is trying to catch us, sir—" interrupted Mulberry, almost apologetically. "I think."

Clark frowned, jumped to the open side door, and looked back.

There in the distance, but closing fast, were a horse and rider. The man was firing his gun into the air.

Clark reacted quickly. He drew his gun and threw a shot toward the rider. Then he leaped to the door at the rear of the car, exclaiming, "No telling how many there are!" He opened the door and disappeared. They heard him shouting, "Train robbers, coming up in back," as he moved through the train.

The gun crew and recruits positioned themselves carefully so they could all see out the side door.

There was about a twenty-second delay. The rider got closer, still waving his gun, which, by then, had to be empty. Then there was a thunderous fusillade from the rear of the train and the rider went down in a tangle of man and horse. Both lay still, accompanied by cheers, until they were lost in the distance.

Everyone in the baggage car had paled, even Jefferson. They took a long while to collect their thoughts, most of which probably concerned Jimson.

Mulberry murmured to Foreman, "Troublemaker, did you say?"

And Jimson said, "I think this calls for a drink."

Since they couldn't kill Jimson, they drank with him.

By the time the lieutenant returned, they were nearly unconscious. Clark had been thinking the matter over—the time sequence, getting the Gatling in position. . . . What was it doing pointing out the door in the first place? Yes, he had some hard questions to ask. But he decided he'd better wait until they were conscious and sober. Judging from the bottles strewn about, he guessed that might take a while.

Racing Elk moved his band steadily northward. They'd stayed east of Denver and Greeley and were now east of the Denver Pacific Railroad on the trail north to Cheyenne.

Racing Elk had spent the previous year carousing, killing, and pillaging on the southern plains. Good hunting and good experience.

His band, the Oglala Sioux part of it, had been the *akicita* of their tribe early the previous summer. The *akicita* societies performed, primarily, as police, or soldiers, within the tribe. They kept order. They were a kind of embryonic civil government. Inevitably, such authority carried with it the potential for misuse of power. And in order to keep any one *akicita* society from becoming dictatorial, the Sioux utilized several devices.

Rotation of authority was one such device. The Kit Foxes policed one month, the Brave Hearts the next, and so on. Racing Elk's society, Seven Rains, policed early the previous summer. It was Racing Elk's first contact with that kind of power, and he liked it. And when the time came to hand over the reins to the next society, he did so, but instead of sinking back into the mass of the governed, he led his society south.

Along the way they'd picked up individuals from other tribes—from friendly tribes such as the Cheyenne, and from tribes that were the Sioux' nominal enemies. And in the southern fighting, Racing Elk had lost men from his own Oglala tribe and gained replacements from others.

Now Racing Elk was headed back north, his band some forty strong. Racing Elk had heard, of course, of the great victory at the Little Big Horn, but he'd also heard of some subsequent reverses. He knew not where Crazy Horse was, exactly, but knew that Sitting Bull was up near the Canadian border somewhere, unbeaten and unbowed. He meant to join him.

They'd stolen two wagons for the trip north. The wagons were laden with goods seized in the south, and were driven by braves dressed in white men's clothes. The greater part of the band rode in columns flanking the wagons, keeping out of sight. And while those flanking braves were under orders to stay in concealment, to maintain that distancing, there were frequent exceptions permitted, for among the wagons' contents were seven white women. They involuntarily serviced the braves. It was not a bad way to travel for the braves, but lousy for the women.

They crossed the border into Wyoming.

Then, from the deepening dusk on the outskirts of Cheyenne, a man appeared and sought out Racing Elk. He was a tall man, a white man on a tall horse, and he was well-armed and his face was scarred.

"Racing Elk. It has been many moons."

Racing Elk knew that. He waited to hear what he didn't know.

"You plan to pass through Cheyenne and drive straight north," the man said, the question a statement.

Racing Elk nodded.

"That is bad. The wagon road is not the best way. There are soldiers."

That was nothing new, thought Racing Elk.

"It would be best to go another way, to follow the railroad that way—" he pointed toward the northwest—"until they turn to the setting sun again—"

"Medicine Bow," said Racing Elk, smiling thinly.

"Near there, yes, and then straight north to the trail we call the Bozeman."

"I call it that, too . . . when white men ask me directions. . . . Why do you tell me this?"

"Because we are friends . . . brothers. . . ."

"I will think about it. You will ride with us?"

"Only into Cheyenne," he smiled. "I want to see this bold gesture you are planning. It is the way of Racing Elk."

Racing Elk shrugged at the empty compliment, and then settled down to wait, for his "bold gesture" was not going to be executed until well after nightfall. It may have been bold but it wasn't insane.

When the time finally came, Racing Elk sent his mounted braves off to circle the city. Then he boarded the first wagon and rode it straight into the center of Cheyenne.

It was very late and there were few people about to pay much attention to a couple of wagons driven by weary travelers who drove with their hats pulled down over lowered heads. It was not really a risky trip, but Racing Elk enjoyed it.

Halfway through town the white man leaned from his horse and whispered into the first wagon, "Have you decided which route you will follow?"

"I have not yet decided. But your words have made sense." What he didn't add, though, was that he'd never run from a battle, nor done hardly anything else, simply because it was the sensible thing to do.

The white man knew he'd said and done all he could. He turned his horse away and tied it up in front of a hotel.

two

It was earlier that same summer day and Stretch Dobbs couldn't believe his luck. All he'd intended to do was ride into town, guzzle some beer, and maybe blow a few cents on one of the ugly prostitutes—the uglier the cheaper. But here he was, him and his horse, surrounded by a bunch of pretty Cheyenne maidens.

There were seven of them, jabbering among themselves excitedly and gesturing at him. He didn't understand the language but could tell from the gestures that they wanted him to go with them.

Stretch looked around. Where the hell was there to go? You could see for miles and there wasn't anything *to* see. These were the High Plains of Wyoming and there was grass, grass, grass, rolling damn near to the horizon. Way off to the north and northwest you could make out the Big Horns, but these Indian gals weren't thinking of *them*, were they?

Stretch was close to six-foot-seven and proud of his height. He was also proud of his strength, though it lay dormant much of the time. But beyond that he forgot about pride. He wasn't very good at doing things, not real skillful, and his best buddy Malone claimed he was dumb. And since he couldn't figure out how to change Malone's mind on that score he guessed he was. But by God he was tall, and he could really see. So he looked around some more.

Outpost Number Nine was a mile out of sight to the rear. The friendlies' settlement, Cheyenne mostly, was off to the

15

right, the south, he could make out the tipis. They couldn't want him to go there, Windy was the only one who ever went *there*. Town was straight ahead. And to the left, the north, rolling fields of grass. He remembered once chasing a jackrabbit that way. Damn thing disappeared into one of them gullies. . . .

A smile broke on Dobbs' face. He dismounted. "How," he said, raising a palm.

The girls giggled and closed in on him. He looked down on them circling around his waist, bemused, reminded of his own childhood games. Maypoles, it was.

He rested his hands on his guns, just in case any of them got some funny ideas.

But they didn't, they just started dragging him by his belt off through the grass, north.

He started hooting, brushing at their hands, galloping along with them. His horse, abandoned, started to amble along in his wake. Stretch, remembering the horse, looked back, but when he saw the beast following he forgot about him.

He'd only run about two hundred yards when he had to stop and pull his boots off. The Cheyenne girls started cackling all over again. He sure wished he knew what they were saying. But pretty soon, running again, he didn't care if he knew. He didn't have the breath to converse.

They gamboled merrily on for about another half-mile— "Gawdamn! We must be halfway to Canada!"—before stopping. Stretch was gasping like a lungshot buffalo. And his feet hurt; going without boots hadn't hurt him less, only differently. He sat down, rubbing his feet, sucking in great draughts of hot, dry air.

They were down in a draw. The High Plains were covered with them, except that when you were up top, looking around, you never knew they were there. Hostiles could run along them for miles, sneak right past whole regiments in full daylight. Stretch figured these "hostile" maidens were right at home.

He studied his feet. One big toe was poking out through a grimy sock. He hoped the girls weren't too fussy. He felt hands on his neck and shoulders, massaging. Ah, that was nice.

His eyes slowly rose and then popped wide open. There, smack-dab in front of him was a buck-naked girl, black thatch between her legs, young brown breasts dancing in the late-day sun. Suddenly his pants were too tight.

16

The other girls were in various stages of undress. These dusky beauties were all business. Stretch started to bend forward to undress himself, to catch up, but his forward movement was arrested by the feel of cold steel against his throat.

His eyes rolled downward. A *bayonet* for crying out loud. Most useless piece of equipment the army owned. Only ones who knew what to do with them were Indians. The Indians *loved* hand-to-hand combat; Sergeant Wilkie'd told them that. Indians didn't think much of guns. They'd use them if they had to, and most often they did have to, but real glory came from hand-to-hand combat, with hatchets, spears, or knives.

All that ran through Stretch's mind as he stared down his nose at the gleaming steel. Hand-to-hand combat was about the last thing he was thinking of just then.

The undressing had stopped, and a few of the Cheyenne girls showed surprise, dismay. Apparently the knife had not been in the plans. One girl said something with a plaintive sound. And another voice snarled a reply just over his head.

What the hell? The voice carried little femininity; had some hostile buck come creeping up on them? He rolled his eyes up, gently leaning his head back.

'Bout the meanest looking Cheyenne maiden he'd ever seen. He wondered how he'd missed spotting her.

A tug on his shirt combined with pressure from the blade brought him slowly to his feet and upright. This was his chance. This little bitch could hardly reach his neck with him standing. But suddenly she'd sprung on his back, legs clasping his middle, arms around his neck, knife still in place. "Carry me," she hissed.

"You speak English?"

"Carry me."

"Sounds like English to me," mumbled Stretch as he grabbed hold of her legs. She then rode piggyback a ways down the draw.

"Stop here."

She really knows the language, thought Stretch.

"Lie down."

He did so, noticing she'd picked a spot with a lot of sandy mounds. She said something else in Cheyenne. He wondered what she was saying. He found out.

The rest of the girls suddenly fell on him, pulling his clothes off. "Hey," he squawked, "*I* coulda done *that*."

He was naked. A trifle embarrassed, but hell, he'd seen *them* naked a few minutes ago. 'Cept he wondered why they weren't naked anymore. . . .

More commands from the hostile bitch and his arms and legs were pulled in different directions, spread-eagling him. Hell, what kind of game was this? He noticed the girls weren't smiling anymore. Game? Stretch began to worry a bit. And he *really* began to worry when he discovered he'd been staked out. Immobilized.

Torture! Indian torture! That bastard Sergeant Wilkie'd told them about *that*, too. Stretch began to hope he lived long enough to pass it along.

The knife had left his throat, and the knife-wielder walked around to where he could see her. She didn't look half bad, thought Stretch, if you could forget she was a killin', torturin', Indian bitch. "What's yer name, gal?"

"I am not *gal*. I am Cheyenne woman. I am Whispering Grass."

"Howdy. I'm Stretch Dobbs. Soldier. Mounted infantry. Army of the West." It didn't seem to impress her much. "You kin let me up now. This has been a pretty good game, but I think—"

She began to undress. Which didn't take long. Once the painted hide dress was dropped there wasn't anything else.

Stretch's mouth dried up. Funny kind of torture, he thought. He looked around. The other girls had vanished.

Whispering Grass dropped to her knees between his legs. He craned his neck, grinning to hide his worry. She rubbed stuff on his testicles. Then she started scooping and Stretch felt warm soil pushed into that same genital area. Felt kind of nice.

She gripped his pecker, gently. That felt even nicer and his member stood tall. His head fell back in a kind of blissful swoon as her mouth closed over it. What *torture*, he murmured. But sure hope she ain't planning to bite.

Suddenly there was a sharp pain, like a sting. What the hell?! But her tongue got active and he forgot about it . . . until the next sting.

Stretch wondered what the hell she was jabbing him with. Big old needle, it felt like. Just what kind of crazy bitch was this he was dealing with?

Ow! Another one, dammit. He wished she'd— But her

tongue began to describe a clever, circling pattern on the head of his pecker. . . .

Private Maximillian Malone and Windy Mandalian left Outpost Nine together. Not because they were such great friends, but rather because both were going the same way: Malone toward town to join Stretch, and Windy toward the friendlies' village.

Windy was Easy Company's chief scout and a good one, but a quiet one; the sign he read told him more than he ever told anyone else. A man of few words. But all who knew him knew that the few words he did speak had best be listened to. He was a dark-skinned man with features that almost looked angry to start with. The son of an Armenian fur trader and a French Canadian mother, his high cheekbones, flat facial planes, and hook nose were cause for suspicion. The word was there might be a touch of Cree blood in his maternal ancestry, and Windy never disabused anyone of that notion. And the fact that he enjoyed socializing with the friendlies lent support to the notion.

But Windy didn't fraternize with *Indians* exactly, or generally, only with squaws and maidens. He'd found them very congenial, eager to please—especially when there weren't any horny warriors in the vicinity—and remarkably inventive. The suspicions regarding his own ancestry amused him, since he thought there were a whole mess of Cheyenne and Sioux that had a touch of Windy in *their* blood.

"Where you headed?" asked Malone.

Windy just looked at him.

"Thought so," said Malone.

They rode on some more.

"Glad you're so talkative," said Malone. "Don't know what I woulda done out here without a lad like you to talk to."

Probably talked to himself. A number of guard corporals and officers of the day had come upon Malone walking his guard post in the dead of night, holding a brisk conversation with himself. The various officers wished he wouldn't do that. Malone would usually hear them, above his own prattle, at the last possible moment, and throw down his Springfield and spit out a challenge so fast that the officers were sure his damn gun was going to go off one of these nights. And if it did go off, Malone was sure as hell not going to simply be found guilty of manslaughter, fined two dollars and five cents (the five cents for the wasted bullet), and transferred to another outfit. No sirree. Malone would get rapidly "transferred" to the Happy Hunting Grounds, no questions asked. The officers agreed on that. Only First Lieutenant Kincaid suggested they not go sneaking up on poor Malone.

Of course, Malone knew better than anyone how close he'd come to blowing some commissioned heads off. Therefore, he never walked guard with a loaded gun. But no one knew that. And he could load faster than he could talk, if he had to. He was a fighter, born and bred, head to toe. The Civil War never knew what it missed, ending as it did when he was only ten.

Maximillian. That came from his mother, German and the strongest woman he'd ever known. His father'd been a skinny, cantankerous, contentious Irish ne'er-do-well. He'd gotten his fighting spirit from his father and the strength to win from his mother. Both were dead, him in the War, her right after.

"I'm gonna meet Stretch in town," said Malone, and Windy nodded.

"We'll be getting ol' Stretch laid, just as sure as Kelly's green." Malone slipped easily in and out of a brogue. He smiled now in anticipation, and glanced at Windy.

Doubt was writ, however subtly, on Windy's face.

"Don't think I can, do you? Listen, I got this raggedy-ass gal in town what'd french a buffaler fer a shot of whiskey."

"Sounds like she has taste."

Amazing, thought Malone. He talks. "Too much fer Stretch? Don't you believe it. Ain't you never seen him do his buffaler imitation?"

Windy shook his head sadly and considered picking up the pace. Malone simply wore a person down.

Just then, Windy spotted a bevy of Cheyenne beauties, some quite familiar, approaching through the grass from the north. They crossed the trail right in front of the two riders, squealing and chattering. Malone eyed the girls keenly. As a rule, he wasn't too fond of friendlies, no matter what shape or size, but . . .

"Now maybe I'm getting an idea about what you're up to, Windy me boy, me bucko," said Malone. "Maybe I'll just tag along with you."

An expression of distaste clouded Windy's features for a moment but was quickly replaced by a look of intense concentration. His eyes narrowed. Malone caught the look. He'd seen it on the trail before, doing soldier-work. "What's wrong?"

"Them gals. Sounded like we wasn't the only whites they'd seen recent." He looked northward, scowling.

"So what? They was jes' young fillies. They *was* young, wasn't they?" Sometimes you couldn't tell, or Malone couldn't. If Windy'd told him they were a bunch of crones, he wouldn't have argued.

"Them gals got funny games sometimes." Windy kneed his horse gently and it swerved north. "Take a look."

Malone had to yank his horse to turn him. Malone was not a natural or enthusiastic rider to begin with. He was infantry, a footsoldier. The fact that they stuck them up on horses to get them to a fight didn't change that. And the soldiers weren't assigned a particular horse; they got a different one every day. And this one wanted to be shown who was boss.

He had to kick it with his heels repeatedly to get back up close to Windy. It was goddamn tiring. And he hoped he wasn't going to have to outrun any hostiles. "Hope you know where you're goin'." He scowled. Partly because the saddle wasn't any bargain, either. McClellan. With its goddamn slot down the middle you had to ride pretty careful or you'd wind up ruptured for sure.

Malone scanned the distant horizon. God sure was ambitious when He made this land. And though Malone's heart may have been with the footsoldier, he sure was glad he didn't have to *march* any scouting patrols out there. Stretch might manage okay, but... He leaned forward and patted his horse, and almost ran into Windy. He hadn't seen the scout's raised hand.

"What's up? Hostiles?" he whispered.

Windy didn't say anything, and Malone wondered why he bothered asking.

Just ahead of them the land dipped down out of sight. Could be a whole goddamn war party sitting down there, just waiting fer them.

Suddenly Malone thought he heard a kind of moaning, but a *familiar* kind of moaning—them raggedy-ass whores in town made noises just like that—'cept this one was kinda deeper. But seeing where they were, it was a pretty funny noise to be hearing, either way. If this was an Indian trap, it was a new one.

Windy kneed his mount forward a bit. Malone kneed his, too, but it didn't move at all. So he got off and walked up beside Windy.

Then he heard, "Ow! Hey, what the hell you think yer doin' with that needle? Or whatever you got."

Stretch! He'd know that dumb voice anywhere. He and Windy went forward until they could see down into the draw.

And there was Stretch, staked out, a naked Indian gal bending over his midsection. Stretch was breathing hard.

A faint smile creased Windy's lips, but Malone exploded, "Holy Jesus, what's she doin' to him?"

Stretch climaxed gloriously just as Whispering Grass spun her head around to stare at Malone and Windy. Then she scrambled off to the side and snatched up the bayonet.

Some kind of noise came from Windy, but Malone's draw was automatic and his Scoff leaped from leather like a rattler. Forty-five-caliber thunder filled the draw.

Whispering Grass turned a flip backwards and landed in a heap.

Malone looked at Windy and found himself staring into the business end of Windy's Winchester. Model '73. A real nice piece, a carbine. Malone had always admired it, but not at this moment. He remembered that Windy might be part Indian.

His look took in Windy's finger on the trigger, watching for that telltale knuckle-whitening. He might be able to get his Scoff around fast enough. Malone's breathing shallowed considerably.

Finally the carbine lowered. "You didn't have to do that," Windy said.

"Whaddaya mean?" squawked Malone, relief washing over him, "she had a knife, she was gonna cut Stretch."

Windy looked disgusted. And when they got down and looked at Whispering Grass, Malone didn't feel too good.

"Hey!" cried Stretch. "Hey! What's goin' on, cut me loose, damnit! Ow, What the hell?! I thought she was *stickin'* me with somethin'!"

They cut him loose. Windy explained, "They had you staked out on an ant hill. Them's bulldog ants bitin' yer balls."

"Ants! shrieked Stretch, and he danced around, slapping and brushing at his testicles. Until he danced over near the Indian girl's body. He slowed suddenly and gaped in dismay, then almost horror.

"That some new kinda fandango you invented, Stretch?" asked Malone, forcing a grin. He glanced at Windy and his expression sobered. "What'll we do with her?"

"I'll take her," said Windy.

"Did you . . . know her?"

"Yep. She warn't bad . . . jes' wild . . ."

"I really thought she was gonna use that knife."

"I don't wanta hear no more."

Stretch, well sobered, was almost dressed, pulling on his pants. Carefully.

"Where's yer horse, Stretch? We didn't see none."

"Up the draw, prob'ly. She made me carry her down here. Guess we was lookin' fer these ants. She didn't hardly weigh nothin'."

Windy heaved Whispering Grass up over his saddle and they went up the draw. They found Stretch's horse wondering where everyone had gone. Windy looked around. "The whole bunch stripped you here, huh?"

"Yeah," Stretch replied sheepishly. "But the rest took off when I got staked. Guess they was scairt." His eyes got a faraway look. "Glad y'all didn't come *too* soon."

"*You* came jes' in time," said Malone, grinning again. "Yeah, I saw you, like Ol' Faithful, you was."

Stretch sprang up on his horse and, with a yelp, sprang right off. "I think I better walk."

"You better," said Windy. "You woulda been a hospital case soon. When you get back to the post, you better have someone take a look."

"Some nice *white* gal," suggested Malone, and Stretch blushed.

To describe Outpost Number Nine as commanding the high ground is a bit misleading, since *all* the land for miles around was high ground, all at about the same level, five to six thousand feet above sea level, the High Plains. Rolling brown prairie for about as far as the eye could see, it actually got green for a while in the spring, but most times it was brown, when it wasn't covered with snow.

On that rolling prairie, Outpost Nine sat on one of the higher rolls, a slight rise that gave them an unobstructed view for about a quarter-mile in all directions.

It wasn't called a fort, since forts were just for regimental headquarters or higher, but it was built like one. Heavy, solid timber, tarpaper, and prairie sod, with a rammed-earth foundation. The company housing, about twenty feet deep, was built right into the walls. The roofs formed single, linked, rectangular sod pieces and were the ramparts along which the guards walked their posts. It was a pretty economical arrangement. And it was the home of Easy Company.

Easy Company's commanding officer, Captain Warner Conway, sat at his desk studying a map. It was a map he'd drawn himself, from memory. It depicted the Battle of the Little Big Horn, with the disposition of cavalry and hostile forces as he understood them. He scratched his head. Maybe he'd left something out, but as far as he could tell there was nothing Custer could have done, in the way of brilliant strategy, to keep himself from getting killed. Except not gone there in the first place.

Conway hadn't been there, but it had only happened the year before, and it was still a hot topic of conversation and of controversy, and it fascinated him. He'd even run a patrol up there to the Greasy Grass, far outside his legitimate sector, under the pretext of chasing hostiles, just to get a look at the killing ground.

It hadn't been the most comfortable of forays, quite aside from the actual hardship of the ride. Crazy Horse was probably still out there somewhere and eager to show someone else what he'd learned about military tactics. Lucky all those Indian tribes didn't like each other much more than they liked the white man. Put them all together under one good leader, and there'd be hell to pay.

Conway sighed. He was in his mid-forties and he'd been a captain longer than he cared to remember. The classic means of advancement was a great victory in the field, and every commander worth his salt lusted for such an engagement. But, looking down at his map, Little Big Horn was one he was glad he'd missed. It sure as hell hadn't done much for Reno or Benteen.

Captain Conway stood up, rolling his map and shoving it into a pigeonhole above his desk, and walked from the room. A tall, upright man with good military posture, he walked with a rolling gait. He'd spent quite a few years on his feet, in this man's army, in the infantry, and he walked like it.

Acting Master Sergeant Ben Cohen—Easy's first sergeant—

24

and Corporal Bradshaw, company clerk, looked up as Conway appeared in the doorway connecting his office with the orderly room. Sergeant Cohen caught the captain's eye and fingered a button near his waist. Conway sighed and buttoned the offending button. He'd loosened it at his desk. His shirts were feeling a tad snug of late. They must have shrunk.

"Thank you, Sergeant," he said, smiling. "Is it that you have someone for me to discipline, which I can't do very well with my undershirt hanging out."

"Nothing so far, sir," replied Cohen, returning the grin. "I got hopes, though. Men are gettin' a bit restive. They'll do 'bout anything to get out of work details, even fight Indians."

"Wouldn't we all."

"Yes sir. But lackin' that, I figger one or two of the boys will bust out soon. Matter of fact, Tompkins up top reported thinkin' he heard some gunfire not too long ago."

"Did you send someone out?"

"Tompkins *always* thinks he hears gunfire."

Conway frowned. "Is Tompkins one of the youngsters?"

"Nope. Older'n me. A War veteran. He was under McClellan, havin' a nice, dainty war, and then along comes Grant and he had to fight his ass off. It's a memory that stays with him."

"He's a good fighter, then?"

Cohen's grin widened. "One of the worst."

Conway's frown deepened. "I don't understand it. We should have a crack, efficient outfit and instead we're getting deluged with green recruits and men that should have been pensioned off— No. No. I do understand it. Washington's gone crazy after what happened to Custer. They're going to give us ten men for every Indian."

"That's right, sir. And it's costing them a bundle."

"And they're the ones that keep saying the lid's on promotions because money's too tight."

"You just hang in there, sir. You'll get that gold oak leaf."

Conway stared into the distance. "Almost forgot what one looked like. These bars *are* beginning to look a little tarnished, wouldn't you say?"

"I figger the order's already been drawn, *Major*, jes' waitin' to be sent."

Captain Conway smiled. "If only you were in Washington, Sergeant. But since you're not, be sure to let me know if a war breaks out. I'll be in my quarters."

He left the orderly room, turned right, and strolled south toward the Officers' Quarters.

He'd almost reached his door when there was a commotion by the front gate. He looked over.

Two soldiers had just entered, one riding, the other walking and leading his horse. A very tall man. Dobbs, it was. Walking in an odd way, too. Conway decided to look into it.

Sergeant Cohen had also decided to look into it. He'd surged from the orderly room and he and Captain Conway converged on Stretch Dobbs and Private Malone. A few other soldiers were standing around.

Dobbs and Malone had headed for town. They hadn't been gone long. What were they doing back? Had they run into something? Tompkins, up top, eagle-eyed the surrounding landscape, his rifle ready.

Sergeant Cohen looked from Dobbs to his horse and back to Dobbs. "What the hell's going on?"

"Don't feel too good, Sarge," said Dobbs, abashed.

Conway asked, "What's wrong with this man, Sergeant?"

Malone piped up, "Stretch almost got his pecker bit off."

Conway and Cohen glared and chorused, "What did you say, *private*?"

"Stretch almost got his pecker bit off, *sir*!"

"Neat trick, Dobbs," Cohen said. "What'd you do, take a leak on a rattler's nest?"

Dobbs swallowed hard. "Not exactly, Sarge. See, I was ridin' along toward town when all of a sudden a whole bunch of wild Indian gals come up out of a draw. I pulled up sudden— jes' to keep from runnin' 'em down, y' know—and they surrounded me and pulled me off my horse. I didn't want to shoot 'cause they was jes' gals. Anyway, one of 'em pulls a bayonet on me 'fore I knew what was happenin', and the next thing I know, they've got me staked out on a bulldog ant hill. The rest of 'em run away, but one real mean one stayed behind and started doin' terrible things to my privates. . . ."

Malone snorted, but was silenced by a withering glare from Sergeant Cohen, who then turned to Dobbs and said, "Sounds like a terrible ordeal, Dobbs. Maybe we oughta have Dutch take a look at the, uh, wound."

Stretch went pale. Sergeant "Dutch" Rothausen was the company mess sergeant, and served in a pinch as chief medical officer. His formal knowledge of medicine was slim, but he took great pride in his ability to perform a clean amputation.

Conway shook his head in exasperation. "Never mind, Private Dobbs, I'm sure you'll be just fine." Then he said to both Dobbs and Malone, "You men can stand at ease."

It was meant as a rebuke, since neither Malone nor Dobbs had come to attention for the captain. But the two privates mistook the sarcasm and tried to become even more at ease. They almost fell down.

Things were getting out of hand and Conway, with a nod at Sergeant Cohen, turned away and headed back for his quarters. Soldiers seemed to line his route, snapping to attention and saluting all along the way. His arm almost fell off, returning the salute. He nearly suspected a conspiracy.

Cohen said to Malone, "You're lucky I ain't feeling mean. Since when don't you come to attention?"

"No one called attention, Sarge."

"No one's gotta. Now you two clear out."

They cleared out. And Lieutenant Matt Kincaid came strolling up. "What was that all about, Sergeant?"

"Let's go back inside, sir, it's hot out here, I'll explain."

And he did, on the way to the orderly room. Kincaid was as much amused by Captain Conway's behavior as by Stretch's close call. "What happened to the girl?"

Cohen stopped, looking at him. "The girl?"

"The Indian girl who was doing all the deviltry."

Cohen spun on his heel and roared, "Malone!"

Malone popped out of the barracks door.

"What happened to the girl, Malone?" roared Cohen.

"Dead, Sarge," yelled Malone right back. "I shot her. Windy took her home."

Cohen's face fell and he turned back toward the orderly room, his shoulders slumping.

"Windy let him do that?" wondered Kincaid.

"Maybe not," said Cohen. "Malone's hot-headed *and* fast. Saw that knife he talked about and shot before Windy could do anything." He shook his head sadly. "Well, Windy's got her. It'll be all right. Sad, though...damn!"

"Exactly," said Kincaid.

The lieutenant was a tall, lanky man in his thirties. A good-looking gent in a rawboned way, he was supposed to be quite a hand with the ladies, what ladies he ever got to lay a hand on. There weren't many. A few passing through, but that was

27

about it. All the worthwhile locals were spoken for. And Kincaid was a gent, a real gent.

Kincaid, like the rest of the men, wore two guns. Only one was issue, the Scoff, or Schofield Smith & Wesson .45. The other was a pearl-handled Colt Peacemaker. It was his only affectation. But he still took some ribbing from the other officers.

"What about those new recruits we're due, any word on them?"

"Nope," said Cohen, but then, entering the orderly room, he repeated the question for Corporal Bradshaw.

Bradshaw stared at the telegraph equipment for a moment, as if it might be holding out on him, then said, "No, Sarge, not recent."

"Well, we don't really need them," said Kincaid, echoing Conway's words on the matter. "Custer getting killed really lit a fire under the brass back East. They figure if we can't kill them all, we'll crowd them out."

"Never met an Indian I couldn't beat," groused Sergeant Cohen.

"They don't fight with their fists, Sergeant. And you never met Crazy Horse." Then Kincaid went on, mumbling, "Wish I knew where Crazy Horse was. I'd ride him down myself."

And get yourself a promotion, thought Cohen. "Hear tell he might be up around Pine Ridge. Fort Robinson, maybe." These fellows would ride down the setting sun if they thought it might mean a promotion. "How long have you been a first lieutenant, sir?"

Too long, Sarge, too damn long. . . ."

three _____

It was well after midnight when the Union Pacific train pulled into Cheyenne. Lieutenant Clark kicked his dozing crew and the recruits awake and hustled them and the Gatling, with its carriage, and limber, out of the baggage car. From another baggage car came a brace of horses.

Evinrude, onetime farmer with an eye for decent horse-flesh—working horses anyway—said, "That's not a very impressive pair of horses."

"They'll do," said Clark curtly. "They're not for riding, just hauling the gun. I'll requisition riding horses, if the escort hasn't brought any. But you're right, they are not true draft horses. They're condemned cavalry horses, too worn out to keep up with a cavalry troop."

The rest of the men, gummy-eyed and thick-witted from sleep and booze, stood about.

"Now then," said Clark, "where's that damn escort? There's supposed to be one." He turned in a slow circle, eyes peeled. "It's pretty damn late, but they should've left *someone* up. Anyone see anything that looks like an escort? A troop of soldiers? *One* soldier?"

"Cav?"

"No. Mounted infantry."

No one saw anything.

Cheyenne, with its more than 2,500 souls, lay sleeping around them. A few saloons were still open, but most of the town had turned in.

"I suppose we could spend the night," Clark said. "Wait for the escort to show up."

"That's what we're goin' to do, sir," said Trash.

"No, we're not," Evinrude corrected him. "We've wasted enough time as it is, and I don't feel like taking forever to get there."

"Who made you boss?" Trash said.

"You can stay overnight if you want, but you'll stay alone," Evinrude told him.

"Where are you men headed?" Clark asked.

"Medicine Bow. It's a ways on down the line. Then north, I figger."

"Well then, you'd better hustle back on board, trooper—"

"Trooper's *cavalry*," snarled Jimson, "sir."

"—Err, soldier . . . And—" It took an effort of will, considering Jimson— "good luck."

"Thank you, sir."

"But I do think we will stay over," muttered Clark, talking himself into it.

"I wouldn't, sir," advised Mulberry.

"Why not? You want us to go on alone? That's hostile country where we're headed."

"There might also be some hostiles coming up behind you, too."

Jimson tried to kick Mulberry.

Clark caught on. "Oh. Yes. I'd forgotten about that, and I'd been meaning to talk to you. There weren't any hostiles back there, were there? Or train robbers? Or *road agents*?"

Silence.

"Damn," said Clark. "Damn damn damn. My first action, gunning down a cowboy and a bunch of cows."

"*Two* cowboys," Mulberry amended.

"An honest mistake, sir," said Evinrude.

"What kind of excuse is that?"

"The lieutenant's right," said Mulberry. "The brass won't like it. By the time the escort gets here, there'll probably be word up along the line, and the escort commander . . ."

It took a few moments for the implications to sink in.

"My *commission*!" cried Clark. "I'll end up in *chains*."

Which made Jimson realize the kind of shape *he'd* be in. "You better get the hell out of here, sir," he urged.

Gunner Foreman didn't like the drift. "'Scuse me, sir. That

30

still doesn't make it any less Indian country up there. I think we'd better wait."

"Damn the Indians. We'll travel at night, sleep forted up by day. Indians don't attack at night."

"The hell they don't, sir," argued Foreman. "They don't *charge* at night. *No one* does, horse is apt to step in a goddamn hole. But they love to *raid* at night. Sneak up and cut your goddamn *throat*."

"To hell with them," Clark practically screamed. "We're armed, we've got the Gatling, we're *going*."

The gun crew exchanged worried looks.

"Now let's go find some horses and move on out."

Before they could move, though, a stranger spoke to them. He seemed to come out of nowhere. "Couldn't help overhearing. You soldiers are headed north?"

The recruits, who had started for the train, now edged back.

Foreman waited for Clark to answer, but in vain. "Yep," the gunner said.

"We're expecting an escort," said Clark.

"Ah. Better yet. Due soon?"

"Already due," Foreman said dourly.

"I see," said the stranger, drawing it out. He rubbed his dark, stubbly chin. He had real dark skin, in the dim station light, but the cast of his face was white. His eyes were hardly visible due to a squint. Black vest, plain shirt, denim britches, fancy boots, fancier spurs, one Colt slung haunch-high on the right, another stuffed in his belt. He carried a Henry repeater in one fist. His face, besides being a white man's and squinty-eyed, was kind of ugly, hard and unpleasant, a lot of angles, all wrong, and heavily scarred. Greasy hair poked out from under his Stetson. He might have been a buffalo hunter—he smelled like one—or a trapper or a scout or almost anything. What he definitely was, was another gun for the trip. "Name's Scarborough. Creed Scarborough. Scout, Indian fighter, you name it, I done it."

Jimson leaned close to Mulberry and said gruffly, "Heap big medicine."

Mulberry didn't think he was funny and didn't answer. He saw the man as a killer. An Indian-killer, maybe, but still a killer. It almost made Mulberry shudder. He was not a physically courageous man.

"Well, Mr. Scarborough . . ." Clark began indecisively.

"Creed, if you don't mind. Now it seemed to me you was headin' out anyway, escort or no escort, ain't that right? Headed north? Fort Smith? Keogh?" Clark's eyes gave it away. "Well, I know the way, the ol' Bozeman. Was closed for a long time, due to Indians, but it's open agin now. I can point you in the right direction. And these ain't toys I'm packin'. . . ."

"Well . . . Creed . . . I guess that will be a suitable arrangement." Relief swept over Lieutenant Clark—a problem met and conquered. "So, anytime you're ready."

"You get your horses. There's a livery just down the street that the army deals with. Wake the ol' bastard up, and I'll meet you there after I clear up some business." He grinned. "Say goodbye to a sweet little lady."

Just then the train started moving and Jimson, Mulberry and Evinrude had to hustle to get aboard.

When they looked back, the squat, heavy bodies of Foreman and Willoughby somehow managed to speak their despair; they couldn't make out the faces.

"They got themselves a good guide, anyway," opined Jimson.

Mulberry couldn't find a way to argue with that, but now that he'd met the real West, and somehow Scarborough was "real" to him, he found it made him nervous.

At noon the next day, the Union Pacific train chugged into Como. During the night it had gone due west, south of the Black Hills, then started northwesterly, passing through Laramie and a passel of other towns before it turned west again to cross the Laramie Plains.

It was pretty high up on those plains, considered part of the Rockies, and the air was thin, taking some getting used to. And at night it was damn chilly. The recruits bound for Easy Company had a fitful night of sleep and were stiffer than railroad ties when the sun finally came up behind them and began to warm things up.

"How much further we gotta go?" grumbled Jimson, still curled up on a seat.

"Orders say Medicine Bow," said Evinrude, scanning them once more to be sure. "That's the next stop. This here's Como we're coming into."

"How come you know so much?" asked Trash.

"I asked around. I couldn't sleep too good."

"That's 'cause your old bones don't bend as good as mine."

"You're not stiff?"

"Hell, no—" He tried sitting up. "Jesus!"

Evinrude grinned.

"Where's Mulberry?"

"He didn't sleep at all, not a-tall, till about an hour ago when he almost fell over. He's down at the front of the car. Worried something fierce, he is."

"How come?"

A conductor came through shouting "Como." Mulberry sat up suddenly and almost fell into the aisle. He blinked, then stood up and stomped to the rear, moving as if to stir some life into dead limbs. "He say Medicine Bow?"

"No. Como. Next stop's ours." Evinrude checked the orders again.

"Hope those orders are better than the ones the gun crew had."

"Warn't nothing wrong with them orders," said Jimson as the train ground to a halt. "Somethin' wrong with the *escort*."

They were settling down for one last snooze when the coach door opened and a soldier entered, a first lieutenant. "You the gun crew?"

Jimson's eyes snapped open. Then he shot to his feet. "Ahten*shun*!" And he grinned, snapping up a salute, as Evinrude and Mulberry fumbled their way to a standing position.

"I said, are you the gun crew?" the officer repeated.

Jimson's hand slowly slid down to his side as Mulberry, whose head throbbed painfully from having stood up so suddenly, said, "The Gatling crew? No sir, they got off at Cheyenne."

"Cheyenne?"

"That's what the orders said. Lieutenant Clark had me read them just in case he'd made a mistake."

"*He'd* made a mistake?! Those bumblers back East, the Department of Army, they can't get anything right. That gun was supposed to come *here*. I've got an escort waiting. Damn!"

He stood there fuming.

"Excuse me, sir," said Mulberry. "*We're* supposed to be getting off at Medicine Bow . . ."

"What for? Nobody gets off at Medicine Bow. Where you headed?"

Evinrude scanned the orders. "Outpost Nine. Easy Company."

The train started with a jolt. The lieutenant jumped and

33

pulled a chain and the train stopped with another jolt. "You get off right here, damnit. *This* is where you pick up horses."

"Horses?" queried Jimson.

"Yeah. You do know how to ride, don't you?"

"Like an Indian," claimed Jimson.

"Oh, yeah? Well, then, try not to kill your horse. They don't grow on trees. Now get your stuff and let's get off."

An hour later, Jimson, Mulberry, and Evinrude were astride horses, riding north in the company of Lieutenant Bracken and a ten-man escort, plus a tarp-covered wagon.

"You'll stay with us awhile," said Lieutenant Bracken, "then I'll have a couple of soldiers take you to Outpost Nine."

"Aren't you going to go get that gun crew?"

"I telegraphed headquarters. Someone else will."

"What's the wagon for, sir?"

Bracken shrugged. "We weren't sure what was involved with this Gatling, what kind of extras they were bringing."

Evinrude nodded and looked around slowly. Couldn't see much, not east anyway; they were riding next to an embankment. But he didn't care. He was sleepy and bored.

"What brought you West, soldier—Evinrude, isn't it?"

Evinrude thought for a moment, and then, as his mouth was opening to reply, he saw a hole magically appear in the middle of Lieutenant Bracken's forehead. Then, simultaneously it seemed, Bracken's eyes opened wide, his head snapped back, his campaign hat went flying, and a resounding *crack!* reached Evinrude's ears.

"Jesus!" breathed Evinrude, staring at the empty space where Bracken had just been.

Bedlam broke out as soldiers scattered for cover, diving from dancing horses, and the air filled with the sounds and smell of battle.

Evinrude's mount started spinning around, seriously spooked. On one go-around, Evinrude saw Mulberry, not too far away, frozen atop his horse, which was standing spraddle-legged, eyes rolling. Then Evinrude was thrown from his horse. The impact brought him to his senses and he started crawling.

But which way to crawl? There were guns going off every which way and the smoke was so dense he could hardly see a thing. Something plowed up loam in front of his nose. He reared up on his knees and the forage cap flew from his head. He dove back down. You couldn't win.

Lieutenant Bracken, fatally lax, had failed to position point and flank men. Thus the attack was a complete surprise and the squad was totally contained. Fortunately, the attack had come from just the one side, the side with cover, and those who weren't hit in the first volley were able to gain some kind of cover of their own and fight back. But they would never have survived a crossfire.

Frequent whoops and cries told them it was an Indian attack, undoubtedly Cheyenne, some small, renegade outfit looking to count some easy coups.

A fire arrow flamed overhead, but missed the wagon. And then another one missed. But two more hit the target and the wagon's canvas tarp slowly burned as the firing became more sporadic. Finally the wagon was a charcoal shell, not giving too much protection to the men still crouched behind it, men who preferred searing heat to bullets.

Some yips and whoops...

And then there was silence....

Mulberry had burrowed in so deep he figured he must have swallowed half the plains. Lord knew, his mouth felt dry enough.

His Schofield S&W .45 had never left its holster.

Those lying with their heads to the ground, like Mulberry, could hear the hoofbeats as the attackers rode off.

Heads began to rise, men slowly got to their feet.

One soldier cautiously climbed the rise and reported that the plains beyond were empty.

They collected themselves, counting the dead.

Three soldiers, besides Bracken, dead. Three wounded, but none very seriously. Jimson and Evinrude survived. Jimson had shot off all his ammo and then used the ammo from a body lying next to him. Evinrude, Civil War vet, had prayed like mad.

Finally someone asked the obvious. "What the hell was that all about? They had us *cold*. And they didn't hang around to finish us off, collect some scalps?"

The speaker, a corporal and squad leader, was truly mystified.

But another soldier grumbled, "Don't complain. Help me load Bracken on his horse...poor bastard."

"That horse won't mind."

"I'm talking about *Bracken*, you idiot."

35

four _____

"Use your reach, Stretch. Jab 'im, jab 'im. *Move*. On your toes."

The man giving the orders was Second Lieutenant Price of Easy Company's First Platoon. He claimed to have done some fighting at the Point and was therefore an authority. The First Platoon's sergeant, Gus Olsen, didn't figure Price could fight his way through wet grama grass. But who was he to tell an officer he was full of it, even if the officer was Price.

The afternoon at Outpost Number Nine had started out boring, which wasn't unusual. If they weren't out campaigning, searching for the elusive Mr. Lo, and then fighting like hell to keep from getting killed, they were being bored to death.

All the petty details First Sergeant Cohen could think of had been taken care of, and then some. A private could practically *eat* off the stable floor; the dirt and dust in the mess were usually unbeatable, but noonday grub presented a soup that for once was not covered with a grit-slick; the orderly room looked like it came straight out of a catalogue; the tack room's leather was shiny and supple; you could see your reflection in the Company shovels; the blacksmith had so much wood laid in, he could barely move around the smithy.

It sometimes got absurd. The previous day a new enlisted latrine had been dug. A First Platoon private, Wolfgang Holzer, felt like he'd dug it all by himself, and since his co-diggers had been Malone and Spuds Felson, he probably had. In any event, once the latrine was set up and ready for use, Holzer

36

had eyed the first man waiting in line and advised with glum solemnity, "Pliss. Do not use, pliss. You use diss vun und vee haff to dig annuzzer."

So, faced with boredom, idle hands, and a restive company, Ben Cohen had come up with a boxing tournament. It was not a new idea. It seemed that any time the top kick could not think of a way to keep them busy, he came up with a boxing tournament. All it meant was that a lot of privates would end the day hurting.

It was a natural diversion for Cohen. When it came to fisticuffs, he was accepted as top dog in the Company. And he kept his rep in the course of maintaining discipline.

Companies generally liked to avoid courts-martial. Besides the red tape involved, it looked bad on the company's record; sloppy command. So most companies, Easy included, preferred to wash their own linen.

Usually that involved strenuous physical exercises—pushups until arms were like wet noodles, walking guard in full battle regalia plus pack and two rifles. But there were rare times when the subject resisted the company's punishment, actually *defied* the top kick (and this was distinct from the army regulation that allowed a man to quietly refuse company punishment and demand a court-martial, which regulation, though theoretically sound, didn't work anyway, because the first sergeant would merely say, "All right, Private, but you're restricted to quarters until the court-martial is convened." And then, after a month restricted to quarters, the court-martial would be forgotten).

In any case, when met with defiance, Sergeant Cohen invited the subject out behind the woodshed, so to speak.

During the boxing tournaments, though, Cohen remained benignly above it all. He supervised. And, if the truth be known, made mental note of weaknesses. He'd been able to reduce the Third Platoon's prime troublemaker, Skokowski, to abject whimpering simply by knowing that Skokowski, who had a head and jaw of Pennsylvania granite, couldn't take a body punch. Ben had bored right in, pounding the gut and ribcage.

At the moment he was noting that Stretch Dobbs didn't have the foggiest notion of what to do with his amazing reach, besides hanging it out in front. He was vulnerable under it. Combine that with lousy footwork and . . . Cohen quit making

37

mental notes. The day that Private Dobbs refused his well-earned punishment would be the day Sitting Bull learned how to crochet.

"Dance," cried Lieutenant Price. "Dance!"

Cohen had to laugh. Stretch had two left feet, and together with the recent injury to his 'delicates,' well . . . He wasn't doing badly, though, stumbling around in a circle, keeping his left almost touching Broadhurst's nose. . . .

Broadhurst kept trying to duck under Stretch's lead and flail away at his midsection, and maybe slip a few in below the belt—*he* knew where Stretch was tender. But every time he tried to get under, Stretch would leap back, stabbing down at Broadhurst's head. Broadhurst couldn't have reached him with a ten-foot pole.

The men grouped around the rough square were laughing. Lieutenant Price was beside himself. He'd *coached* Private Dobbs and they were *laughing*. Broadhurst was from the Third Platoon and Lieutenant Smiley was in his corner. Price found Smiley a bit overbearing. Smiley'd come up from the ranks. Price wished he'd go back down. If Broadhurst got in a lucky punch . . .

And just then, Broadhurst *did* get in a lucky punch. Stretch, dancing backwards as always, tripped and flung his arms wide to regain his lost balance. Broadhurst dove in, whacked at the gut, and then hooked a left onto Stretch's nose.

Stretch went backwards even faster, righted himself, sensed blood streaming from his nose, and let out a fearsome cry. He rushed Broadhurst, flailing like a windmill. Broadhurst tried stepping inside the wide, wild swings, but Stretch, finding Broadhurst so conveniently close, simply started pounding him on the top of his head.

Stretch's strength was just decent in repose, but prodigious when aroused. Broadhurst began to get shorter. He tried to back off, crouching, but Stretch stayed right with him, steadily reducing his height. Until Broadhurst folded completely, sitting on the ground, covering the top of his head with his gloves.

"Knockout!" screamed Lieutenant Price, leaping across the "ring."

The ref, Second Platoon's Sergeant Chubb, said, "I'm not so sure."

"Well, I am, *Sergeant*."

Rank did have its privileges, thought Chubb.

38

"The hell it is," said Lieutenant Smiley. "My man's not near finished."

Broadhurst gave Smiley a look, and then immediately fell over on his side.

Cohen, grinning, said, "Begging your pardon, Mr. Smiley, but it looks like Private Broadhurst's had enough. He may have to fight Mr. Lo some day, remember."

Smiley could only scowl. After all, it was Cohen's tournament.

Just then, there was a shout from the guard above the main gate. "Riders approaching."

The men started scrambling, hoping for a war party. Things were really boring.

"How many?" yelled Cohen.

"Five."

The scrambling slowed to staggers. Pretty damned small war party.

The front gate was opened and the five riders entered. Jimson, Evinrude, and Mulberry looked around at their new home.

"This is a *fort*," said Evinrude. They'd only seen the one eastern side when approaching.

"Sure looks like it, don't it?" agreed Jimson.

"Only regimental headquarters and above rate the title 'fort,'" explained Mulberry.

Jimson glared at him. Bloody know-it-all. Every step of the way he'd had to listen to Mulberry lecture on various features of the countryside, even all the different types of *grass*, for crying out loud—gama, buffalo, bunch grass, even something called cheat grass that wasn't near as good as it looked when it first came up nice and green. Jeez. Trash now knew more than he'd ever wanted to know.

Mulberry even said the Indians that attacked them weren't wearing the right color warpaint, that Cheyenne liked certain colors, Sioux other colors, stuff like that, and that the Indians who'd attacked them were wearing mixed colors. Christ. Maybe they'd run out of the right colors.

Besides, how come he was the only one who saw anything? Hell, probably because he was sittin' up on his horse like a dunce when everyone else dove for cover. "I seen you back there in that fight, mister. You're some fighter, you are."

What had brought that on, wondered Mulberry, and he sought an appropriate response. "Second lieutenants are the

39

only ones called 'mister.' You'd better watch that."

Evinrude, looking around, could have sworn he saw a couple of men wearing what looked suspiciously like boxing gloves. He wondered about it. Like many back East, he'd heard the expression 'punching cows.' . . .

"We'd better report," he suggested.

"Where?" asked Jimson.

"I guess over where that sergeant's standing looking at us. The one with the three stripes. Guess he's the top kick."

"He looks big," said Trash.

"*And* mean—let's go."

They rode toward the orderly room.

"Holy Christ, do you see what I see?" Trash's tone of near-reverence was one usually reserved for high-class brothels.

Flora Conway, the captain's lady, was standing outside the CO's quarters, watching the new men ride up. Though in her late thirties, she was still a stunning beauty and her age didn't show until you were up close. Real close. She kept out of the sun and her complexion was like cream.

"Kin you 'magine what her tits must look like?" croaked Trash.

Evinrude swallowed. Mulberry choked.

Her hair was swept high, her breasts pushed up, and her ground-length dress clung to her slim figure. Trash could hardly be blamed.

The welcoming smile she showed them, small but visible, was seen by Trash as one of invitation.

Since Flora was childless, she'd naturally come to regard the men of Easy Company as her "family." She mothered them, calling all "dear" indiscriminately, and there wasn't a soldier on that post who wouldn't have traded his own blood mother for her.

Victorian-bred, from Maryland, her proper public reserve was usually enough to dampen the misguided ardor of anyone save those driven near-frenzied with lust. Into which category Trash fell naturally.

"God, kin you 'magine that b'tween sheets?" drooled Trash.

"Can you imagine yourself facing a firing squad at dawn?" inquired Mulberry dryly. "That's almost certainly an officer's wife, no enlisted man's toy."

"A woman's a woman, me bucko," replied Trash. "Never

seen an officer what owned a pecker worth salutin'." He grinned.

"Did I hear you right, soldier?"

They'd arrived at the orderly room. Trash looked down to the side. His distraction had been such that he'd been unaware of anything except Flora. Now he found himself nailed by the hard gray gaze of Lieutenant Matt Kincaid. Just one look at Matt, and Trash told himself that this man was *all* pecker.

"No sir!" cried Trash. "At least, sir, I don't see how you *coulda*—" His mind raced, searching for a way out. "—We was jes' discussin' our last stopover?... 'fore comin' on out here?... havin' a *peck'a* trouble in this here *saloon*?..."

Kincaid's eyes narrowed, but he didn't say anything.

He's gonna buy it, thought Trash, he's *gotta* buy it. A firing squad at dawn, that wasn't no joke.

Kincaid still stared. Finally he said, "Go on in."

Relief washed over Trash and he hit the ground lickety-split, trying to salute while still airborne. But by the time he'd landed, Kincaid had already turned away and was heading into the orderly room. Kincaid was the company adjutant and had an office next to Captain Conway's.

The three men entered the orderly room; Evinrude and Mulberry were careful to let a little distance grow between them and Jimson.

Sergeant Cohen was hunched up in a forbidding manner behind his desk. When you hunch up a man Cohen's size and add a heavy scowl, it's forbidding. He'd caught a little of the discussion outside through the open door. He hadn't heard what led up to it, but he'd heard Kincaid, and Matt didn't use that tone of voice very often. Only when he was about to kill.

Cohen thrust out a hand and Evinrude was extending the travel orders when Jimson came to attention, threw up yet another salute, and hollered, "Elmer 'Trash' Jimson reporting as ordered, *sir*, but Trash is the one I prefer, *sir*!"

Cohen's eyes widened, and Evinrude and Mulberry cringed. Cohen then slid into a momentary posture of weary resignation as a voice from the adjutant's office said, "Jesus Christ Almighty."

Cohen finally looked up, saying, "You men *did* receive some roody-mentary training before comin' out here, didn't you?" Then his voice began to rise. "I am *not* an *officer*. I am

41

a sergeant. You do *not* address NCOs as 'sir,' you got that?"

Jimson nodded vigorously. Evinrude and Mulberry edged a little farther away.

"And where do you two think you're going?" snapped Cohen, nailing them to the floor.

He flicked the papers, the orders. "Privates Elmer Jimson...Elmer...Privates Trash Jimson, James Evinrude, and...Edward Mulberry the *Third*?" his voice rising at the end. "And how do *you* want to be called?"

"Edward Mulberry, Sarge, and—" descending to a mumble— "you can drop 'the Third.'"

Cohen took a deep breath.

"Welcome to Easy Company. If you keep your mouth shut and your ears open you'll find us firm but fair. If you fuck up you can give your soul to Jesus because your ass will belong to *me*! I am Sergeant Cohen and I am the first soldier. When I say froggy I expect you to jump. If you think you can whup me I'll be glad to take off my stripes and show you the error of your ways. If you're ready to soldier, go over to the kitchen and tell them I said to coffee and grub you before you report to your squad leader."

They turned and started moving out the door.

"Hold it!" They stopped and turned. Sergeant Cohen eyed them. His voice did not sweeten easily, but he tried. "You would like to know what squad leader you are to report to, wouldn't you?"

They stood dumbly.

"I'm putting you in the Second Squad of the First Platoon—"

From the adjutant's office came a weary "Oh, shit."

"Your squad leader's name is Corporal Wilson. Your platoon sergeant is Sergeant Olsen. Your platoon leader is Second Lieutenant Price. And—" now he smiled—"your adjutant, the officer you've already met, Lieutenant Kincaid, he usually rides with the First Platoon. Any questions?"

"Yeah, Sarge," said Jimson. "How soon can I transfer out?"

The query was so bold, so absurd, the first sergeant had to smile. "Also, you will keep your eyes on the bulletin board posted outside this door. The various details are posted there every evening, no later than five...guard, KP, stable...*latrine*.... You boys keep your eyes on that list—your names will appear there very, very soon." He waved them out.

They stood outside the orderly room, hanging onto their duffels.

"Now where?" asked Trash. "Seems he coulda told us."

"Over there, left," said Mulberry. "Barracks. Mess. Kitchen's probably down there in that far corner."

"I shoulda known," said Jimson, shouldering his bag.

"These posts are usually laid out the same," said Mulberry. "I made a study of it. Like over there, by the gate, under the lookout tower, that'll be the guardhouse—"

"Your home away from home, Trash," said Evinrude, "you keep it up."

"You guys," sneered Trash. "You gotta get smart. They *like* their men with a little salt. You saw Cohen smile there at the end, didn't you?"

"He was just glad to be rid of us," suggested Mulberry.

They strode across the parade toward the mess and barracks.

An hour later they came out of the mess, full of soup and bread and coffee, to find the boxing tournament under way again.

Stretch had retired undefeated. His testicles were acting up. Of course, his only opponent had been Broadhurst, who was nursing a headache. At the moment, Malone was pounding the stuffing out of the Third Platoon's Private O'Reilly, who laid his glasses aside for the occasion and could barely see Malone. Felt him plenty, though. Lieutenant Smiley's eyes were glazing over. But he had his biggest man, Thompson, waiting in the wings—"Trouble" Thompson.

O'Reilly went down again and decided to stay there.

Lieutenant Price beamed at Malone. True, he'd never had to coach Malone, just unleash him, but glory still reflected.

"Who've you got next, Mr. Price?" asked Smiley with unnerving sweetness.

But Price wasn't paying attention to such shadings of tone. "I think Weatherby's about ready," he said blithely, motioning forward a tall young man with lank, flaxen hair.

Weatherby brushed the hair from his eyes. "I am?"

"Get the gloves on, son." There weren't many Price could call "son," but Weatherby was one of them.

"I've got . . . Thompson," said Smiley.

Weatherby did an about-face, but the rest of his platoon wouldn't let him escape. And the two fighters laced up.

Evinrude looked on with interest. Trouble Thompson reminded him of a horse he'd once owned. Same size. Probably the same disposition. Evinrude had once had to stop the horse with a kick and discipline him with a sledgehammer right.

The fighters were bare to the waist. Alex Weatherby was hairless, but Thompson had enough for both of them.

The fight went on for as long as Weatherby's legs held out. But finally Weatherby's friends, and members of the Second Platoon, all real sportsmen, caught hold of Alex and threw him at the frustrated and enraged Thompson.

Thompson practically lifted Weatherby off the ground with a flurry of body punches, snapped his head every which way with another quick series of hooks and crosses, and finally slipped a sneaky elbow to the jaw that sent Weatherby to dreamland.

There was a reason for the elbow. With Weatherby lying at his feet, Thompson loudly complained, "You can't do nothing, wearing these here pillows."

"Knucks!" arose shouts from the Second Platoon. "Bare knuckles!" The Second Platoon was not fighting on this day, so their enthusiasm for "knucks" was understandable.

"Sounds okay," said Sergeant Cohen, interest rekindled.

Thompson stripped the gloves off with a roar and awaited his next opponent, or victim. McElroy, a onetime Boston cop, was selected but was quickly retired with a closing eye. Four more opponents followed in quick order. The First Platoon was getting decimated.

"Don't forget us," shouted Trash Jimson in Lieutenant Price's ear.

Price jumped a foot, came down as Trash was belatedly yelling "sir," and demanded, "Who the hell are you, soldier?"

"New men, sir. We're in your platoon."

"Are you now?" oozed Price. "And who might you be?"

"Private Trash Jimson, sir." Evinrude added his name more quietly. Mulberry disappeared.

"I've got Private Jimson here, Mr. Smiley. Who've you got?"

"Why, I've still got Thompson. He hasn't been beaten, has he?"

"Isn't he tired?"

"If he'd had to do any fighting he might be," said Smiley, and laughed.

Price launched Trash toward Thompson with the hoarse advice, "Try to dig one in his balls."

All Trash dug was the ground. He didn't know how to run away, or even back off. He gave Thompson's ribs a rattling, making the man wince, but kept being knocked down. *And* kept getting back up.

On his ninth trip to the turf he was grabbed by the ref, Sergeant Chubb, and pinned down. "TKO," said Chubb.

"That's it," called Sergeant Cohen. "Save him. I've got plans for that boy."

"Now who?" wondered Price, his voice barely audible.

"I'd like to give it a try, sir," said Evinrude.

Price looked at him a bit more closely. "Aren't you a bit old for this kind of thing, soldier?"

Old? Evinrude leveled a hard look at him. Price waved him forward.

Evinrude shed his shirt. His muscular torso seemed covered with scars. Some were old gunshot wounds. Others were knife slashes. He took a deep breath. It'd been a long time. That ambush had caught him by surprise. But now he was beginning to feel like his old self.

He moved to meet Thompson. He flicked out a jab that Thompson seemed to duck his head into. Then another, and another.

Sweat flew from Thompson's head in a fine spray. Thompson got mad and came in swinging.

Evinrude caught most of the blows on his shoulders and arms. But some slipped through. And Thompson could hit.

Evinrude leaned in close and worked on the body, and then he tied him up.

Chubb stepped in. "Okay, let's not have too much of that stuff."

Evinrude stepped back. He was inclined to adopt the classic boxing stance, but felt it might be a tip-off, so he waited with his fists held in at his chest.

He started popping Thompson from long range again. Until the man once more got mad and charged, after which they fought at close quarters and then waltzed each other around.

They separated. Evinrude smiled to himself. He thought he had Thompson's rhythm now, and figured he knew how long it would take before he'd charge.

Finally, Thompson dropped his head a fraction and launched forward. But Evinrude was ready. For a second, Thompson's head and chin were out leading the charge, one fist coming around in a wide arc and the other one cocking, and in that brief second his chin encountered Evinrude's short, straight right.

Thompson dropped like a ton of buffalo chips.

Evinrude looked amazed. "Hey," he said, "I only stuck my fist out, tryin' to slow him down. He ran right into it. He's not *hurt*, is he? He's probably just exhausted."

The exhausted Thompson was out for ten minutes.

Smiley then sent man after man, each more reluctant than the preceding, at Evinrude. Evinrude sent them all back, consistently baffled by his own amazing luck.

Cohen had watched closely, beginning to get itchy. The man might be a good match. Ben didn't often get directly involved in these things, just on occasion to set the record straight, or teach a lesson. This might be such an occasion.

He didn't think Evinrude was just lucky. Not that many men in succession would have thrown their heads and guts at his fists, even though Evinrude was always retreating, seemingly on the run. No, the man was clearly a good counterpuncher. But still a brawler. A "natural" maybe, with good instincts, but without schooling in the finer points. Which didn't mean a lot of dancing around, for that was not Ben Cohen's style, but rather how to get your knockout blows through a good defense, or draw a counter-puncher onto the offensive. For instance, throwing a lead right that misses, but when the opponent then throws his own right at the exposed target, stepping inside and hooking over that right to the chin. Especially easy if the other guy drops his shoulder when throwing that right. If he doesn't, digging to the body.

He hadn't seen Evinrude doing any of those things.

Of course, Evinrude hadn't had to, but Ben Cohen, in his hunger, in his eagerness to demonstrate the science of *punching* if not boxing, overlooked that little point.

He pushed through the ring of soldiers. "You're not getting much competition, are you, Evinrude?"

"Almost more than I can handle, Sarge," replied Evinrude, pawing the ground as if in embarrassment, foolish behavior in a man no longer young. He'd reached the age where a man should know what he could and couldn't do and faced up to it. At least that's the way it was out West. Maybe it was different back East, but in the Western territories false modesty could earn you bullets buzzing by your ears, and that was only if the man encouraged by your modesty was a bad shot.

Though his eyes and intelligence told him differently, Ben Cohen automatically took the man at his word. Maybe it *was* luck of a kind. "Well, since I haven't had a workout for a while, why don't I try that luck on for size."

In the back of the crowd, where he was still well hidden, Mulberry suppressed a grin. Up front, Jimson laughed out loud.

"What the hell are you laughing at, soldier?" demanded Cohen.

"Oh, Christ, *nothin'*, Sarge, really *nothin'*."

"Ain't you had no sense pounded into you yet?"

"Yep. Sure have, Sarge. Yep. Yes indeedy."

Ben Cohen stripped to the waist. His bulk and fatless musculature even bettered Evinrude, but he sadly lacked scars. A few places where the skin puckered, courtesy of two bullets and one arrow, but compared to Evinrude's battle-scarred body it was as smooth as a young gal's tit. Just as white, too, attesting to the fact he was the top sergeant, that he rarely left the post on patrols in the scorching sun and damn sure never stripped down to dig holes. "I'll take it easy on you, Evinrude. That is, unless you happen to slip in a few lucky punches."

Cohen was about to get the show rolling when he heard Trash taking bets, making book. Even with the odds three, four, or five to one in Cohen's favor, promising a small payoff, the men were backing him . . . and that was nice, real nice . . . but Jimson was taking every bet and calling for more. How the hell was he going to pay off? It gave Cohen pause. He eyed Evinrude. "You gonna bet?"

"Good Lord no, Sarge. The man's insane." And, to be honest, he did appear to be considerably upset by Jimson's hustling.

Cohen nodded and threw an overhand right.

Evinrude took it on the cheek but rode with it, cushioning the blow.

Cohen snapped out two quick lefts and came in under, but Evinrude slid away to the side. Cohen turned to follow and caught two quick lefts himself, right on the snoot.

Cohen kept waiting for Evinrude to lead, to throw that right—or even a left—and maybe drop a shoulder so he could

47

hook over it and show the old boy something. But Evinrude never did, at least not for a while, content to pop away with lefts and keep moving. He moved surprisingly well for a big man. But then, Cohen did too.

Finally Evinrude did throw his right—Cohen had given him an irresistible target—but he didn't drop his shoulder hardly at all and the heavy blow Cohen countered with, slipping Evinrude's right and leaning in and hooking over, glanced up off Evinrude's brow. It was enough to make Evinrude back away fast, shaking his head, but not square enough to down him. But Cohen had his man, now. He moved in.

Evinrude stood his ground, ducked under a left lead, and pounded a right to Cohen's ribs. Cohen dropped his elbow in, protecting the ribs, but still pawed with the left hand. Evinrude quickly shot a right over that feeble, pawing left, caught the chin flush, and the Fourth of July went off in Ben Cohen's head.

Evinrude looked stricken as Cohen went to his knees. But when Cohen went that far and no further, Evinrude marveled. The blow that had shaken hell out of a horse had only sent Cohen to his knees, dazed. And now Jim Evinrude was confused. What was worse, knocking out the top sergeant or finding out that the damn man was nearly indestructible?

Sergeant Cohen dimly realized that Evinrude had neatly suckered him; he'd drawn his guard down and crossed over *his* left. The bastard *did* know how to fight. Him and that bastard Jimson, they'd suckered the whole damn company.

Sergeant Cohen got to his feet amid a deathly silence, except for Jimson jumping up and down and yammering.

Evinrude spied Mulberry beyond the inner circle. Ed Mulberry looked alarmed and was shaking his head slowly.

Cohen suddenly came at him, and from then on it was a bloody, knock-down-drag-out battle. Evinrude concentrated his heaviest blows on the body while Cohen was head-hunting. Evinrude hurt and weakened the top kick, but Cohen was the one who drew blood.

The pace slowed. Cohen no longer bothered protecting his head. Why Evinrude wasn't going for it he didn't know, but he wasn't about to complain. It was his midsection against Evinrude's jaw, a jaw that the term "iron" didn't really begin to describe.

Finally, Sergeant Cohen saw an opening. Evinrude must have known he was wide open and seen the blow coming, but he couldn't seem to get out of the way. The blow landed flush and Evinrude went down and the goddamn biggest collective sigh went up that one could imagine.

Evinrude woke up in the barracks. Other members of Easy's First Platoon were there, but only Mulberry and Jimson crouched by the bunk.

"Finally," said Jimson, "he's awake. Jesus Christ, Jim, what the hell did you think you were doing? I'm broke. And *then* some. I owe most of next month's pay, too. Ten miserable dollars out of a miserable thirteen."

Evinrude looked at him. Boy, the sympathy was really gushing out. "Ed. Hand me my sack, will you?"

Mulberry reached the duffel for him and Evinrude dug into it. He came out with money, counted out ten dollars, which didn't leave him much, and gave the sum to Trash. "Sorry, Trash, I done my best. Take care of them debts."

Trash grabbed the money, looked at it for a second, then said, "Boy, Jim, you look like hell." And then he was gone.

Evinrude adjusted his position, groaned, and said, "It ain't my fault he bet. And it wasn't my idea for the sarge to fight."

Mulberry said gently, "I understand, Jim. You did the right thing."

"The only thing I could have done," said Evinrude, half-rising.

Mulberry nodded. "Can't beat the first sergeant and expect a decent life, not even in that kind of fight."

"How do I look?"

"As Trash said, like hell."

Evinrude lay back muttering, "With this face, that's no big difference." Then he rose up again, pushing his face close to Mulberry's, making Mulberry flinch involuntarily. "But I could have beaten him, Ed—"

"Shhhhh." The less said the better.

"But I could have."

"I know, I know," said Mulberry hoarsely. "Ten different times. I'm a student of the art."

"You?!"

"I said *student*. I didn't say I fought. But I know boxing. You had him cold, anytime you wanted."

Evinrude lay back, a smile growing. "I hope his ribs hurt as much as my head."

"Hey, Evinrude." Trash came up grinning. "Guess what?

You gotta dig a latrine tomorrow. All by your lonesome."

"That bad?"

"Don't sound like fun."

"What have *you* got?"

Trash's face fell. "Stables. Guess that means horseshit."

"Guess it does. Well, what the hell, latrines have gotta be dug and horses followed around with a shovel by *someone*."

Wolfgang Holzer was seated across the room. He hadn't heard much, and what little he'd heard he hadn't understood completely—English was a hard language—but "latrine" he knew. "Effenrood," he called. "Dot Sergeant Cone, he luff you. I'm digging latrine already. Yoost opened yessertag... yessertag?... yesserday. He make you dig speziale latrine. Yah, he sure luff you."

five ─────────────

By nine o'clock the next morning, Evinrude was already thigh-deep in the hole he was digging. At the moment he was toiling in the shadow of what he thought of as "Holzer's latrine," but soon the sun would rise up over the low wooden structure and then it'd be fun. His head still ached some, but mostly it was surface pain, bruised and discolored flesh about the eyes and especially his cheekbones. He looked up to watch a bird circle overhead and then fly off. He'd have to learn what kind of birds they had in Wyoming. Mulberry probably knew already; he'd ask him. The bird was gone. He bent back to his task.

Sergeant Cohen came out of the enlisted mess, took a long, slow look around the parade—it was empty—and then moved very slowly and carefully over to where Evinrude was digging.

He stood at the edge of the hole. Evinrude glanced up at him, then back down. Cohen opened his mouth to speak several times, but no words came. Finally he said, "Don't dig too deep, Private, the Chinese might complain."

Evinrude paused, but decided not to grin.

Cohen raised his head and eyed the sun that was rising fast. It'd be damn hot soon, High Plains or no. He studied the far wall. Finally he muttered, "You hurtin' as much as me?"

Evinrude didn't have to be hit over the head with an olive branch to recognize it. "I figger you got the worst. It's only my face, and the only thing I use that for is smiling and I haven't had anything to smile about. You gimme that body of yours to work on, I don't figger you slept too well last night."

"I didn't sleep at all," said Cohen, flat out. "Every time I turned, it hurt worse...." And it didn't feel too good standing up, either. He sighed and, with an effort, brought himself to ask, "Why didn't you put me away when you had the chance?"

Evinrude didn't look up. "What makes you think I could?"

"'Cause I been thinkin' about it, and you could've."

Evinrude still didn't look up. "Maybe...but a soldier doesn't even *try* to put the first sergeant away, unless he's stupid."

"Huh...I see.... Well, now you know what *I* think about that fight...but if I hear that anyone else knows what I think, you'll be diggin' a goddamn *moat* around this post...you and that Jimson. I don't know how many times you an' him have worked that scam...."

"Hey, Sergeant." Evinrude looked up, his red face showing anger even if he didn't feel it. "I *lost*, remember?"

Sergeant Cohen stared down at him, then turned on his heel and hobbled away.

Ten minutes later, Privates Malone and Felson showed up at the pit, Spuds toting a shovel.

Malone said, "First sergeant wants you in the orderly room, fast, Evinrude, and I pity your ass— Hey! You ain't got this hole even part dug."

Evinrude climbed out of the pit, handing Malone his shovel. "How much money you win yesterday, soldier?"

"Name's Malone. And I won some. Why?"

"'Cause me and this punched-up face won it for you, so shut up." And he walked off.

The moment Evinrude stepped into the orderly room, Cohen said, "Bradshaw, run over to the mess and drink some coffee until I call you back."

Bradshaw left. Cohen hoisted himself slowly out of his chair, went to a cabinet and opened it, and took out a bottle and a couple of grimy, mismatched glasses. "How much?"

"Whatever you can pour, I can drink."

"Where're you from?"

"Maine."

"Mmmm, gets cold. Bit of juice warms you up."

"You've been there, have you?"

"Been through. Where'd you learn to fight?"

"Army. In the War. Found out I was good. I was a champeen for a while."

"Who with?"

"Meade. Then Grant."

"Didn't fight much, then, I'll bet."

"Beg pardon?"

"I meant *boxin'*.... So how come you're still a private?"

"Not still. *Again*. I got out, went home, after a while things happened, here I am again."

"What things?"

Evinrude pursed his lips, sipped his drink.

"The law lookin' for you?" pursued Cohen.

"Don't think so."

Cohen made no further comment on the subject. Instead, he said, "It ain't a bad life out here." He sipped at his drink. "Well, now that you been innerduced to the West, how d'ya like it?"

"You mean this fight? I was introduced yesterday."

"How do you mean?"

"That ambush."

"*What* ambush?"

"Didn't you hear? Indians?"

"That was *you*?" He'd heard something, but not much. "Tell me about it."

When Evinrude finished, Cohen got up and put the bottle away. "Go back and rest your face. You may have to tell it again. Kinda doubt it, though. But go by the mess an' tell that lazy Bradshaw to get his ass back here. He ain't gonna goof off on company time. You tell him just that an' watch his eyes."

Evinrude left. He told himself he should be satisfied. A good peace had been made. But he wished the sergeant hadn't asked about possible pursuit from back East. He'd thought a few times about that himself.

Some 2,500 miles east of Wyoming, an elegant carriage was being drawn along the rutted streets of Mellanee, Maine. The spring mud had finally dried, but the ruts were still making travel arduous.

The driver kept his eye out for the local constabulary. He'd been told of a small sign saying "town marshal."

He finally saw it alongside the door of a small, white,

wooden building, one with a high, steeply-pitched roof. The driver leaped down and opened the carriage door. Albert Meyerling got out.

The town marshal, a sturdy man in his forties named Jack Purdy, didn't see many visitors up his way, at least few so elegantly attired. He welcomed this one. But the welcome didn't mean that the visitor was any less suspect. Not so easily did Jack Purdy betray his New England heritage.

"I'm Albert Meyerling."

Purdy pursed his lips.

"From New York City."

Purdy stared expressionlessly.

"My nephew was killed here."

Purdy still waited.

"Phil Meyer?"

"Ah."

"Ah? Ah, what?"

"Ah, yes, Phil Meyer was killed here." He'd been about to offer coffee but decided not to. "Quite some time ago."

"I am a patient man. But my sources have recently told me that the man has scarcely been chased, much less caught and brought to justice."

"He was chased," muttered Purdy. "Chased out of Maine, anyway, but I don't know about that justice."

"And why is that?"

"Your nephew killed a man himself."

"In a fair fight."

"He used an axe handle, mister."

"It was still fair."

"You weren't there." Purdy once more checked out the elegant clothing. "Your nephew was a logger, was he?"

"He was summering here—"

"It was near winter."

"Just an expression. And he'd been here since the summer. He was trying to become a man."

"Didn't make it."

"You dare to be smart?"

"Nope. Stating a fact. And the man that killed your nephew . . ."

"Then you know who did it?"

Purdy thought it over. Old Jim Evinrude was long gone, God knew where, but sure as hell far.

54

"I am not without power, sir," said Meyerling. "I am personally acquainted with the governor of this state. He has promised full cooperation in righting this foul wrong."

"The man that killed your nephew only used his bare hands. And he'd suffered enough. The boy whose skull your nephew split with an axe handle was his son. And if your nephew was still alive, you'd be spendin' your money gettin' him out of prison. His killer just did everyone a favor. Your nephew was a bad piece of work." Purdy hadn't strung that many words together in the preceding six months, maybe more. He felt exhausted.

"I want the name of that man, Marshal."

"Get it from the governor. He's your friend, I ain't."

Meyerling's thin lips smiled coldly. He was the kind of man one underestimated. Despite the patrician features and the faintly sallow complexion, he was a tough man. "I will, sir, with pleasure *and* with ease."

"You're wasting your time. Jim's sure dead by now, or gone to China." But Purdy was wasting *his* time, his breath.

"Least he didn't get the name out of me," he told himself after Meyerling was gone. And he hoped old Jim had covered his tracks.

That same day the early sun lit the eastern slopes of Wyoming's Rockies. Buzzards circled. Their focus was a point on the North Platte wagon road just south of the cutoff to Fort Laramie, which lay some thirty miles to the northeast.

The buzzards dropped, still circling. On the ground lay five bodies, four white men and one black man. The bodies had been stripped down to their underwear, save for one man who'd evidently worn none. Out of one body stuck an arrow. They'd all been scalped. And that was it. No signs of horses, wagons, guns, nothing.

Some twenty five miles north along that cutoff, an armed escort from Fort Laramie had just settled into a fast but not too exhausting pace as it rode south toward the Wagon Road. The escort assignment had been transferred to Laramie since it was closest to the gun crew's adjusted route north.

The officer leading the escort didn't expect to have any trouble finding the gun crew—monster gun and soldiers, hard to miss them—if the timing was right. Which meant reaching the wagon road fork before the gun crew passed. If they didn't, if the gun crew had already passed, then they'd be riding south while the gun crew rode north to their rear, getting farther away every minute, still unguarded. And while Mr. Lo had been quiet of late, the first thing a man learned to expect from the Indian was the unexpected. And a lone gun crew might just provoke the unexpected.

Evinrude's face felt a whole lot better the next day. And Sergeant Olsen said he looked half-human. But when he tried to smile, he found he was not yet fully recovered.

Jimson rolled from the sack saying he never realized horses dumped so much. "You'd think they might wait till they got outside, out in the paddock."

Mulberry groaned, straightening slowly from the sod floor where he'd tracked down a boot. "Wait'll you hit KP. That mess sergeant's a maniac."

"Tasted okay," said Jimson.

"That's because he's a perfectionist."

"How come you're standin' so funny?"

"I may never straighten up again."

"Git any writin' done?"

"I dropped my writing tablet in the water. My fingers had no *feeling* left in them, they couldn't hold onto anything."

The men of the First Platoon were galvanized by the bugler's blowing grub call. All, that is, except Mulberry who, after a full day in the mess, wasn't in any hurry to rush back.

Mess Sergeant Dutch Rothausen's offering of creamed chipped beef was met with something less than ecstasy. It was only the fifth time in the last seven days. Rothausen had the makings of a fine chef. He was mean, demanding, tempestuous, temperamental, and fat. He made sure everyone worked harder than he did, and he worked pretty hard himself. He just didn't have much to work with. Just so many miracles could be fashioned from chipped beef.

He'd tried to plant a vegetable garden once, and did so, but one night he'd been caught dipping into the enlisted latrine for fertilizer. No amount of learned discourse on the advantages of human waste over horse manure could save the garden.

"What this post needs is a vegetable garden," said Mulberry, poking at his chipped beef.

"That's a fine idea," said Evinrude.

"Yeah," agreed Jimson, adding, "Hey, this stuff is good."

They caught several of the other men eyeing them strangely.

After eating, the men had time for a second cup of coffee. At least the coffee was good. Well, strong, anyway, and available twenty-four hours a day. Jimson opined that the coffee was the best he'd ever tasted. And that got him some more looks.

After coffee, the men had time to get back to the barracks for last-minute sprucing before assembly was blown. And then, with the sound of the bugle fouling the air (Bugler Reb McBride had good days and then he had some bad days; he'd had his lip pounded in town three days earlier and it was still sensitive) a race began. Intangible points were to be won by being the first platoon to fall in at attention. Mulberry found himself running faster than he had in several months, just to keep up. And the First Platoon might have been first except that Edward Mulberry III, racing like the wind but blindly, fell in with the wrong platoon.

The officer of the day said "Report" quietly to the First Sergeant, who passed it along a lot louder. Various "allpresentandaccountedfors" rattled around the parade. In time the routine part of assembly was finished; the officers walked off, and Sergeant Cohen addressed the men.

"Right, stand at ease. . . . You men that don't have details, I've got a surprise for you. Reports have reached me that there are *bumps* in the road to HQ." He grinned as the news sank in and groans went up. "So, we're going to have a road-grading party. And then, since this modern army of ours depends on fast communications, and you all know what this past winter did to the telegraph wires and some of the poles—"

"A goddamn bunch of *buffalo* did that, Sarge," cried someone.

"—we're gonna stick up some new poles and string some brand new wire, how's that sound?"

Cohen grinned some more at the hissing and booing his statement elicited.

"Awright, awright," he finally shouted. "Shut up and listen! Privates Jimson, Evinrude, and Mulberry fall out with Sergeant Olsen. The rest of you just hang in."

The three privates joined Olsen and formed up in front of Cohen.

"Olsen, take these men to the armory, have them sign out some rifles, and take them out to the range and see how they shoot."

What they used for a rifle range was about a quarter-mile from the post, a flat two hundred yards to a slight rise, against which they set targets, or pasted new targets over old stands.

Back at the firing line, just in case they didn't already know, Olsen explained the workings of the .45-70, single-shot, "trapdoor" Springfield.

At the end of the Civil War the army found it had a huge number of new muzzle-loading rifles on its hands, which had been made obsolete by the breech-loading cartridge rifles just coming in. Rather than throw all the muskets out, they had them converted to breech-loaders that took cartridges, the only drawback being that they could only take one cartridge at a time. There were any number of conversions of the Springfield rifle—the Miller, the B. S. Roberts, the Mont Storm, the Needham—but the one they had at Outpost Nine was the Allin conversion. Of course, Olsen didn't tell them all that, just showed them how the gun worked.

"How come we ain't got repeaters?" asked Jimson.

"Only ones got repeaters out West are Indians and highwaymen."

"And that's the way it should be," said Lieutenant Matt Kincaid.

Jimson jumped; where'd *he* come from?

"Evens the odds up some," continued Matt. "The last thing the army'd want to do is take unfair advantage of poor Mr. Lo, our local primitive."

"Where'd that Mr. Lo come from, sir?" asked Evinrude.

"Maybe you heard back East, 'Lo, the poor Indian'?"

Mulberry found that information reasonably interesting, but he was a bit more concerned about his own skin. He didn't know if Kincaid was kidding, but the lieutenant's spirit and confidence made him nervous. "Didn't I read, sir," he ventured, "where a commander out here boasted that with just his six hundred men he could whip all the Indians, or local primitives, in the entire Northwest—"

Kincaid dreaded what was coming next.

"—and wasn't that commander General Custer, sir?"

"I believe it was, soldier, except that when Custer got

through splitting his forces, he was facing Crazy Horse and Gall with only 225, and that's different."

"Then Custer could have beaten Crazy Horse and the whole Northwest if he didn't get out-generaled by Mr. Lo in the process, is that it, sir?"

Who the hell recruited this man? wondered Kincaid. "We all have bad days," he said, smiling a wintry smile.

"As I understand it, sir, you generally ride with the First Platoon."

Kincaid stared at Mulberry. "I'll try to keep my bad days to a minimum, if that's what's worrying you."

"It *is* something to think about, sir."

"What concerns *me*, soldier, is how well you can handle that Springfield."

"C'mon," said Sergeant Olsen, and led them the few paces to the firing line. On the way he whispered to Mulberry, "Don't mess with him. He's fair but tough. And he's army, remember that."

Jimson shot first and showed he could hit the target, two out of ten smack-dab in the bullseye.

Evinrude was next, settling himself slowly into the sitting, legs-crossed-and-folded, position. He aimed and fired.

He was dead on, but the Springfield had a nasty kick and his tender face felt it. On subsequent shots he tried holding his face off the gun a mite, but the gun still kicked and hit his face even harder.

"I can see yer face is hurtin', Private," said Olsen, "but you ain't gonna help it that way. Jes' lay yer cheek inta that stock, press it right up agin' yer thumb, that'll be best."

Evinrude cursed under his breath. It was humiliating to be treated like a raw recruit, especially when he knew how to shoot as well as Olsen. If it only didn't hurt so much.

But he swept his mind clear of pain and put the last five shots dead center.

Mulberry's turn. He took his Springfield, sat down, loaded it, aimed, and fired.

"Clean miss."

Evinrude and Jimson looked surprised while Mulberry stared hard down the range. He borrowed Olsen's field glasses, squinted through them, then made ready to shoot again.

"That's a Cheyenne out there, soldier," said Kincaid, "and *he's* shooting at *you*."

Mulberry fired.

"Missed again."

"Goddamnit, soldier," snarled Kincaid, "he's shooting at *me*."

Mulberry fired.

Olsen peered through the glasses, then turned to the lieutenant. "Sorry, sir. You better duck."

"Damnit," said Kincaid, and he snatched the rifle from Mulberry. He grabbed a handful of .45-70 slugs, shoved one home, aimed for a fraction of a second, and fired. Then he reloaded and fired, reloaded and fired, four more times.

Olsen dropped the glasses. "You beat the hell out of that bullseye, sir."

Kincaid, jaw clenched, thrust the rifle back at Mulberry.

Jimson and Evinrude had steppped back a few paces and were standing with their heads together.

Mulberry took careful aim. Kincaid watched closely. The gun was true, and as far as Matt could tell, the beggar was steady as a rock. Unless he was cross-eyed. . . .

Mulberry squeezed one off.

Olsen dropped the glasses, looking unhappy. "I don't know where that one went. It's the bullseye you're aimin' for, right?"

Mulberry didn't look up, just reloaded, sighted again, and squeezed.

Olsen didn't say anything, just looked at Kincaid and raised his eyebrows.

Mulberry squeezed off four more. Nothing.

Olsen was about to stop Ed, tell him to put the gun up, when Kincaid, standing to the rear, held up his hand.

With Mulberry's next shot, his tenth, the target seemed to leap a bit, then fell over.

"Well," said Olsen, "you musta hit *somethin'*."

Evinrude and Jimson smiled. Kincaid wasn't sure he believed what he thought he saw.

"As you can see," said Mulberry, "I wouldn't be much good in combat."

"Maybe we can find you an office job," said Olsen. "Ol' Four-eyes need any help with the clerkin', Lieutenant?"

Kincaid worked his mouth around like he was chewing tobacco. Finally he said, "Take 'em on in, Sergeant."

•   •   •

Back on post, Sergeant Olsen reported to First Sergeant Cohen, "Evinrude and Jimson's okay, but Mulberry couldn't hit the floor if he fell outta his bunk."

"That's a problem. Maybe he can cook," Cohen suggested.

"I dunno. I guess I wouldn't like to eat anything he cooked, either."

Lieutenant Kincaid entered the orderly room.

"The lieutenant was out watchin', he could tell you," Olsen went on.

"What'll we do with Mulberry, sir, seein' as how he's in the First Platoon?" Cohen asked.

"You worried about me, Sergeant? Don't. Leave him be."

Later on, Captain Conway was walking toward his quarters when he bumped into Kincaid. "Hear you've got a dead shot in the First, Matt."

"Word gets around. Well, as a matter of fact, I 'spect I do."

Conway didn't understand that, and he usually understood Matt. Matt was like him. Army. And Matt knew what fighting was about—how a platoon, a company, was only as strong as its weakest member. The mess team took their firing practice each month, the same as everybody, but nobody bothered counting their scores, and that's why they worked in the kitchen. Matt's casual approach worried Captain Conway. Maybe being stuck so long in grade was finally getting to him.

Conway looked up to find Matt still standing there, smiling at him. What the hell did he have to be so cheery about?

six _____

Captain Conway entered his quarters and called, "Flora?"

"Warner?" came the reply from the other room.

Warner Conway scowled. "Who else might you be expecting?"

Flora appeared. Her black hair was piled high, as it usually was, with a short fringe of curls capping her lovely face. The hair was let down at night, and then pretty often it got tangled. Conway smiled.

"What are you smiling at? Is there something wrong?" She felt her hair.

"Nope. Just thinking how lucky I am. If I didn't have you here with me I think I'd go crazy."

"Well, we know what to do when you feel like you're going crazy, don't we?"

Conway nodded and smiled. But the effort of getting undressed and then dressed all over again, he just didn't feel up to it. And it wasn't something that Flora usually suggested, not at this time of day anyway. It took her long enough to get dressed just once during the day.

She suddenly put a finger to her lips, shushing him, as a knock sounded at the door. He frowned. What was going on?

Flora opened the front door and said, "Well now, aren't you all just perfect *dears*," and she meant it.

Malone smiled as he staggered in the door hanging onto two buckets of steaming water. He was followed by Privates

Spuds Felson and Wolfgang Holzer, similarly loaded down. Holzer paused, setting his buckets down, to doff his forage cap and proclaim, *"Guten Tag, Frau Conway. Du bist schoen."*

Jimson rammed into him from behind. "Goddamnit, kraut, move it." Then he saw where they were. "Holy Christ. Didn't know— Morning, sir." He dropped his buckets, saluting.

"It's afternoon, Private," Conway wearily corrected.

"It is?" He picked up the buckets. "Gosh, time flies." Then he noticed, behind the door, Flora. His eyes bulged and he surged on in.

"Into the bedroom, please," instructed Flora. Turning to Warner, who was staring at Jimson as he passed, Flora said, "I'm learning German, Warner. Private Holzer just said good day and that I'm beautiful, isn't he a dear?"

The men came back out of the bedroom. "One more load should do it, ma'am," said Malone.

"Lessen' you wanna drown," added Jimson, following that up with "Ow!" as Felson kicked him in the ankle.

"Danke Schoen," said Flora, *"Herr Holzer."*

Holzer stopped, raising an admonitory finger. *"Nein. Herr Private Holzer."* Then he grinned and ran out the door.

"A real ladies' man," said Conway.

"Oh, he's sweet. And I said thank you, did you know that?"

"I know, love, I know. We had Germans at the Point, Germans in the War, Germans . . . I never thought it was a pretty language, you know."

She smiled at him. "Well then, Captain, use your influence and get me some French privates."

Conway shuddered. He started to take his uniform off.

"Not *now*," said Flora. "The men will be back soon."

"I wasn't planning to greet them buck naked, m'dear, just my shirt. But perhaps you're right, I'd better wait until they're done. For that matter, what *are* they doing?"

"A bath, silly. It's summer and we girls have to bathe more often to stay fresh for our men."

"I thought you just had a bath."

"I did."

"Fresh, huh? Does that mean Maggie and that Fletcher woman and the enlisted wives are about to troop in here to join you?"

Her laughter was gay. The soldier walking his guard post on the roof wondered what the hell might be going on, what

Persian delights might be in progress. He'd seen the water being hauled. But bathing was not something that sprang readily to mind. He hadn't washed fully since the previous September, so the water was something of a mystery. And here came some more.

The men entered with their buckets. Holzer went through his German routine again and Flora replied, simply, in kind. She didn't know much as yet, but what she knew she had down cold.

"You! Private!" Conway called as the water-haulers trooped back out.

"Me, sir?" answered Jimson.

"Yes. That man you showed up with yesterday, the one that looks like a teacher. Do you know if he speaks French?"

"Prob'ly sir. He knows just about everything."

"Aha. I'll have to speak to him."

"Should I send him over, sir?"

"No! No, I'll take care of it. You may leave."

"Yes, *sir!*" Jimson snapped to attention so crisply it hurt, whipped up a blindingly swift salute, and was gone before Conway realized he'd been saluted.

"I may get you your Frenchy after all."

Flora smiled. "Come. Scrub my back."

He followed her into the next room, the bedroom, where a large tub sat, half-filled. Flora stripped slowly. Conway stood ramrod-stiff, only his eyes moving. Occasionally his eyes shifted upward to follow the muffled progress of the guard overhead. It occurred to him that the guard was walking a very limited post. This one, if he was covering the entire route, was *running* the other parts.

He eyed the stove in a corner of the room, and the stovepipe that ran up through the ceiling. He supposed sound carried through it.

"What in the world are you looking for, dear?"

She was standing naked. He was reminded of the wisdom of choosing a dark-haired woman to wed. Milky pale as she was, the dark triangle of her sex fairly leapt at him. The rich cocoa nipples swam before his eyes as she turned to and fro slowly. He was not a man who savored subtleties, the gray middle grounds, infinite shadings of color and tone. Plain, stark contrast was more to his taste. A simple yes or no.

"Yes," he said.

"What, dear?"

She raised a leg to step into the tub. "Aren't you going to scrub my back?"

"With pleasure, dear, with pleasure."

The trouble was, there was no way to identify the bodies—five naked, scalped bodies that buzzards had begun to gnaw on. It was necessary to wrap them in blankets and then ride like hell for Fort Laramie. There they would spread the word of new hostile activities and also try to determine whether or not the five were indeed the missing gun crew. They took the bodies with them in case a second, or third, closer examination was necessary to make a positive identification.

Twenty-four hours later a wire would arrive from back East, containing detailed descriptions of the five men in the crew. The descriptions tallied. The corpses were a green second lieutenant, two young but experienced gunners, and two teamsters. There would be no doubt.

Flora and Warner Conway lay wrapped in each other's arms, his eyes closed, hers open.

Was he napping, she wondered?

He wasn't. Rather, he was savoring the moments just past in his own private darkness. It made him want to retire right then and there and spend the rest of his days in bed with Flora.

Wonder how she'd like that? He smiled. Probably like it very much, if he knew his Flora. She'd received a proper Victorian upbringing, there was no doubt about that, but the constraints it placed on her public sensuality only seemed to lend fire to her private moments. It had always mystified him, where she'd acquired her amazing ability in bed. It caused him no suspicion or jealousy, since he knew that she'd been a virgin when they'd married and he'd had no reason to believe she'd ever been unfaithful to him. Had his own proper Victorian shyness permitted him to ask, she would have told him the truth, which was simply that her intense desire for him had sensitized her to every nuance in the rhythm of his passion. The fact was that their deep love for each other had made them both formidable lovers.

They'd made love avidly but stealthily. Noise was not a part of Flora's private abandon, just an occasional moan, and Conway had been too conscious of the soldier overhead, undoubtedly circling the stovepipe, to raise his voice above a whisper.

He opened his eyes. "The next time the promotion lists come down . . ."

"I know. If you're not on it, you'll . . . you'll just keep on being the fine soldier you are. You won't complain, you won't whine. . . ."

"You think I should complain?"

"No. There's no money in Washington, that's what you've said."

"None for us, anyway. No promotions, no new guns. The cav's got repeaters, you know."

"I know, dear," she said, smiling. "You've told me."

"But they can pay the wages of a lot of green troops. They're sending us more than we need. It's not as if we were under siege or something."

"Mmmm, how exciting."

He blinked. "And I'm worried about Matt. I think the pressure, the frustration, may be getting to him."

"Maybe he needs a night in town."

"Probably, but it might take more than that."

"Do you want to take a bath, dear?" she asked. "That water's probably still warm, and not *too* dirty, and you're . . .

Private Peters heard the splash and muffled voices. He'd been moving from one stovepipe to the other, trying to catch some better sounds, walking like an Indian, casting a glance every so often to see if any of the real thing were sneaking up on the post.

"Private Peters!"

He stared goggle-eyed at the stovepipe. Jesus! Caught. How the hell did he know he was up there, that it was *him* up there?

"Private Peters." The sound had a weary edge to it now, and was accompanied by footsteps.

Peters whirled. Approaching him were Corporal Medford, that day's corporal of the guard, and Private Thompson—Trouble Thompson—stomping along like a damned elephant.

"You're supposed to be *walking* your post, Peters, not standing around that—" His eyes narrowed as he suddenly realized who lived beneath.

"I was, Corp," protested Peters. "Just got a stitch in my side, that's all."

"A stitch, huh? Well, I think I've got a few exercises that will take care of that. Take over, Thompson."

Thompson grinned at Peters.

Corporal Medford decided to grind it in. "Anything *special* you noticed, Private Peters, anything Thompson should know about?"

"Yeah," said Peters, disgusted with himself but faking excitement. "There's a huge war party just over that far rise. I figger any minute now..."

Corporal Medford started walking off as Thompson eyed the far rise and there was the sound of splashing from below.

Damn, Conway swore to himself, watching the water seep through the rug and into the hard-packed earth below. Wallow in mud before going to bed now. He'd righted the tub before more than half had spilled out. He knew he shouldn't be so excitable, but all that stomping around overhead...

He felt like killing Private Peters. Almost gave him a heart attack, to say nothing of invading privacy. But he guessed he'd have to leave Peters to Medford, which was probably best. Or worst. He remembered the time one of Medford's squad had come down with a social disease. Medford was all for having the man hanged. And that was mild, compared to what he wanted to do to the girl. Ah, yes, Peters was in safe hands with Hellfire Medford.

God, if there was only some *action*.

At four-thirty, Reb McBride blew a facsimile of grub call. And later, as the sun dipped below the horizon, he blew retreat and the colors were lowered.

The men gathered afterwards in the sutler's store and wondered if Reb would do as bad a job on taps that night as he had the night before.

"We gotta keep Reb out of town," said one man. "He'll fight anyone that thinks the South didn't win."

"The South won, huh?" said Jimson. "Where is he? He'll blow taps out his asshole when I git through with him."

"Jesus, another one. You sit on him, Ev, if he starts actin' up. Reb blows the charge. We don't fight if Reb ain't blowin'."

Evinrude placed a fatherly hand on Trash's shoulder. Trash tried to wriggle free but couldn't, and then quit trying. He'd lost all that money on Ev for damn good reason and wasn't about to mess with him. If only he hadn't gone and thrown that effin' fight, Trash'd be sittin' pretty. . . .

"Howdy, sir."

Kincaid had poked his head into the store, which was one place where they didn't have to drag themselves to attention. Kincaid nodded, looked around, then withdrew.

"Any of you boys interested in re-peatin' rifles?" inquired the sutler, Pop Evans, a wily old hustler.

They were interested, but couldn't touch them. It wasn't the same as the extra sidearm. "You got some?" Jimson asked.

"Kin prob'ly git some."

"Who'll you sell 'em to, Injuns?"

"Me?" All innocence.

"'Long with a few cases of Hardy's Irish."

"That ain't no joke, son," said Pop Evans, scowling. "There's sutlers that'll do just that. But me, I wouldn't sell to no Indian that was gonna kill any of *my* boys. Naw, I'd ship 'em north, or run 'em over to Pine Ridge. . . ."

He grinned a yellow grin. They knew he was kidding, or at least they hoped he was.

Kincaid let himself out the front gate, explaining that he just needed to walk for a while.

He moved away from the post in the pale moonlight—it was an early half-moon.

He passed the picket guard some hundred yards out, and proceeded on, but not without caution.

He didn't think there was any real danger, but he hadn't lived as long as he had by being careless. He was packing the Colt as well as the Scoff.

He walked quickly and directly, not like a man just out for a stroll. He knew where he was going.

He stopped, squinting. Was that a movement? He thought a dark silhouette had changed shape. He looked just to the side of the dark silhouette, having learned that, at night, you could see something better by not looking directly at it.

The silhouette, a low clump of earth and grass, wasn't moving. Nothing. He walked on.

At length he came to the firing range. He got his bearings and then walked down the range.

More movement. He frowned. He was edgier than he thought, if his eyes were starting to play tricks on him.

He got to the end of the range, to the rise against which the targets were set.

He found the one that had fallen over. He bent and inspected it closely, lips pursed.

He stood up and began to retrace his steps. He heard a sound, a guttural, choked cry. Adrenalin shot through him and the Scoff leaped into his hand. He crouched, turning slowly.

Nothing.

He began to advance slowly in the same direction, toward the post, and toward that sound.

A dark shape on the ground. Matt drew closer, slowly. The shape gained definition. A man, lying on his face. But still just a dark shape, with a touch of light around the shoulders—a kerchief. Goddamnit, it was a *soldier*. That fool guard had come out after him. But what?. . .

He looked around. Nothing. But Indians could look like nothing when they wanted to. However, they were probably long gone, having counted their coup, namely this poor beggar. If they hadn't run for it, they'd have to come out into pistol range and he'd nail the bastards. He ran forward to the still form.

Just as he was bending down, he was wondering what it was that was wrong. Where were the holsters? Where were—

The shape suddenly twisted, rising up toward him. He caught a glimpse of high cheekbones, and the glint of a knife headed toward his belly.

The night seemed to explode with sound as he felt the knife hit and begin to thrust into him. His first bullet, reflex, almost a panic yank-and-squeeze, took the tip of the Indian's nose off. The second blew out the back of his head.

Matt looked to see two dark shapes rushing at him from both sides, screaming their heads off, already close. His Scoff thundered across his body one way as the Colt cleared leather and fired.

The two Indians danced like marionettes in the hands of a spastic master as the heavy .45 slugs ripped into them.

And it was over.

Matt stood, the Indian's knife hanging from his waist where it had buried itself in his leather harness.

He met the patrol on his way back in—six men drawn from the guard roster, headed by Corporal Medford. "There're some hostile bodies back there a ways, Corporal. Bring 'em in."

Approaching the post, Matt saw many men moving atop the walls, silhouetted against the light night sky. He'd have to mention that. Mr. Lo would have fun picking them off.

He entered the post. Captain Conway bore down on him, astride his favorite gray gelding. Matt realized that Conway had been ready to ride out himself.

Conway brought his horse to a prancing stop. "What the hell's going on here, Matt?"

"Got jumped, sir," answered Matt, noticing that the captain's kerchief was askew. "Had to jump right back. Three dead ones back there."

"Any more?"

"I don't think so, sir, or I would have had them to deal with too. Sorry."

"Who were they?"

"No idea, sir."

"Where's Windy?" asked Conway, knowing Cohen would be within earshot.

"Over with the friendlies, sir. I'll send a squad."

Captain Conway sat astride his horse, thinking and nodding absentmindedly, a bit disappointed.

Then he slid off the horse and gave it to a soldier to return to the stable. He looked at Matt and gave a kind of smile. "I thought for a moment there . . ."

Matt smiled back. "It does kind of get the blood racing."

A few minutes later the patrol rode in with the dead hostiles. And an hour later, Chief Scout Windy Mandalian arrived.

"Had to practically pry him loose from them squaws," said the corporal in charge. "Whole lot of caterwauling."

Windy took a look at the dead Indians. He didn't say anything.

"Well?" asked Captain Conway.

"Jes' a few more dead injuns," said Windy, his voice flat. Conway nodded. When Windy acted this way, it was no

70

use pressing him on the matter. He'd explain when he felt like it. But there was perhaps a clue in the fact that he almost never referred to an Indian by anything but his actual name, or tribe. Sometimes "hostile." But never just "injun."

"Part of a war party, Windy?" asked Lieutenant Price.

"Mister—" began Conway.

"Nope," said Windy. "Jes' some bucks, some poor, proud, misguided bucks. From the village, likely. Young, too."

"You know them?" pursued Price, and Conway didn't try to stop him. Might as well have it out now.

"One."

"And?"

"He was fourteen and a brother to the girl Malone shot and killed."

A moment's silence.

"But Malone was defending Stretch," protested Price.

Windy hadn't been speaking directly to Price. But now he turned and stared at him. "I was *there*, Lieutenant."

Kincaid found Mulberry in the stable, where the man appeared to be studying the horses. The stable was lit dimly by two coal-oil lamps.

"Can't see much," Kincaid said.

"Enough," Mulberry replied, then turned and peered through the dimness toward Kincaid. "Oh, good evening, sir."

Silently they both watched the milling horses.

"It's amazing when you think about what it takes to keep a place like this alive," said Kincaid. "These horses are all grain-fed."

"I was wondering."

"Makes a difference. They'll outrun those Indian ponies; they're grass-fed, just grazed. But of course grain has to be hauled in, as does everything else. There's a wagon train due in tomorrow... or the next day... or the day after that. Depends on what they're using to haul the wagons—horses, mules, or bulls. Horses and mules are fast, but you have to grain them. Bulls are slower than maple sap after ten hours of boiling."

Mulberry seemed to grow more alert. "Where are you from, sir?"

Kincaid allowed himself a smile. "Thought that might catch

your ear. Connecticut, actually, but I spent a lot of springtimes farther north. Ever taste maple syrup boiled and dripped on snow?"

"You've got to boil it a long time."

Kincaid nodded. "You have, then?"

"Ayup," said Mulberry, mimicking a Maine twang.

"Anyway," Kincaid went on, "wait till you see this train. Whichever animal they use, there's usually about ten or twelve animals pulling three or four wagons hooked together. That's a team. And there'll likely be ten or twelve teams in the train. That's something to see."

"Yessir," Mulberry replied, aware that Kincaid wasn't here to talk about maple syrup or wagon trains.

Kincaid saw that it was time to come to the point, so he did. "I just went out and took a look at that target you were firing at today," he said.

Mulberry gazed at him steadily, and Kincaid went on, "You see, my curiosity was aroused. When you were shooting, you were as steady as an outhouse, and you're not cockeyed, so I couldn't help wondering how you could miss so consistently. So, as I said, I went out to take a closer look, and I saw where you sawed off that target at the bottom with...what was it, ten or twelve shots?"

"Ten, sir," Mulberry replied evenly.

Kincaid folded his arms across his chest. "So maybe you'd like to tell me why you want to be given a job where you won't have to do any shooting."

Mulberry sighed. "Begging your pardon, sir, that isn't exactly right. I don't want to do any *killing*. I didn't ask to be assigned here, sir."

"None of us did, Mulberry. And I think there are very few of us who relish killing. I know I don't, and I had to do some just a little while ago."

"Is that what that shooting was, sir?"

"'Fraid so. I was jumped by three young braves trying to prove their manhood, while I was out at the firing range examining your target."

"Sorry to hear that, sir," Mulberry said.

Kincaid shrugged. "Wasn't the first time, and I'm damned sure it won't be the last. Anyway, the point is, you didn't have to do what you did. You could have missed entirely, which was what you were trying to give the impression you were doing. But I think the answer has something to do with *pride*. You're good, soldier, very good, and you just couldn't help *showing* how good you are. So I want your story, Mr. Edward Mulberry the Third."

"Aha. You mean, what's the aristocrat, the scion of wealth, doing in this man's army, shoveling out horseshit once every two weeks... or every day, if an illiterate first sergeant feels I should—"

"Sergeant Cohen is not illiterate."

"I didn't mean him, exactly... sir."

"Go on."

"There's nothing much to say. Mine was an old family with a military tradition. And like in Europe, the eldest son carries on the military tradition and the other sons run the businesses. I was the eldest son. And the weakest. And the one least interested in the military. I didn't like war."

"What'd you think of the Civil War?"

"I was too young then."

"What do you think of it *now*? Was it worth fighting?"

"I... I... I don't know."

"Your family had a passel of niggers?"

"God no. We were Northern... Massachusetts... I told you that." He looked at Matt. "All right, we had holdings, in the South.... They were profitable....

"Family wanted me to go to West Point. I wouldn't. I was old enough to say no and I wouldn't. A brother went. And I was nothing. Nowhere. So I read a lot... and I shot. I enjoy guns. That's funny, isn't it, but I do like them. Not to hunt, I can't kill, but... I just like them."

"And you're good."

"And I'm good, yes sir, in fact I'm *very* good."

"There's that pride." Matt laughed. "But you don't think you could kill if you *had* to?"

"I can't foresee a situation.... You see, that's not what I came out to do, just the opposite. I... I was an outcast, in my own family. And I read about the life out here, the Indian wars, and I understood how the Indian must feel, being *pushed*, so I thought maybe I could help, maybe I could do something... to save both sides."

"As a *private*?"

"I know. I hadn't thought it all the way through. I was excited. My *family* was excited. That's probably why I did it, really, I wanted to impress them. They think I'm out here killing savage hostiles. They think I'm a *hero*. But I've found something out, I think. I'm a coward. Always knew it, I guess."

Kincaid had gotten a little more than he'd bargained for. He thought about it awhile. Finally he said, "You want me to get you out of here? I think I can."

"No." Mulberry gripped the wooden railing against which he was leaning. "I've nowhere to go. This is it, this is my . . . home."

Kincaid had never heard the word "home" sound quite so ugly. He didn't know what to say, or if there was anything *to* say. "Well, do me one favor," he began.

"Sir?"

"The next time you're out shooting, do better. I don't want to have to go out in the middle of the night again."

Mulberry smiled, then said, "I'll think about it, sir."

Kincaid began to leave. "Oh, sir," called Mulberry. Kincaid turned. "Could you keep all that to yourself, sir?" asked Mulberry. "About the shooting and the . . . the coward part. The other men. . . ."

"I don't normally gossip with the enlisted men, soldier, but yes, I'll respect your confidences . . . as far as I can."

"Thank you, sir."

seven _____

Corporal Medford strolled along the roofs that formed the perimeter guard post. He'd started at the gate, above the guardhouse, and moved north.

The moon had long since disappeared, and it was pitch black. Starry, but black.

He'd corporaled the guard often enough to know where all the blessed stovepipes were, and in the course of circling all the post, he stopped by each one of them, knowing which room each one dropped down into. And he listened. Yes, the man's strict, puritan fervor had an underside.

He didn't hear much at any of them—snoring, mostly, some groans—but what could one expect at 3:30 A.M.? About the most you could expect would be to find some guard fast asleep, but he hadn't even found that. Damn!

He heard a noise, a door opening, a distant "Halt!" and then, "That you, Pete? Jeez, you nearly scared the piss outta me . . . almost saved me a trip." And then a shadowy figure moved out on the parade toward the enlisted latrine.

That's a change, thought Medford. Half the men just stepped outside the barracks door and cut loose. He'd caught a few in his time, had them squirting down their legs. Served them right.

Medford had almost made the full circle and was nearing the front gate, where he'd climb down, enter the guardhouse, and help Sergeant Breckenridge rouse the guard relief.

Light splashed onto the parade. Medford looked west to

where the orderly room door had opened. Lieutenant Smiley appeared and set off at a lope for the enlisted barracks. He vanished for a while, but when he reappeared he was hustling someone along. It was probably Corporal Bradshaw. And in the light from the orderly room door he saw that it *was* ol' Four-eyes, in his skivvies.

Medford, standing just outside the guardhouse, held his pocket watch up to the dim light coming from a window. Three-fifty. Better start waking the relief. But—

Now Smiley and Bradshaw came out again and split up. Smiley heading toward the officers' quarters, and Bradshaw toward the barracks.

Three-fifty-five. He couldn't wait any longer. He went into the guardhouse, nudged Breckenridge, and the two of them woke the ten-man relief. He'd formed them up outside and was about to march them to their posts when the air was rent by a godawful version of reveille.

What the hell was McBride doing? Had he gone nuts? Medford checked his watch again. Four o'clock on the button. He held it to his ear. It was ticking properly.

Reveille ended. Smiley was standing just outside the orderly room. Medford heard him call, "Do it again, Reb."

"My *lips*, sir."

"Do it again ... and do it right, this time. Maybe no one recognized it."

Reb McBride did it again, cursing the Union with each spare breath.

Lights began to slowly glow and grow in various windows as kerosene lamps were lit.

Captain Conway, Lieutenant Kincaid, and Lieutenants Price and Fletcher emerged from their quarters in various stages of dress. Conway, who'd had the most time, was most completely attired. But even he was struggling with his harness.

Conway cursed, not because of the harness, but rather because Smiley's pounding on the door had caught him practically in *flagrante delicto*. Lucky as hell Smiley hadn't simply charged in, as was his occasional and irritating habit. And Flora, poor thing. He had the impression that she was still moaning and tossing as he was on his way out the door. He was mistaken, of course, but it had been a rather abrupt change of plan. And it had been *her* fault. She was the one who'd fondled him awake.

76

He laughed now. It'd been tough getting his pants on over his hard-on.

Conway, Kincaid, Price, Fletcher, Cohen, and Bradshaw, now dressed, converged on the orderly room.

Smiley handed Conway a sheet of paper as he entered. Conway read it and snapped, "Bradshaw."

"Sir." Bradshaw stared at him through thick lenses.

"Get back on that wire. Ask Headquarters for fuller information. In my name, tell them I'm here."

He waited, staring at Bradshaw until the telegraph key started clacking. Then he stepped to the door and yelled across the parade, "Mess!"

No response.

"Let me, sir," said Sergeant Cohen, and he stepped to the door and bellowed, *"Bailey!!"* The walls damn near came down.

A distant, "Yohhhh," and then a slightly lower, "Jesus. That you, Sarge?"

Cohen glanced at Conway, who said "Coffee," and Cohen repeated it at the previous ear-shattering level, adding, "And some grub!"

Everyone in that orderly room was now wide awake. And the telegraph operator at HQ wondered why "coffee" suddenly came over the wire. He'd ask for a repeat on that one.

Conway looked around at his men. "Indians," he said tersely, trying to mask the shameful jubilation he felt. "We'll wait till we get the full picture."

As they awaited the return wire, each man's pose and look reflected his thoughts and feelings.

Captain Conway couldn't stop pacing, even with a mug of coffee in one hand and a hard roll in the other. Crumbs fell from the hard roll as it was squeezed repeatedly.

Kincaid was absolutely still as he deliberately repressed excitement. He was the officer who most frequently lead the men out on patrols or skirmishes, but he knew how itchy Conway had been, and this might be something special.

Lieutenant Smiley's eyes gleamed. He'd been born to fight, to command, and had always shown it. They hadn't pulled him up out of the ranks for fun.

Lieutenant Price, on the other hand, was a trifle edgy. Theory at the Point was one thing; facing a howling, painted attack might be another.

Lieutenant Fletcher, the Second Platoon's leader, was usually a calm man who took whatever came with fair composure, the kind of officer who'd be outwardly satisfied with his rank until, suddenly dissatisfied with nonpromotion, he'd quit rather than complain and go off and open a store or run a ranch. He was the kind of man who didn't make waves, but who also couldn't handle waves, and who had enough sense to get out before he drowned. The problem that was making him fidget at the moment was that his wife had recently arrived and he was just beginning to feel comfortable back in the saddle, so to speak, and a long campaign was just what he didn't need. Maybe Price could take his place. Of course, Price was a dodo, and a green dodo to boot, to say nothing of obvious shortcomings in fighting spirit.

As for Sergeant Ben Cohen, he knew he wasn't going anyplace, but since, in the event of a campaign, a few men were going to have to pull the shit-details and duties for the many that were gone, he was not going to be a popular man, and so he wore a frown. But then, the army wasn't a popularity contest, and those who thought it was were soon gone. Except for someone like McClellan.

But then, McClellan hadn't lasted that long, either. Cohen wondered idly where the general was just then. Politicking, the last he'd heard.

The telegraph started making noise. And Four-Eyes Bradshaw started writing words down.

The clacking finally stopped and Bradshaw handed Captain Conway the sheet of paper. Conway studied it for a few moments. Then he looked up at his men.

"Indians raided a gun crew, traveling north out of Cheyenne."

"Platte wagon road?"

"Mmmm. Officer and four men, all killed, scalped and stripped. Laramie had quite a time, apparently, getting definite identification. Indians left sign, an arrow in one of the men. Cheyenne. The gun crew was hauling a Gatling. Now the Cheyenne have it, with all the ammo and everything that goes with it."

There was silence. Mr. Lo armed with a Gatling wasn't fun to contemplate.

"Maybe they won't know how to use it," ventured Price, who'd seen one but never worked one.

."What's to know?" answered Smiley, who had. "Drop a magazine into the hopper and start cranking. It does the rest."

"Your attitude regarding this matter," said Conway, with the faintest suggestion of a smile, "seems rather cavalier."

"No, sir," replied Smiley. "I just don't see a war party running around dragging this thing—it *is* a regular Gatling, isn't it, not one of those cav Gatlings?"

"I would assume so," said Conway. "It was meant for General Miles up at Fort Keogh."

"Yeah, Miles," said Smiley, grinning. "He'd know what to do with one, too." He saw that the rest weren't savoring this the same way he was, except maybe Conway, who wore a benign look, and Kincaid, who was damn near grinning. "The point is, it's damned heavy. They ain't gonna be *running* around anywhere with it. They'll probably head for someplace specific and fort up there."

"But in any case," Conway said, "the question is *where* they're headed, and then we've got to beat them there."

"I'd say northwest somewhere," said Smiley. "Chief Joseph's supposed to be up there with his Nez Perce. A Gatling would be to Joseph what cannon were to Napoleon."

"I appreciate your colorful analogy, Mr. Smiley, yet even Napoleon probably had second thoughts about dragging his cannon to the Russian front," Conway said.

"But he did, sir, and for a while he did good with them."

"But he got beaten," Conway pointed out. "Joseph's smarter than that."

"Northeast, then," offered Lieutenant Fletcher. "Up toward the Red Cloud Agency in Nebraska—Crazy Horse is supposed to be somewhere around there—or over in Dakota, the Pine Ridge Reservation. Wouldn't have any trouble recruiting an army *there*."

"Possible," said Conway. "And Mister Smiley's idea about Chief Joseph is also just as possible. But by the way, Mr. Fletcher, what makes you think Crazy Horse is at the Red Cloud Agency?"

Fletcher looked surprised. "Those buffalo hunters that rode through last week. When they were leaving, I told one to watch out for Crazy Horse and he laughed and said Crazy Horse was at the Red Cloud Agency, having, if I may quote him, the crap bored out of him."

Captain Conway looked stunned. Crazy Horse's death or

capture had fit neatly into one of his fantasies. And Kincaid didn't look very happy either, for much the same reason.

Conway exploded, "What the bloody hell is going on? Camp Robinson's right there, right by the agency. Colonel Bradley commands Camp Robinson. He's a friend of mine, he'd tell me something like that."

"Does he know you're here, sir?" inquired Fletcher. "We haven't been here *that* long, just feels that way. Word travels slow sometimes."

Conway smiled wryly. "That's all we need, a Cheyenne war party presenting that Sioux maniac, Crazy Horse, with a Gatling. But be that as it may, there's a third possibility—that they're heading straight north. Sitting Bull's supposed to have gotten into Canada recently." He eyed Fletcher. "Those buffalo hunters didn't tell you anything different about *that*, did they, such as that Sitting Bull's about twenty miles north of here and riding hard our way?"

Fletcher shook his head, afraid to smile.

"Then we'll assume he's still in Canada, and if *he* got hold of a Gatling . . ."

Kincaid looked stricken. "The Queen would never forgive us."

"And I wouldn't blame her," said Conway. "What the hell was a gun crew doing out there by themselves, anyway?"

"When our new men arrived at Como, sir," said Ben Cohen, "there was that escort waiting there for the gun crew—"

"But the gun crew'd gotten off at Cheyenne," Conway cut in, "and started north. And the escort was ambushed—"

"Indians probably realized the gun wasn't there," said Kincaid, "and rode off looking for it. . . ."

"And found it," concluded Conway. "But what I can't understand is how the hell they knew there was a Gatling being shipped?"

Apparently no one else could understand it either.

"Well," said Conway, "however *that* turns out, we've got a job to do. Fort Laramie's taking an eastern sector; Fort Fetterman's taking a northeast sector that'll include Pine Ridge and the Red Cloud Agency; Fort Casper will throw up a skirmish line in case they head northwest—unlikely, but they may be thinking of sneaking up the Bridger trail."

"That'd be a hell of a trip," said Kincaid, "with carriage and limber."

"Agreed. But HQ's trying to cover all possibilities. We've

got the sector straight north, a part of the Platte wagon road, which some folk are *still* calling the Oregon Trail, and then up the Bozeman Trail. That's probably their most likely route, whether they're headed for Canada *or* for Chief Joseph. We'll try to get them before they get to the Bozeman. If we don't, and they *have* had a head start, we'll just run them down....

"Headquarters is feeling pretty bad about this. The mood seems to be that it's their fault, which is stupid since Washington cut the orders wrong, but—"

"You got all that from that telegraph message, sir?" asked Fletcher, unable to control his amazement.

Conway blinked at him. "It was there. You just have to ... know how to read those things. Anyway, headquarters really wants this."

"What are *they* covering?"

"The area between here and the Platte road that we're *not* covering. It's closest to them, and if Mr. Lo's lost all his horses they might have a chance, get lucky, but I figure the Cheyenne moved north fast, which leaves us as the best bet."

"Why'd it take so long to get the word out?"

"Took a long time to positively identify the bodies. I think I said that."

"Long time ago," muttered Fletcher.

"They're sure it was Cheyenne?"

"The arrow."

Matt frowned. "Just one?"

"That's all they said."

There was suddenly silence. They seemed to have run out of questions. Except for one, the big one. Matt asked it.

"Who's going, sir?"

Captain Conway avoided looking at Matt. "I'll take them, two platoons, Second and Third. The First will stay here with Matt." He finally looked at Kincaid. "Sorry, Matt."

"It's all right, Captain, I had it figured."

"Mr. Smiley, Mr. Fletcher, get your men ready. They're probably wondering what the hell's going on." He glanced toward a window. "It's just starting to get light now. We'll want to move out as soon as possible. Sergeant Cohen, set us up with rations, three days' worth—a wagon, but light, we'll be riding hard. If we run short we'll resupply at Casper or Fetterman. And I want Windy. Anybody know where the hell he is?"

"Over with the friendlies, most likely," said Sergeant Cohen. "I'll send a man."

"Okay. Let's get cracking."

When Flora saw Warner, there was fire in his eyes.

"Warner," she said quietly. "You're going out to fight, aren't you?"

"Damn right I am."

"Warner—"

"Oh. Sorry about the rough language, dear. Must've thought I was still with the men."

"It's not the language that bothers me. You're a man. I expect the occasional damn. It's the fighting. . . ."

Warner Conway was surprised. "You've never said that."

"I've always felt it."

"You married a soldier, love."

"I'm scared."

"When I courted you, all I talked about was fighting."

"Mmm, I know, my brave, valiant hero. Charging into battle, banner gallantly held high, laying waste to the Union's enemies."

"I don't remember saying *that*."

"Oh, darling, when you were talking like that, all I could see was you charging into my bed. . . ."

"Banner held high?"

"Mmmm."

"Damn it, Flora—sorry again—but glory be, Flora, if I'd known what you were thinking, I wouldn't have had to waste so much time courting."

"It was fun, though, wasn't it?"

"You didn't hear me complaining, did you?"

"You're complaining now, Warner."

"Not really."

"Do we have time, Warner?"

"Good gracious, no. A fine thing, all my troops mounted up and ready to go and me in bed with my wife. . . . I'll tell you, Flora, if I can stop these rascals—"

"Rascals?"

"Killers," he amended. "If I can stop them, there's no way Washington'll be able to stop a promotion, *no way*. Then perhaps a tour back East, visit Maryland, your folks. . . ."

"They're dead, Warner, remember?"

"Well, drop by the cemetery, then..."

"Warner."

Her robe fell off. She ran her fingers through her black, tumbling hair, then reached out to him....

The Second and Third Platoons were forming up on the parade, the men standing with their horses, several of which were pawing the ground; they wanted action as much as the men did.

The men of the First Platoon were standing just outside the barracks, their mood mixed. Some said they wished they were going; others kept quiet. Jimson and Malone were honestly infuriated at being left out of the action. Somewhat sobering, though, was the word that had just leaked out about the missing Gatling.

"Lord," breathed Jimson, "It'd be murder, goin' up against *that* thing."

"You ever seen one?"

"Seen? I've *fired* one. Hell, I fired the one that was stole."

Malone looked dubious. He'd found Jimson to be about as full of hot air as anyone he'd ever met. Jimson got excited.

"Yeah. Ask *them*, they kin tell you it's true."

Mulberry and Evinrude, standing nearby, both nodded.

A nearby soldier exclaimed, "What? Miss Mulberry saw it? Lady Mulberry?" There was a ripple of laughter.

"Aw, cut it out," said Stretch, who'd found Mulberry a nice fellow to be with; he didn't make fun of Stretch as most of the others did.

"Bottle it," growled Evinrude, and they did, his being the voice of sledgehammer authority. Evinrude then slid over next to Ed Mulberry and said, "They been ridin' you pretty good. It ain't fair. You may have to fight one of them."

"Fight?" Mulberry looked surprised.

"Pick one you can beat."

Mulberry's expression showed how impossible that was. "I just can't handle it. I've never lived with men like this. They're too rough. I'm not saying that's bad, just that I'm not used to it."

"We've been in the army near six months now."

"But we were always on the move, not isolated like this. You could always lose yourself in a crowd."

"Maybe next time on the range you better shoot yourself

some bullseyes. Me and Trash know you can do it."

"I don't like that, Jim. They'll wonder why I can't shoot an Indian. What'll I do, Jim?"

"Beats me, Ed. Sure beats the hell outta me."

There was a sudden movement, a shifting of men and horses. Captain Conway had emerged from his quarters and was jogging toward the orderly room.

Conway entered the orderly room only to encounter Matt Kincaid's knowing grin.

Conway scowled, wondering who else had guessed.

"Windy couldn't make it, Captain," said Sergeant Cohen.

"Why not? What does he think this is, a picnic?"

"'Parently he's pretty sick, over with the friendlies."

"I'll bet. With some squaw wrapped all around him to make him feel better."

"He sent a couple of fellows that've scouted with us before," Cohen said. "The River That Forks and Son of Bear with Limp."

Conway stared at Cohen. "I'll try to remember."

"Just 'River' and 'Bear' should do it."

"Good, 'cause that's all they're going to get. Mr. Fletcher? Mr. Smiley? Let's move them out."

And so, on that chill early-summer morning, in the Territory of Wyoming, with the sun just lifting off the horizon, Captain Warner Conway led some sixty men of Easy Company out the gate and north toward what he hoped was a rendezvous with destiny.

eight _____

The horsedrawn carriage moved slowly down Park Avenue. The horse was spirited enough and the wheels well-oiled; the problem was the street itself. Cobblestones. Dirt was preferable, but got messy in winter and rain.

Albert Meyerling sat back in the carriage and made a mental note. The city's streets were terrible. He could hear the wheels grinding on stone and the horse stepping carefully. He'd have to speak to the mayor. The least New York City could do was have decent streets.

He could remember the day he could leave his home in Gramercy Park and race to work down hard-packed, earthen streets, the coachman's coat flapping in the wind, sometimes losing his hat. And sometimes Meyerling had ridden up there with the coachman, laughing as people scattered. You couldn't drive like that anymore. There were laws. Ah, the price of civilization.

At length the coach drew up before a stone building on Church Street. The home of Meyerling & Sons, Ltd. Albert Meyerling entered the building and climbed to his office on the second floor. The first floor would have been easier, but he wished to be above the common herd. The third and fourth floors were for the energetic clerks and the aging failures whom he kept on because, in these hard times, he could underpay them and still get their experience, which didn't amount to much, but it was better than having to constantly train new men.

Meyerling ran an empire, mostly textiles, some lumbering and furniture, but a very promising new venture in shipping.

Half an hour after his arrival, his secretary entered, carefully closing the door behind her. "A gentleman wishes to see you, sir." She laid negative emphasis on "gentleman."

"Who is he?"

"He *claims* to represent the Fishkill Detective Agency."

"Claims? Is he fat, with curly red hair all over his head and face, and surly and given to smoking foul cigars?"

"Indeed, sir."

"Then he *is* the Fishkill Detective Agency, and a loathsome specimen of the breed, but effective. Show him in, please."

The round man with red hair was shown in.

"Grout. Sit. You have word for me?"

"Sure do, guv. Evinrude's not in China, which woulda cost a pretty penny, an' he ain't dead, which woulda cost less... *unless* he died in China." He produced a surprising giggle. "Naw, the scum's in Wyoming."

"Exquisite. What is he doing there?"

"He's in the army, guv. Army of the West, one of Phil Sheridan's little boys in blue."

"Where, exactly?" Meyerling had a pencil poised.

"How about showing me some money, guv?" Grout had already said too much, damn it. With Wyoming and the army as leads, Meyerling could find him easily himself. If Meyerling got cheap, the only thing Grout could do was wire Evinrude and tip him off. And, by God, he would.

His intent might have been writ on his forehead, what little there was visible below the red tangle, for Meyerling, after a searching scrutiny and some thought, calmly asked, "How much? Seventy-five dollars, as I recall."

"There warn't no set amount, guv."

"But there were, and are, limits. That is always implied. A man of business such as—"

"Hunnert, guv, I'll let it go for a flat hunnert. And that's cheap."

Ha. The man had a reputation for shrewdness. Meyerling thought Grout had probably made a lucky guess (or several; only one had to pan out), wired an inquiry to the Department of the Army in Washington, and *voila!* Cheap, indeed. He'd have me think his nose was to the ground all the way to Wyoming. The man was ridiculous.

He reached into his drawer and withdrew money. He counted out a hundred and laid it on the desk.

Grout picked it up smoothly and pocketed it with a casual, professional motion, at ease now. "He's at Outpost Nine. An infantry company." He told him the battalion, regiment, division, took it all the way up to the President. "It ain't hard to find."

"Thank you. I'll find it. You can go."

Grout went.

Meyerling settled back in his chair, savoring the prospect. Then he summoned a messenger.

"Run down to the police station, boy—" he called all such menials "boy," even though this one looked eighty if a day— "and ask Commander Bleecker if he'd care to drop by once he gets a free moment." If Bleecker cared about his future, he'd find that free moment very quickly.

But apparently not that quickly, assuming his "boy" had run Bleecker down with anything like dispatch, or hadn't suffered a heart attack on the way. In any case, when Bleecker hadn't shown by noon, Meyerling strolled out to lunch at the nearby Poor Richard's, a restaurant whose name was perversely appealing to its monied clientele.

Two hours later he was back, and soon after that was visited by Police Commander Bleecker. Bleecker, a tall, broad man, wore a wide smile. But he lost it as Meyerling got down to business.

"That's an army matter," Bleecker said, when Meyerling had finished.

"He committed the crime as a civilian."

"It will undoubtedly have to be a cooperative venture."

Meyerling stifled his irritation. "How would that work?"

"Seeing as how it's that far west, A U.S. marshal would have to investigate—a deputy, actually—make contact with the subject, and then, if he decided it was justified, approach the army."

"If it's *justified*? You're questioning my word?"

"Good Lord, no, I was just outlining standard procedure. I'm sure there won't be any problem. All I need now is a name, a description, and where the murder took place."

When Bleecker left, he had all the information. But he was damn sure going to check it. He'd wire this town marshal, Purdy, get it all down cold. He sure as hell wasn't going to do that prick Meyerling's dirty work, not just on his say-so. And if it didn't turn out to be just as he described, then that skinny bastard was going to have it laid—ever so gently, of course—right back in his lap.

But Meyerling, for all his power and influence, covered his bets. Power may corrupt, but it didn't necessarily blind. He knew Bleecker would jump, but not beyond a strict interpretation of the law. So he decided to make further arrangements.

Late that afternoon he visited another restaurant—a saloon, really—the Chamber Street Chowder House. There he met a Jew named Solomon.

Meyerling hated Jews. But they were useful. In Meyerling's scheme of things, Jews were drawn to anything that paid, to crime because *it* paid. At times, of course, he would run into an argument to the contrary, at which time he would resort to a fall-back position that posited that any business that Jews were allowed to get into, including crime, they made pay. And that argument, by his lights, was a justification for his own use of this man, Solomon, in his current endeavor.

"So," said Solomon, after listening to Meyerling's account, "how may I help you?"

"I want him dead."

"He shall die, legally or illegally. And for that you shall pay, whether or not we are the instrument of that death. And, that being the case, with nothing for us to hold as ransom, you shall pay in advance. You expected that, did you not?"

Meyerling ground his teeth. "How much, Jew?"

"How much do you want him dead?" But that was purely rhetorical, and Solomon got down to brass tacks.

An amount was soon set and arrangements made for payment. Meyerling stood up. He couldn't get away fast enough.

"Check," he called.

Solomon waved the waiter away. "I have an interest in this place," he said. "You should stay for some chowder. It's exquisite."

Solomon watched Meyerling leave, thinking that, purely out of charity, he should have Albert Meyerling removed. But, alas, he had not gotten as far as he had through charity.

nine ————————————

It was Windy Mandalian's hook nose that, as much as anything else, kept him from looking out of place among the Indians. It fit right in. And never more so, possibly, than at that moment, thrust as it was between the legs of an Indian maiden. And it stayed there, only Windy's eyes rising to investigate the disturbance at the flap of the tipi.

Matt Kincaid stood just inside the flap, eyeing Windy with amusement. Windy's folk-medicine cures for various ailments were almost legend. Wait till this one got around.

"Hi, Matt," said Windy, his voice muffled.

"How," replied Matt.

"Not well," said Windy, clearer now, beginning to disengage. He swept a buckskinned forearm over his mouth. He was wearing his shirt. His buckskin trousers were down around his ankles. His swarthy skin—buttocks, thighs, and calves—was nearly hairless, like an Indian's.

"Old Indian remedy?" inquired Matt.

Windy, propped up on his elbows, frowned. He looked down at the maiden who was peeking out at him and Matt from behind the folds of a skirt drawn to her chin. Windy's face cleared. "*Young* Indian remedy," he said, smiling.

He patted the girl on the knee as he stood up and stepped past her, toward Matt, hiking his trousers up to his waist in one smooth movement.

Several hours after Captain Conway's departure, Matt had taken to wondering just how sick Windy was. Maybe it was

89

serious. Matt had ridden over to the village, about a quarter-mile distant, to see what the story was.

"I thought I might find a man near death," said Matt.

Windy nodded. "Figgered I'd miss this little field exercise," he muttered as they left the tipi. "Damn waste of time. But I shoulda known you couldn't take a piss without ol' Windy along to tell you which way the wind was blowin' from."

"They already moved out."

"*They*? Who with?"

"Captain. Something big came up."

"Uh-oh."

"Yeah. He wanted you. Didn't anyone tell you what was up?"

"Nope. Just that they was movin' out. Thought it was just a usual patrol. Aw, hell, Matt, what could happen?"

"Might get his ass shot off is what could happen."

"Gun crew got waylaid over on the old Platte wagon road below Fort Laramie. Mr. Lo. Musta been some war party no one knew about. Been some slippin' up from down south, I hear."

"Yeah. You *hear*, but you no *tell*. The gun crew was hauling a Gatling. Cheyenne got it now."

"Gatling?" Windy whistled softly, and took a piece of cut-plug from his pocket and bit off a large chunk.

Kincaid filled him in on all the known facts as Windy found his horse and the two men mounted and rode out of the village. As they neared the post, Privates Mulberry, Jimson, and Evinrude rode out toward them, reining to a halt as they drew near. "How do, sir," cried Jimson.

"Where you headed?"

"Town, sir. Top kick gave us passes, kind of a re-ward for us doin' nothin' but workin' since we got here."

"Just remember who you are."

Jimson frowned. He'd figured on drinking to near oblivion, but never thought he'd forget who he was. "How's that, sir?"

"You're *soldiers*, and as such, you are representatives of the government of these United States."

"Oh. Yeah. Top kick already told us that . . . *sir*."

Kincaid sighed. Jimson would never make a dedicated soldier. The man's forage blues were almost unsightly. But Kincaid was not a man to harass lightly, for sport. He needed a good reason. Of course, when he had that good reason he landed with both feet. He shifted his attention to Evinrude. "Your face healed enough to take on those women?"

"Beg pardon, sir?"

"Those gals. When they get aroused they're inclined to bite."

"I'll try not to arouse them, sir."

"No problem," said Jimson, and Evinrude flashed him a look.

"Very good," said Matt. Then he eyed Mulberry, the thin man with the soft, serious eyes. "As a student of Western culture, Private, I might have expected to find you among the friendlies over there at the village. They *are* really quite friendly, believe me, as Windy can attest to."

"I'll take your word for that, sir, and yours, Mr. Windy—"

Windy flinched.

"—but I thought I'd need some kind of introductions," Mulberry continued.

"You don't need any introductions," said Kincaid.

"That's what I been tellin' him, sir," said Jimson. "We tole 'im them Indian gals'd be all over him."

Windy eyed Mulberry, his potential competition. He spat a copious stream of tobacco juice. Kincaid gave him a glance and then said, "Right, you men better ride on before those gals get too used." An¹ with that, he rode his horse between Jimson and Evinrude and onto the post. Windy followed closely.

"They sure it was Cheyenne what done it?" asked Windy.

"One of the bodies had a Cheyenne arrow sticking out."

"Just one?"

"How many does it take to kill a man? It was just one, as far as I know."

Sergeant Cohen looked up as they entered the orderly room. "By God, Windy, you're a sight for sore eyes. I figured you were a goner."

"How long am I gonna have to listen to this crap?" Windy said, eyeing them both. "I thought it was just a regular old exercise, I tole y'that, Matt. Y'all want me to ride after them?"

"Captain's got River-that-does-something and Son of a Bear."

"River That Forks and Son of Bear with Limp," Windy corrected. "Can't read sign for shit, but they're good boys."

Cohen half rose behind his desk. "You *sent* them."

"I did?"

"He's joking, Sarge," said Matt, "and in my experience no one jokes worse than Windy." When he joked at all, which was damned rarely. "Something bothering you, Windy?"

"Yep."

Matt stared at him. Then he went to the stove and poured himself a cup of coffee. Windy would talk when he was ready.

Cohen joined Matt at the stove. "Don't know what's gonna kill me first," he said. "This," indicating the cup of coffee, "or Windy jabbering me to death."

Matt frowned. "This isn't bad coffee," he said, though he was willing to concede that his taste buds might have been deadened by drinking the stuff over a period of time.

"Maybe not," said Cohen, "but some of the new recruits think so. Or they're spreadin' the word, gettin' the other men upset. Like Malone, he'll drink about anything, but the other day he yells at ol' Dutch that he heard the Injuns had stole a pot of coffee to dip their arrows in. Dutch about had a fit. He's just *waitin'* for Malone to get KP." He grinned. "An' Malone tol' me he'd kiss my ass from now to Christmas just to make sure he *don't* get KP."

"He said that?"

"Not so no one could hear, 'cept me," Ben assured him. Then, looking alarmed, he added, "not that I took him *serious*."

Matt smiled. "I ran into Evinrude on the way to town. How are *you* feeling these days? *He* didn't look so bad."

Cohen's eyes narrowed. The better he felt, the less he remembered. "I think I musta been sick."

"Matt," Windy spoke up, "where'd you say that ambush was?"

Matt crossed to the map on the wall, the 1876 Rand McNally & Company map of Wyoming. "Right about here," he said, jabbing a finger at the map.

Windy studied the map. "You kin see that land's all flat, flat as a poker table." He shook his head. "No one's gonna take an arrow there. Can't get close enough without bein' seen. And any hostile worth callin' hostile's got a rifle, repeater most likely."

"At night?"

"The rest got shot with bullets," Windy pointed out.

They thought about it.

"An arrow got left behind deliberately," surmised Matt.

"They weren't Cheyenne," concluded Ben Cohen.

"Probably anything *but* Cheyenne. Sioux maybe, but not likely. 'Member, ain't no love lost b'tween a lot of them tribes. Iffen they didn't have whites to kill, they'd be killin' each other. They're warriors. That's what they live for... and die for."

Matt went to get more coffee, but the pot was empty.

"Bradshaw," ordered Cohen, "run get some more coffee."

"Right, Sarge."

"And tell 'im to give you the stuff the Injuns *don't* dip their arrows in."

"*I* ain't gonna tell him that, Sarge," Bradshaw gasped.

"Get a running start, do it on your way out the door."

Bradshaw left, more than a little apprehensive.

"Where do you think the captain is?" wondered Cohen.

"Right about here, I figure," said Matt, "and whipping the hell out of those horses, if I'm not mistaken."

"Th' arrow business didn't bother him?" wondered Windy.

"Don't think he gave it a thought," said Matt. "He was too excited. Like a kid. Been champin' at the bit so long, achin' for action."

"And driving *me* nuts," added Cohen.

Just then, there was a big boom from out on the parade.

"Dutch's bloody shotgun," said Ben, looking a mite worried.

Bradshaw burst in, his eyeglasses askew, hanging onto the coffeepot. "Next time," he panted, "*you* do it."

Outside, a loud voice asked, "What the hell you shootin' at, Dutch?"

"Gaw-demmed Injun-lover," bawled Sergeant Rothausen from the far side of the parade, "with eyeglasses!"

"Aw, hell, Dutch," said the first voice. "You don't have to *shoot* him. *Feed* him, that'll do the trick."

Matt was scratching his head. "What really bothers me is, if they were going after the Gatling, in specific, how'd they know it was being shipped?"

93

ten ━━━━━━━━━━━━━━━━━━━━

The band led by Racing Elk was, by that time, well
up the North Platte wagon road, heading for the Bozeman.
They'd moved steadily, but slowly and carefully. The previous
night they'd slipped past Bridgerstown, wondering why the
white man had put the road on one side of the North Platte
River and the town on the other. If nothing else, it made it
easier to slip by. The only thing that had worried Racing Elk,
while they passed, was that the women might cry out.

There wasn't much chance of that, though. The women
knew what would happen to them if they raised a cry. Thus
far, as community property, they had been spared undue violence, although the constant demands of the warriors had
exhausted them, and the five older women were suffering from
the psychic trauma brought on by the violation, not so much
of their bodies as of their entire system of ethics and values.

The younger women—girls, really—fifteen-year-old Josie
and sixteen-year-old Clara, had fared better as a result of the
natural resiliency of youth.

In another respect the two girls were lucky. Josie was the
favored of Racing Elk and Clara of Eight Moons, Racing Elk's
second-in-command. Permission had to be granted before either girl was used by others. And though neither the chief nor
Eight Moons ever refused a request, the mere fact of favoritism
had an inhibiting effect and many of the braves would opt for
the old "cows" instead.

The worst part of it, Josie had thought that previous night as the wagons rolled past Bridgerstown, was having to listen to the other women suffer. She both understood them and didn't understand them. If only they could learn to accept. . . .

But she'd known they couldn't, and she'd decided that if she ever got the chance, if she could get a knife from one of the braves and hide it, she'd put the women out of their misery.

When that solution had occurred to her, the previous night, she'd thought it awful, but now, some miles and many anguished moans later, she didn't.

The moon, three-quarters full, had dropped from the sky. The wagons had pulled off the road and stopped, and Josie forgot about killing as Racing Elk crawled in to be with her. She didn't mind him. He was gentle.

By noon the next day, about when Matt was wondering how Mr. Lo had known about the Gatling, Racing Elk and his band had made another twenty miles.

The forward scout approached the wagons from up the trail, riding hard. Racing Elk rode in from the west flank to meet him. They conferred. Then Racing Elk whipped his horse back to the west flank while the scout rode to the east.

Moments later Eight Moons rode like a wild man from the east, across the road and after Racing Elk.

A cry came from the side and the wagons were halted. Racing Elk rode up and gave the four disguised wagon drivers careful instructions. Four more braves arrived and climbed into the wagons, lying down among the women. They weren't bent on sex, though—Josie had to squirm to get a knee out of her side—rather, they were checking the loads in either their Winchesters or Spencer repeaters (an army command in southern Colorado was *still* looking for an overdue shipment of Spencers). There were even several Henrys among the war party, courtesy of a wagon train that had tried to cross the Staked Plains earlier that year.

About fifteen more braves then rode up and stood their mounts in a circle around the wagons, some thirty yards distant.

Racing Elk sent a brave on ahead to the farthest rise. He rechecked the positioning of his men and was satisfied.

Then he waited.

At length he spotted the forward scout leaping onto his pony and waving his rifle. The scout then urged his pony into a run, not toward Racing Elk, but angling off southwesterly.

Racing Elk grunted a command and the braves surrounding the wagons began to ride in a circle, firing their weapons toward the wagons.

Naturally they fired high, as did the braves in the wagons in answering the "attack."

Racing Elk saw a soldier appear on the far rise, mounted. The army's point man, or scout. Then the man disappeared. Racing Elk smiled; it wouldn't be long.

Corporal Fineman got back to Mr. Brockington, the lieutenant commanding the Third Platoon of mounted infantry out of Fort Fetterman, and reported the skirmish up ahead.

No time for niceties of strategy. The enemy was bunched around the wagons; a straightforward charge would do the trick. The bugler sounded the charge.

Brockington's men appeared on the rise, spreading out for the charge—two squads in a line, the third bringing up the rear.

Racing Elk watched the dragoons bear down on them. The soldiers hadn't started firing yet, but would very soon be within range. At the last moment Racing Elk gave a cry and he and the "attackers" turned their horses and rode hellbent over the tall grass toward the west.

Lieutenant Brockington, smelling blood, roared commands. His first and second squads, the front line, led by himself, swerved to take off after the fleeing Indians. The Third Squad, the rear reserve, continued on to secure the wagons. Once they got to the wagons, they stopped and turned as one man, to watch the pursuit as it developed to the west.

The other two squads, thundering over the plain, trying to keep the war party from reaching the hills and safety, had only a brief moment to see and recognize the long line of Indians that suddenly rose from the tall grass before them, to guess what was happening and try to react. Then the Indians, standing steady or kneeling, sent sheet after sheet of riflefire into their charging line. The army charge came to a crashing, bloody halt.

Back at the wagons, the Third Squad's mouths fell open in wonder. And the Indians in the wagons fired into their backs.

One soldier, his mouth still open, had a bullet enter the

back of his head and exit from that open mouth, followed by a rush of blood.

Racing Elk, having stopped when his ambush had been sprung, began to ride back, swiftly checking for survivors.

One. Just one. A soldier who'd been riding on the northern flank of Brockington's charge, the right side. He reined his horse to the side and thought of making a run for it. But, sensing death was upon him, or angered beyond clear thought, he flung himself from his horse, brought the horse to a lying position, and began to return fire from behind the prone animal. He knew that was the way it was done. But what he'd forgotten, or didn't know, was that that was the way it was done by *cavalry*, not by infantry, mounted or not. The cavalry *practiced* firing over prone horses, accustoming their mounts to such doings. The infantry didn't. And in this particular instance his horse, spooked, regained its feet in a flash and thundered off to safety. The soldier was left kneeling, aghast, staring down twenty-odd braves, and was still that way when his body was riddled by bullets. He was the last to fall but one of the first to lose his hair—and he was the last so honored for a while, because Racing Elk ordered that the entire area be checked first for additional army forces.

A half-hour later, though, Racing Elk turned his men loose, and approximately thirty U.S. Army soldiers lost their scalps— and anything else they had of value, except their rifles. The wagons were already filled with rifles, and better ones than the dragoons were carrying.

Indian ponies were traded for army horses, as were the horses pulling the wagons, horses that, without their grain, had been steadily weakening.

A desultory attempt was made to tidy the scene of the slaughter. Racing Elk did not delude himself that the battle would go undetected for long, but the more delay the better. He had the bodies dragged from the vicinity of the wagon road and spread out over the plain. They were hidden from human eyes but, of course, not from buzzards, a few of which were already floating overhead. Sooner or later someone would want to know what the buzzards were so busy feasting on. Such investigations were not idle activities undertaken by the normally apprehensive traveler, but rather by an army scout sent specifically to track down the missing patrol.

There was another way in which Racing Elk was fortunate. Brockington and his men had already been out on patrol when word had been received at Fetterman of hostile activities and the missing Gatling. Therefore, not only was Brockington critically cheated of the extra caution such news might have given him, but Fetterman didn't have any idea where he was exactly, and would not be keeping close tabs on him, as it was on the patrols it had sent out right after word had arrived. Furthermore, the North Platte wagon road wasn't even in their sector of surveillance.

Racing Elk, not fully realizing the extent of his good fortune, looked the field of battle over, traded a thin smile with Eight Moons, and then gave the signal to move on.

eleven _____

Jimson, Mulberry, and Evinrude reached town midway through the afternoon and tied up their horses in front of the Drovers Rest.

Drovers Rest Saloon & Grill w/ Rooms & Amenities (which amenities amounted to a porcelain pitcher, wash basin, and chamber pot) was the second oldest business in town after Burt's General Store, a three-storied wooden structure. The town wasn't all that big, and it looked like the best bet to the three soldiers. They were about to step inside when Jimson exclaimed:

"Damnit, Ed, how come you gotta come to town lookin' like a raw recruit?"

"Because I am," answered Mulberry peevishly. "What's wrong *now*?"

"Gimme yer knife, Ev. 'Cause, Ed, not only do you only got one gun, but the one you do got ain't prepared right."

"Where'd *you* get that extra gun?"

"I ast around fer an extra, bought it."

"Thought you were broke."

"I'm owin'. *Now*, you gotta cut off this flap, like this, fer a fast draw . . . an' then cut out the bottom so the damn thing don't fill up with water."

"That's absurd. I don't plan to outdraw anyone, and I'm not going swimming with it on. . . . Now I'll just shoot my own foot off . . . or my knee."

99

"Jes' so you don't shoot *mine* off. Now let's git inside an' do some drinkin'."

At the bar, Jimson and Evinrude called for shots and beer, Mulberry asked for coffee. The bartender's eyes narrowed.

"Hey, don't start him drinkin'," said Trash. "He gets too ornery when he drinks. An' he ain't too steady with the gun."

That wasn't what Whitey, the bartender and proprietor, wanted to hear. The last dedicated coffee-drinker he'd served had shot out all the front windows and then tried to shoot Sheriff Cummings. It had been a real nice burial, but nobody'd coughed up anything for the windows. "Coffee'll take a while. It's in back, gittin' thick."

Mulberry, trying not to laugh at the wild reputation Trash was giving him, looked around and decided that the Drovers Rest was not the cheeriest-looking saloon he'd ever seen. Long and dark, with unpainted board walls. Silent drinkers. Intense gamblers.

"Ain't you got no music?" asked Jimson.

"Sometimes," answered the white-haired Whitey, "when he ain't too drunk to play—or too drunk to hear. Coupla boys hadda throw him out last night, it got so painful."

"Great," said Trash. "What kinda people you got here?"

"In here? The usual. Worthless, bad-ass drunks."

"Maybe if the booze was better, they wouldn't be so bad-ass."

"That stuff's prime. Wait'll you try to take a pee."

Trash didn't like the sound of that. "Where're all the gals?"

"Well, I'll tell yuh . . . you're new, aintcha?" He smiled. "You're gonna find there ain't too many gals around, fewer women, *no* ladies, and a bunch of breeds and squaws you gotta be a little careful with."

"Sneak a knife in yuh, huh?" guessed Trash.

"Worse. Dee-sease. That booze don't do nothin' compared. They mess you up so yer pecker'll go off like the Fourth of Joo-ly."

"Any way of tellin' ahead of time?" asked Evinrude.

"You got a nose, aintcha?"

Jimson's eyes widened. "You mean you gotta stick yer *nose* in there?"

"You sayin' you never done that?" inquired Whitey sweetly.

"*Hey*," sneered Trash, "whaddya take me for? I usual jes'

100

dip a finger. I don' favor gittin' all thet close to somethin' I ain't sure of."

"Waaal, you kin be sure of *them*, fella, I kid you not."

"What is there to do around here?" wondered Mulberry.

"You're doin' it," Whitey said, then realized Mulberry *wasn't* doing it, that the space before him was empty. "You hang on, I'll be right back with that coffee. An' you two—you drink up. Hear tell an Injun won't scalp a drunk."

"That true?" asked Trash, after Whitey had left.

"I doubt it," said Mulberry. "Scalps are trophies. They signify honor. A drunk wouldn't be worth scalping...present company excepted."

"How would anyone know it was a drunk's scalp?" Trash asked as Whitey got back with the coffee. And sugar.

"Sugar's extra," Whitey said.

Mulberry nodded. "Do you have a spoon?"

"Spoon? You ain't gonna put one of *my* spoons in that. Jes' pour it in."

Ed did, stirred it with his gun barrel, took a sip of the steaming, dark liquid, then stared steadily at Whitey and said, "Perfect."

"What kinda bad-ass drunks you got here?" asked Evinrude.

"Got some o' yer blue-leg buddies at a back table—see? An' yer trappers an' buffaler hunters an' travelers an' gamblers. Got a few bullwhackers, come through with a train, got it settin' out the other side of town. An' lemme see, the good-lookin' gent sittin' back there, I don't know who the hell he is—probably waitin' fer the girls—"

"Girls?" exclaimed Jimson.

"Didn't say there weren't *none*. Some are jes' passin' through. Actually, they *all* say they're jes' passin' through, goin' to Frisco or some such place, but a lot have been stoppin' off here for an awful long time."

"Why don't they take the train to Frisco?" Mulberry asked logically.

"'Cause they're workin' their way West, ain't that clear? They ain't schoolgirls headin' home for the holidays. They jes' go where business takes them, and when they get tired of one place, or strike gold, like gittin' lucky an' nailin' some poor bastard, they move on—ain't nobody wants to live where his wife used to be the town whoor."

"You got any choice ones passin' through right now?" asked Trash.

"I don't know. Few stopped off from the last stage, but they ain't declared themselves."

"I'll help 'em make up their minds," said Trash.

"The hell you will. That face of yours'd scare 'em."

"They're upstairs," guessed Trash. "You got 'em hid upstairs."

Evinrude sighed. It seemed that every time he listened to Trash he got tired. "I'm gonna take a walk around town, Ed. Want to come?"

Mulberry thought they'd seen the whole town when they'd ridden in. "Just some more saloons," he said.

"I thought I saw a sign saying 'barber.' Barbering and massage by beautiful Indian maidens."

Mulberry groaned. "Weren't you listening before? Do you want me to describe the medical treatment for that kind of disease?"

"You don't have to. I been through it." He wandered off.

The coffee was cool enough now to truly taste. No wonder the barkeep didn't want to stick a spoon in it.

"Hey. That *Miss Mulberry*?"

The voice came from the rear table where the blue-legs sat playing cards. A lot of other heads rose alertly and eyes searched for the lady in question.

"It's just that bastard Dayton, Ed," said Trash. "The same one what was makin' noise when the troops rode out."

"You'd think he'd find something worse to say than 'Miss Mulberry,'" said Ed, making light of it.

He did. "Biggest mystery around the barracks is what Miss Mulberry looks like underneath that yoony-form. Don't never bare himself till it's pitch black." Private Jeff Dayton wasn't very drunk, just mean, mean and bored. "Lemme tell yuh, anyone that ain't happy with the gals when they show up might give a think to Miss Mulberry." He grinned nastily.

"That right?" queried a large, mangy man sitting sprawled at another table, a bottle before him. "You sayin' that there brave Injun fighter at the bar would druther fight *squaws*? Maybe *is* a squaw?"

Dayton wasn't sure. He didn't like Mulberry, but he also didn't like buffalo stink. "You gotta understand. I don't think he's *yaller*, exactly. Jes' *real* delicate, ain't that right, Miss Mulberry?"

Ed had no place to hide. And worse, he knew from his voluminous reading what he should do. So, with an effort, he pushed himself away from the bar and walked lightly through a hush toward Dayton's table, toward Dayton's grin. He stopped there and said, "Stand up," and Dayton stood, stepping clear.

Ed Mulberry eyed his man, took a deep breath . . . and then rose up on the balls of his feet and started to dance around Dayton, flicking quick, perfect jabs that almost reached Dayton's nose. Dayton gaped. The roar that had begun sank quickly to a whisper. Jimson groaned and tossed off his whiskey.

Mulberry danced around, trying to figure out how to get close enough to Dayton to actually hit him without coming in range of Dayton's fists. Desperate, he darted in suddenly and managed to touch Dayton's nose before dancing back out of range as Dayton's eyes popped.

Mulberry was dimly conscious of a low sound gathering and beginning to roll through the room. Laughter.

Dayton advanced on him now, also hearing the laughter and not liking it one bit. Mulberry fluttered before him, flinging lefts in his general direction. Dayton practically ran after him, trying to close and destroy.

Jimson edged closer. His natural fighting style was unbridled ferocity, but he was sharp enough to see that wouldn't suit Ed, probably get him killed. "Keep movin', Ed, move 'n' jab."

But the laughter was too much for Ed. Maybe he wanted to get the humiliation over with quick, go out a real man. So it was that he suddenly stopped, planted himself, and whanged a roundhouse right high off Dayton's head.

Dayton roared. Mulberry, alarmed and sobered by his own madness, scurried away. Dayton leapt over a table after him, swinging. He fell, but caught Ed alongside the neck as he did.

Mulberry yelped. And then stood stock-still, shamed by the yelp.

Dayton recovered, closed in, and flailed away, hitting everything from Mulberry's waist to his brow. Ed's forage cap went flying. But the adrenaline was practically blowing his head off and he didn't feel a thing. No pain. And he started wildly back toward where all the blows were coming from.

Dayton waded through the rain of harmless blows and dug two hard rights to Mulberry's gut. Ed grunted and was spun halfway around just as he was letting fly with one that came all the way from the north forty.

It connected, for a change, but with the chin of one of the buffalo hunters who'd strayed too close. The man went down in a table-scattering sprawl. And his buddies went berserk.

Suddenly Ed felt blows coming from every which way and distantly heard, "Get that yella-bellied bastard blue-leg!"

He felt terrible, now that the pain was getting through to him, but Trash Jimson grinned and launched himself forward with a scream that made Whitey drop a glass and Dayton look up to see what all these critters were that his fists were suddenly banging into.

He saw Mulberry sinking into a surging mass of greasy buckskins. "*Hey!*" he shouted. Mulberrry wasn't *that* bad, damnit, and besides, he was *army*. He charged.

And met Jimson head-on, or would have, if a big buffalo hunter hadn't been caught between them.

Now the three other soldiers at the rear table piled in. And so did the rest of the hunters, trappers, a mule skinner, and a few cowboys.

Whitey, standing behind the bar, nervously watching the melee develop and fingering a shotgun, yelled, "Someone go get Cummings." Then he ducked as a chair came his way. The gun went off, blasting into the ceiling.

Muffled screams came down from above.

Jimson was clinging to a gent so greasy he had trouble hanging on. Trash saw an ear and bit it. The man screamed, whirled, and flung Jimson and a piece of ear into another man, a trapper who was jumping around looking for someone to hit. The trapper went off-balance and crashed into a table.

The man sitting at the table was the good-looking gent that Whitey couldn't put a handle on. The trapper looked up from his knees at the gent and growled. The gent unholstered and raised two pounds, five ounces worth of '72 Model Colt Peacemaker and hammered the trapper's head with it. Then he got up and walked calmly to the bar, holding his gun down by his side, found a drink that had been abandoned, and drank it. Then he winked at the uneasy Whitey and surveyed the battleground.

The soldiers, outnumbered at least two to one, and often outmuscled—Dayton was marveling at how easily a bull-whacker tossed him across the room until he hit the wall—were slowly getting pulverized. Half of Whitey was hoping the trappers, bullwhackers, and cowhands would win fast so he could clean up and get back to selling booze. But the other half knew the army would answer any defeat, sooner or later, in no uncertain manner. And the Drovers Rest, just wood and nails, could fall down as easily as the best of them. The only preordained loser in a battle was the battlefield itself. Still, all things considered, he wished the buffalo hunters and their friends would hurry up and get it over with.

But that was when Evinrude pushed in through the batwing doors, followed by Stretch and Malone, who were both grinning and looking for fun.

Evinrude looked on bemused until he spotted a flash of army blue. "Hey! Those are *our* men."

"Holy Mother of Gawd," Malone breathed in true Irish fervor.

"Where, where?" cried Stretch, blinking.

Evinrude grabbed a soldier, spun the man, and hooked, hooked, hooked and then went on to the next.

Malone hit a greasy-buckskinned man successively in the back of the head, the shoulder blades, and the kidney. The man slowed down considerably and Malone shot a boot up between his legs. The man fell writhing on the floor.

Stretch grabbed a bullwhacker from behind, bent on bringing peace. The bullwhacker doubled over, lifting Stretch off his feet, and then gave Stretch a little ride before digging elbows in his side and shaking him off onto the floor, where Stretch got a random kick in the face and had his hand stomped.

That made him mad. He grabbed the first thing he saw—a foot—twisted it, and was pleased by the yowl of pain. Little did it matter, nor did he know, that it was Dayton's foot he'd nearly twisted off.

Stretch then rose to his full height, grabbed the first man he saw, and tossed him toward the bar, where stood Whitey and some sissy gent. Stretch watched the man he'd thrown slide to a stop at their feet and he saw the sissy gent reach down and smartly crown him with his gun. Sissies did have their uses, thought Stretch, looking around for more game.

Sliding in under his gaze, though, was a sawed-off trapper

with a big belly and the weight of a cast-iron stove, who put all that weight into a blow to Dobbs' gut. Stretch's sudden exhalation almost blew the windows out.

The sawed-off trapper, having brought Stretch down to his own level, was planning his next move when Evinrude messed up his brains with a hook that started near the bar. It took the pleased smile off the short man's face and fixed it permanently near the back of his head. And then Evinrude moved methodically on, pleased that nary a finger had yet touched his tender face.

And in this manner the fight came to an end—Evinrude prowling among the fallen, looking for stubborn signs of life.

Just two were left, at the bar, the bartender and another gent. He decided he'd let the barkeep go, but the other gent . . .

That resolve lasted only until Evinrude, bearing down on the Last Man Standing, found himself staring down the barrel of a Colt and hearing, "I'm a man of peace."

Evinrude stopped, saw the slight smile, and said, "Aw, hell, I am too."

"Good. Let's drink to it."

Whitey brought them a couple of drinks.

Sheriff Cummings walked in the door, looked around, and then said to Whitey, "Damnation. I thought it'd *never* end."

"How long you been hidin' outside?" screamed Whitey.

Cummings jerked a thumb in Evinrude's direction. "Since this feller waltzed in. I took a peek and seen I wasn't needed—"

"Wasn't *needed*?"

Sheriff Cummings looked around innocently and said, "Why, no. Wound up pretty neat without me, far's I can tell."

Cummings joined Evinrude and the other man at the bar, and the three kept Whitey busy pouring drinks as the room slowly woke up.

About a half-hour later, Jimson, having downed three fast shots, peered out from swollen eyes and asked Evinrude, "You seen Mulberry? I figgered he'd be at the bottom of the pile, but he ain't."

"*Mulberry* was involved?"

"In*volved*?" cried Trash, and found he had an echo. He looked over his shoulder at the newly lopsided face of Dayton. "Mulberry *started* it, him and this here peckerhead Dayton."

"How was I to know ol' Nancy'd get up on his hind legs?"

106

"Nancy?" queried Evinrude, eyes hardening, head lowering.

Dayton stepped back out of range. Malone and Stretch cruised unsteadily up to the bar. "Sure and it's a drink I'll be needing," blathered Malone, "or two or three or four...." Malone looked around blearily. "And were these bruised ears deceivin' me, or was it the bonnie prince Mulberry that started these bloody shenanigans? If that's the case, he'll be owing me a tooth and poor Stretch here a busted gut."

"And some bastard damn near twisted my leg off," offered Dayton. Stretch peeked around slyly at him.

"Mulberry may have got it going," said Trash, "but Ev here finished it. Mulberry's probably back at the post by now."

Evinrude grinned. "Probably. Now let's do some serious drinking." He turned to the good-looking gent, his new friend. "I'm sorry, but I didn't catch your name before."

"Ben. Ben Crowley. And yours? I know it's Ev, I know that much."

"Evinrude. Jim Evinrude. You want another drink?"

Crowley didn't. Deputy U.S. Marshal Benjamin Crowley had other things on his mind, matters too important to be crowded out by booze. He'd come out from Cheyenne looking for a man, a U.S. Army private named James Evinrude, and he'd found him.

twelve _____

At that moment, far from being back at the post, Mulberry was two flights up on the top floor of the Drovers Rest, trying not to stare at a young woman who seemed to be undressing.

When Mulberry had sunk to the barroom floor he'd tried to think of a prayer, something like "Mother of God, please get me out of here." And whether or not he actually mouthed it, she did get him out, creating and showing him a crawlspace.

He'd crawled and crawled and crawled until he'd gotten through a side door and sunk down at the foot of some stairs. He'd looked up. The stairway seemed to reach halfway to heaven. At least a thousand steps. He'd started up, planning to stop at five hundred and rest. He'd felt dizzy and a little silly.

He'd made the second floor landing when there was a tremendous crash (Whitey's shotgun blast) and all hell seemed to bust loose all around him. Screams, shrieks...

"Hey, *mister*, quit shriekin', willya? Cut it out! What the hell's *wrong* with you?"

Ed Mulberry was kneeling at the foot of a young woman, staring at a dainty pair of high-laced leather boots. He slowly, painfully straightened, asking, "Was that you yelling?"

She stared at him angrily. "Now, yes. But before, that was *you*. It's bad enough, all that noise down there...."

Ed looked around to see where he was. Pain. A groan escaped.

"What's wrong with you?"

"I got stomped." Goodness. He was beginning to sound like Trash. But the words fit. "I got stomped good."

"Probably deserved it."

"Is there anywhere I can sit down?"

Which was how he got to the top floor, to an end room, to *her* room. The next thing he remembered was waking up on the bed, being shaken awake. "What are you doing, sleeping?"

"What?" Oh, Lord, give me strength. . . . Now why hadn't he thought of *that* prayer? *Before* the fight . . . And that fight—had he gone completely insane? "Who are you? And how did I get here? For that matter, *where* are we?"

"Boy, you did get whacked, didn't you?"

"Dear me, yes."

Her eyes narrowed. The last soldier she'd heard say "dear me" had been her brother, and he was dead. Hanged for desertion. "Stomped, you said," she reminded him.

"Stomped? I said *stomped*?"

"Yep. And . . . were you as thin as that before you got stomped?"

"I've always been this thin. . . . That's why I got stomped."

"Name's Pam. That's short for Pamela," she offered.

"Is there anything to drink?" he wheezed.

"Whiskey?"

"Lord, no."

"Just the water in the pitcher there."

He eyed it suspiciously.

"It's clean. The other one's the potty."

This was a plain-spoken girl; he turned and looked at her. His usual manner when addressing women was to look everywhere but at them. But for some reason he didn't feel shy.

Not ravishing, certainly, but something about her appealed to him. It couldn't have been the short, tangled, blond hair, or the button nose, or the too-wide mouth; he had finer, aristocratic tastes. But the eyes weren't bad, dark and large. A lot of rings around them, though, top and bottom. And the neck was okay. And she wasn't fat, rather slender in fact, except for the big b-br-br-breasts. *Jesus*, he couldn't even *think* about them without stuttering.

She smiled. A cracked tooth. That was either good or bad, he couldn't decide which. He found himself getting interested.

"What do you do here?"

"Here? Oh, nothing much," she replied airily. "I'm just passing through."

The words were discouragingly familiar.

"Oh. How long have you been 'just passing through'?"

She looked surprised. "I just got in today. I could have gone by train but I wanted to take my time, really see the West."

"Where are you headed?" asked Mulberry dully. "Frisco?"

"Yes."

"Do you have employment awaiting you there?"

"Yessirree. I'm gonna be a high-priced . . . hostess."

She seemed to regard prostitution as a perfectly legitimate line of endeavor. Her eyes narrowed. "What about you, your *experience*?"

Panic. He shrugged and grinned foolishly.

"You don't like *men*, do you?" She watched him shake his head furiously, caught his eye, and then saw the blush riding. "Hey, mister. Have you ever slept with a woman?"

He mumbled.

"What?"

"Sure," he said, louder.

He reminded her of Paul, her poor, gentle brother. She'd heard that sometimes when men were hanged they let loose in funny ways. It was probably the only time Paul had ever got it off, poor bastard. Paul hadn't even had the nerve to play with himself. "You ever play with yourself? Wake up with your blankets all wet and gooey?"

"*Me*? Of course not," he grumped. "*Stretch* does that kind of thing."

She smiled gently. She'd loved that brother. She moved around the room, touching things. "No," she said. "I haven't had that much experience. Some, sure, but hell, how much do you need? And how old do you think I am?"

"Not very old, I guess."

"Damn right. Young and fresh, and those old geezers out in Frisco are gonna pay plenty for me. Whaddaya think?"

It was not his area of expertise, but he gave it some serious thought. She had a healthy, energetic, tomboyish quality that some old men might find appealing. His own father, though, wouldn't have paid a dime for her, he was sure of that. As for himself . . . but he couldn't bring himself to think about that.

"Thanks," she said sarcastically.

"Oh, no, I think you'll do well. Pretty well, anyway."

"How about you? Would you pay for me? Huh? How about it—I'll give you a good price." She saw the blush rising again. "I gotta get some money or I'll *never* get to Frisco."

"How much?" he muttered, shocked at hearing the words come from his own mouth, however muted. But she expected it, he told himself.

"A dollar?"

"A *dollar*?" he practically screamed.

"Four bits, and that's a hell of a bargain."

Was he really negotiating? "Army privates aren't rich, you know."

"Tell you what," she said, making a firm decision. "We'll do it and *then* you can pay me what you think you should." She thought she knew her man and figured she might even come out ahead. But beyond that, she really wanted this soldier boy who reminded her so much of her brother.

He sat there mesmerized as she started to undress.

"What's your name?" she asked as a mound of golden pubic hair popped into sight. "You do have a name, don't you?"

"Huh? Oh, yeah. Ed."

"Here, Ed, lemme help you get those clothes off."

They worked his trousers down and his erection sprang out like a jack-in-the-box. She grinned and said, "You jus' been foolin' me."

He stared at his own pecker, astonished, not even feeling the rest of his clothes being removed. "When was the last time you ate, Paul?" she asked.

And then they rolled onto the bed. She grabbed, stroked, massaged, tweaked, covered his face with kisses. . . .

"My name's *Ed*, not *Paul*," he muttered.

She finally croaked, "C'mon, get on me, stick it in."

No response.

"Ed? Come *on*."

"I can't."

"You can't? Why does it feel *wet*? Oh, no! You *didn't*! She sat up and watched Ed's pecker slowly going limp on a damp patch of sheet.

"I couldn't help it. I'm sorry."

"You should be." She grabbed his pecker and tried to work some life into it. No use. Suddenly she was angry. "That'll be ten goddamn dollars!" she spat.

He came bolt upright—that is, all but his pecker. And she fell back down. "Oh, hell," she said, "I guess you don't owe me anything."

"Well, maybe *something*. I mean, what there was wasn't bad."

She jumped from bed and hastily started throwing on clothes.

"What are you doing?"

"Sounds like the fighting's stopped," she said, struggling with some snaps. "I'm gonna go downstairs and get me someone, someone with money who can . . ." She turned and looked at him sadly. "Now, Paul—I mean *Ed*—you just get dressed, and if you've still gotta hide, there're some rooms empty up here. Okay? And . . . I'll see you again, won't I? Before I leave?. . ."

Ed nodded dumbly, only looking up when the door slammed.

He dressed slowly, eyes smarting. Why couldn't he have done it right? If anyone found out he was a *virgin* . . .

He stood by the door, tears running down his cheeks. He opened the door and looked out. The corridor was empty. But then, suddenly, there was more noise. A door below had been opened And he heard a voice, an eager, cajoling voice. "C'mon, you big ol' bear.   " *Her* voice. Jesus!

Pamela and her prize made the stairs and she hauled him down the corridor, a big man who looked like he'd been through a meat grinder and stank and didn't seem to be all there, but he'd flashed a big wad of bills. She congratulated herself; it'd been her all-time fastest score.

She approached her room with some trepidation. If Ed hadn't gotten out yet. . . . She pushed the door open cautiously.

Empty. Thank God. "Come on in, big boy." Big Boy made a grunting sound and lumbered in.

Downstairs, the boys had been drinking nonstop. The stranger, Ben Crowley, had excused himself not long after two obvious hardcases, packing iron slung low, had entered the saloon. Ben was now sitting off by himself, watching the two gunsels.

"We better get back to the post," said Evinrude. "We were due back 'fore sunset. We better git while we can still ride."

"Sun's down already?" asked Jimson. He eyed Malone owlishly. "We're gonna hafta *pour* Malone inna saddle."

112

"Sod yeh, yeh bastard," gurgled Malone. "It will shoor be a sawry day win Malone kinna mount a mangy beastie."

Evinrude frowned. "Why does he talk like that?"

"Gets worse when he's drunk," Stretch explained.

"Sounds Scottish to me, almost," Jim pursued.

"He gets mixed up. And it gets so you can't understand him at all. That's when he's talkin' to his sainted mother." Stretch winked. "Then he falls over. We better get goin'."

Once outside, Jimson cried, "Hey, Mulberry's horse is still here."

They realized he wouldn't have taken anyone else's, not Mulberry. They split up to search the town. But fifteen minutes later they met again. Mulberry had not been found.

"Why don't you and Malone ride on out?" said Evinrude. "He looks sick."

Malone was about to deny it when he threw up. Stretch hoisted him up into the saddle and then, carefully staying upwind, led Malone out of town.

"He's gotta still be inside, Ev," said Trash, and led the way back into the Drovers Rest.

Inside, they found the side door and disappeared through it.

One of the hardcases at the bar asked Whitey, "That blue-leg called Ev, just went through the door, what's his full name?"

Whitey eyed the sallow face, the slack jaw, the pendulous lip—the man looked like a dum-dum. But the hard, angry, red eyes that were set too close together made Whitey figure that he'd *better* know the name and fast. "Evinrude," he said. "Name's Evinrude."

Ben Crowley heard the exchange and his brow furrowed.

Trash and Jim worked the third floor, room by room. Nothing so far. They opened the last door at the end of the corridor. Pamela looked up from beneath Big Boy at them, wide-eyed, without a trace of embarrassment. "Sorry," she said, "full up." And she giggled.

"Shit," said Trash. "If that's Mulberry he's doubled in size."

Big Boy's sweaty, matted head swiveled around and tiny eyes glared at them. "What the hell *you* want?" he growled.

Evinrude recognized Big Boy as the third man he'd dropped.

"You shore got a pimply ass," said Trash, grinning.

113

The girl was silently telling them to get out. Cute little thing, thought Trash, eyeing the thigh and bit of tit he could see and the face that was fast becoming contorted.

"Ev! Look!"

A hand stuck out from under the bed, waving discreetly. And then an imploring face peeked out.

"Lookit what?" roared Big Boy, rearing up, turning, almost pulling out and getting off the bed. "What's so goddamn funny?"

Pamela's eyes widened, the mystery of Mulberry's whereabouts solved, and she would have laughed herself if she wasn't scared as hell.

Trash and Ev closed the door. They waited outside, listening, until they were certain that Mulberry was still safely hidden. Then they went back downstairs and waited by a couple of glasses of beer.

The hardcases eyed them, but said nothing. And for the whole time they and the hardcases stood there together, Deputy U.S. Marshal Ben Crowley's hand rested solidly on his gun butt and his gaze never wavered. The backs of those hardcases got to look awfully familiar. He'd even picked his spots, just below and inside the left shoulder blade of each.

Eventually, Big Boy came lumbering downstairs, grinning.

Then Pamela appeared, looked around, spotted Trash and Jim at the bar, and came over, grinning and dodging groping hands. "You boys sure know how to make a gal feel real relaxed," she said.

Evinrude liked her and Trash liked her even better.

"Thet big turd worth anythin'?" asked Trash as Jim glared.

Her grin widened and, after looking around to see where the "big turd" had gone, she said, "Paid a lot more than he was worth. Paid near all the way to Frisco."

"That something special, all the way to Frisco?" asked Trash, visions of unlikely debaucheries squirming through his mind. "I hearda somethin' called 'round the world'. . . ."

"Where's Mulberry?" asked Evinrude.

"I *hope* he's coming down," she said.

He was. He soon appeared and painfully made his way across the saloon to join them. "Stiffened up," he explained.

"*Now* he stiffens up," cried Pamela, and Mulberry almost collapsed in shame. "Well, you sneaky bastard," she went on, "did you learn anything?"

He looked at her imploringly. His fate was in her hands. "I learned the floor's pretty hard, and there's not that much clearance especially when people are bouncing the springs up and down."

"What'd she mean," said Trash, grinning, "*now* you stiffen up?"

"'Cause he got stomped," said Pam quickly. "He knew he was going to stiffen up, just didn't know when."

Mulberry breathed a silent sigh of relief.

"Well," said Pam, "gotta move around. My public, you know...."

"An' we gotta git," said Evinrude. "Top kick'll be fit to be tied."

Trash sobered. "You mean *we'll* be fit to be tied."

Outside, Trash asked Mulberry, "Hey Ed, you do anything with that gal, what's-her-name?"

Mulberry gave Trash a man-of-the-world smile, and then added, "Her name's Pamela."

"How much you pay her?"

Mulberry gave him a *rich*-man-of-the-world look, then said, "We had an understanding."

"Yeah, but how much did the understanding cost? I mean, she said that big turd paid her enough to get her all the way to Frisco."

"He did?" yelped Mulberry.

"Can you beat that?" Trash said in obvious wonderment.

Mulberry looked stricken.

thirteen _____

Racing Elk and his band of warriors traveled north at a faster pace. Since the army massacre, they knew it was just a matter of time before the alarm was raised.

They'd gained the Bozeman Trail. Two forts lay ahead, Reno and Kearney. They'd been abandoned when Racing Elk had traveled south the year before, the Indian having forced the white man out. But now . . .

The whites were pouring West again, in ever greater numbers. They never stopped coming. Maybe the forts were manned once more. He'd have to be careful.

Racing Elk noticed that the braves were not riding in to taste the white women nearly so often. Perhaps the long, hard ride was taking its toll, or the combat had sent their thoughts racing to distant plains, or they were weary of the tired women, who wouldn't eat and lay unmoving.

One of his braves, Two Dogs, had grown sufficiently tired of the unresponsiveness of one of the older women that he had, just that morning, put her out of her misery with his knife. There had been no time to bury the corpse, so it had been left a short distance off the trail. Two Dogs had been reprimanded, of course—not so much for his wanton destruction of community property, but because Racing Elk didn't care to mark their trail with flocks of circling buzzards that could be seen for miles.

At that moment, Racing Elk was riding with the wagons. He'd thought of joining the girl, but it was a bad example, and he could wait for night. Too much of one thing was bad, for the brave as well as the woman.

Racing Elk looked up and narrowed his eyes. The forward scout was approaching fast.

Ernest Finley had called it quits. For a while, anyway. He'd spent the winter and spring trapping up Montana way, in the area around Fort Keogh. He was not your ordinary trapper, Ernest Finley; he'd brought his wife and child along, lodging them at the fort, to which he'd repair whenever the need arose. And, with a handsome and legally bound woman within easy reach, it was surprising how often the need arose—so often that, come fall, another baby was due to arrive.

Ernest Finley had been a trapper for twenty years, married for five, and now, with his final harvest of skins sold and all his earthly belongings in his wagon, he was heading south to sink roots.

Far south. It took a hardy breed to weather Montana's winters, especially when the other three seasons were practically nonexistent, they were so brief. He'd nearly frozen his ass off in both May and September of one year or another. Besides, the trapping life was no way to raise a family.

He, his pregnant wife, and his son, Evan, comfortably riding their canvas-topped wagon behind a team of four strong horses, had kept company with a small wagon train between Fort Keogh and Fort Smith. At Fort Smith, though, he'd let the train continue on West as he prepared to angle back southeast along the Bozeman.

The folks at Fort Smith had wondered if he wouldn't rather wait for some more wagons, to form a wagon train down the Bozeman. The Bozeman was open again, but there were no guarantees.

Ernest Finley had conferred with Nan. They were headed now for a life that she wanted most of all, and so she deserved a say in the matter. She'd never seen anything but tame Indians her entire life, and was anxious to get south and settled. "I don't feel like having my baby in the back of this wagon, Ernest."

"Plenty of women have, Nan."

"But I am not."

And so they'd driven south, alone.

Ernest flicked the reins, scattering flies, and wiped his brow.

It was heating up nicely, thank you, too nicely for a Northern man. Nan, of course, was used to the heat. She was raised in the South somewhere. Austin, he thought, Austin, Texas, near the banks of the Colorado River, though what the Colorado River was doing in Texas beat the hell out of him. Same thing the Mississippi was doing in Minnesota, he figured.

"What's funny, dear?" Nan asked.

"Nothin'. Jes' the Mississippi." He laughed again.

He shaded his eyes. Wagons, in the distance. Two.

He reached back into the covered part, where Nan and Evan sat, and brought out his Remington repeater, laying it on the seat by his side. Then he reached beneath his seat and got his Colt and laid it in his lap. Finley was a careful man.

Damned if those men weren't looking funnier and funnier, thought Ernest, as the wagons drew closer. They were *dressed* normal, could be drovers or teamsters or near anybody, according to their clothes, and their hats could've been pulled down low and their heads ducked because of the hot sun, but that still left a little bit of their faces showing, and that was what made him wonder. Ernest Finley had an eye that could see an eagle before the eagle saw him.

Maybe they were Mexican, with those dark faces, or even niggers—seemed like every third or fourth cowboy he saw was a darkie. And he'd heard tell the army down South was almost *all* darkies, 'cept of course for the officers. Yeah, they could be niggers. Or they could be friendlies. Some Indians were beginning to fit in real good, had a real feel for the white man's ways.

The wagons were close now. He could see the drivers' eyes. Weren't friendly. But weren't *un*friendly. Not really. Yet Ernest Finley felt his scalp tingle.

Finley halted his team as the wagons drew abreast. He smiled. He was ready to stop and talk a bit. But the other wagon, though the drivers nodded, kept right going on past. Finley scowled and wondered whether to waste a smile on the second wagon.

To hell with it, he decided, and so, with his eyes deliberately downcast, he failed to see the guns raised and pointed and only heard the blasts when great holes had already been torn in his throat and chest. Simultaneously, there was a hail of fire from the first wagon into the back of Finley's.

Nan and young Evan died instantly from head wounds.

Racing Elk and his braves then drove the Finley wagon well off the road and down into a draw and cut the horses and Finley scalps loose. Racing Elk took Ernest's and put it into a leather bag, where it joined many others. As soon as this journey was done, he would find a squaw to refine the scalps to smaller bits and sew them onto his war shirt, a practice that was common among the Sioux.

Once the choicer items among Finley's possessions—a glistening, well-kept mouth organ for one—had been transferred to the Sioux wagons, and Racing Elk had congratulated his men on the swift, disciplined operation, the march north resumed.

It wasn't until they were well under way, gone from sight, that the baby inside Nan finally died.

Captain Warner Conway stood by the wagon, having his morning coffee. He twisted and stretched, trying to loosen his aching muscles. Maybe he was getting too old for this stuff.

"Think we'll get lucky today, sir?" asked Mr. Smiley.

How the hell did he know? thought Conway. They'd ridden north to intercept the Platte wagon road, followed it west, and then swung north onto the Bozeman, and they hadn't even *smelled* an Indian, much less seen one. Of course, the chances of picking up sign along the well-traveled Platte wagon road, and the somewhat-less-traveled Bozeman were pretty slim. And there was always the chance that the Cheyenne weren't even heading that way, but possibly east and out of their sector. Damn! It had been a long, hot, fruitless ride. And yet . . . after a long, hard stare to the north, Warner Conway turned and leveled his gaze at Smiley and said seriously, "I wouldn't be surprised, Mr. Smiley."

Smiley sure as hell would, though, if the truth be told. He was even more frustrated than Captain Conway. At least Conway was a captain. Second lieutenants like Smiley and Fletcher were *nowhere*. They really needed action and victories and subsequent commendations. Or at least Smiley did. Fletcher's lack of spirit was no big secret. All the same, Smiley was about to write this one off as a lost cause.

And, as if reading his mind, Fletcher said, "They're probably in Nebraska."

Who the hell needs him, thought Conway, though he tended to agree. But, "I think not, Mr. Fletcher," he said instead.

"Not if Mr. Lo is as canny as we give him credit for." Which also gave Captain Conway an out, should he be proved wrong. He then finished his coffee, took a deep breath, and strode off toward his mount, grating, "Let's move them out."

The camp broke. Lieutenant Smiley sent Corporal Brent and his squad up front, another squad under Sergeant Breckenridge to the left, and he himself took the remaining squad, with Corporal Wallace, off to the right flank. Lieutenant Fletcher and one of his squads rode with Captain Conway in the center. Bringing up the rear were Sergeant Chubb and the last two squads. Together they formed a rough diamond formation, which, viewed from afar, seemed a bit ragtag but was rather precise, terrain permitting.

Reb McBride rode with the captain, and whiled away the time by blowing quiet little tunes on his bugle. At first it irritated the hell out of Conway. But then he'd heard some privates whistling along with the bugler, so he'd ground his teeth and kept silent. And on the third day he'd found himself also whistling along with McBride, such was the power of suggestion and the extent of his boredom.

Smiley came riding in from the right flank. "How long have those tracks been out there, sir, do you know?"

"What tracks?"

"I don't know, but there're a lot. Ghosting the trail, sort of. First time *I've* seen them but, as you know, we've been rotating. . . ."

"Mr. Fletcher," Conway called out.

Fletcher rode forward. "Sir?"

"How long have those tracks been out on our flank?"

Fletcher looked accusingly at Smiley. Then he said, "What tracks, sir?"

"Get the scouts," snapped Conway.

"Chubb!" roared Smiley, and Fletcher complacently took a back seat. Chubb was *his* sergeant, but what the hell.

Chubb rode forward from the rear. "Sir?" he said to Smiley, since he knew Fletcher couldn't yell like that.

"Have a man go bring back a scout."

"Do it myself, sir," said Chubb.

Half an hour later, River That Forks had returned, checked the right flank, and read sign of fifteen or twenty riders. "But not Indian pony. Too big."

"But they're riding like Indians?" pressed Captain Conway.

River That Forks nodded.

"Of course," said Conway, nodding. "Now check *that* side, see how many you find there."

"Fifteen, twenty, I betcha."

"Don't bet, go see."

"What are you thinking, sir?" asked Lieutenant Smiley.

"War party. Got some men dressed in those uniforms, driving that carriage and limber, trying to sneak by as soldiers. Got the rest riding the flanks, out of sight. That's the only thing that makes sense."

"Not bad."

"No, not bad, and it's got the element of surprise. By the time anyone realizes that they're *not* soldiers, it's too late . . . unless it's a whole damn platoon they run into."

Hoofbeats from the south had them all twisting in their saddles. A single rider approached fast.

The rider, an unfamiliar soldier, rode in among them and, after saluting, handed Captain Conway a folded piece of paper.

"Where're you from, soldier?"

"Headquarters, sir. It's from Fort Fetterman."

"Why didn't Fetterman contact us directly?" The fort was a lot closer than headquarters. But he knew the private couldn't answer that. He shook his head. "If we were camped right outside Fetterman's gates, they'd route a message to us through headquarters." He unfolded and read the paper.

He looked up. His voice was calm, belying his excitement. Finally, he knew the enemy. "I'll have to amend that statement I made a little while ago. They've already run into a platoon from Fetterman, on the road south of the fort, a good ways south."

"And?"

"And, Mr. Smiley? They wiped it out. All dead. And not one sign of a single Indian casualty."

"Any . . . atrocities?" wondered Fletcher.

Conway frowned. That was a newspaper word, for the public. The army savaged hostiles and the hostiles gave it right back, often in spades. Both sides expected it. There was a lot of fatalism west of the Mississippi. "Atrocities" sounded worse than they were. Dead men didn't feel anything. Torture, of course, was different. But that, too, was a double-edged sword.

"No. No sign of torture." He suspected torture was what Fletcher meant. "No, just an efficient killing. The best guess now is that it's Racing Elk, coming back from down South where—I think we've all heard this—where he really raised hell, always one step ahead of the army. Oglala . . ." He showed a wintry smile. "The Sioux keep coming up with them, don't they? Wonder where they've got *their* West Point?"

"You aren't making a serious comparison, are you, sir?" inquired Fletcher, all too aware of the appreciative glint in the eye of up-from-the-ranks Smiley.

"I certainly am," said Conway, a graduate of the Point. "And I think you and Mr. Smiley had best inform your men. It might help to know who they're facing. They haven't been looking that sharp."

Nor have you, thought Smiley, but hell's bells, hadn't he himself been pissing and moaning to Sergeant Breckenridge just that morning? "Yes sir! Right away, sir!"

"What about the Cheyenne arrow, sir?" asked Lieutenant Fletcher.

"Fake," said Conway confidently. "The Sioux being cute, that's all."

The morning seemed to pass faster, now that eyes were sharpened and guts tightened.

Along about noon, River That Forks waited for the Captain to ride up and said, "Looks like they stopped here to rest."

They were off the trail a short distance.

"They camped spread out, same formation."

Conway smiled. He appreciated discipline. "Gun tracks?"

"Maybe. Something heavy. But more than four wheels."

"A wagon besides?"

"Tracks confusing," said the scout, "but maybe eight, ten wheels."

"Gun carriage, limber, and a wagon. It has to be that." Conway glanced up at Fletcher. "No reason they couldn't have brought a wagon north."

Later that afternoon the man riding out front for the point squad spotted buzzards circling and dipping into a gully alongside the trail. Trouble Thompson was probably the biggest target in all of Easy Company, a distinction of which he was all too aware, but he didn't hesitate to investigate. He only wondered why the hell the scouts hadn't.

He found the chewed-up body of Nellie Fairchild, born in North Carolina forty-eight years earlier, a recent emigrant West with her husband and family, and most recently an occupant of Racing Elk's first wagon. She'd been the one lying closest to Josie.

They let River That Forks handle the body. After examination, the scout said she'd been knifed to death, stabbed once in the side. Then she was buried.

"Wonder who she was?" muttered Lieutenant Smiley.

"It's not who she was but *what* she was that matters," said Fletcher, a trace excitedly. "She was *white*. Racing Elk's got white women with him."

They'd all been thinking that. But it didn't bother them very much. Fletcher seemed to be the only one who was really upset. Indians grabbing white women wasn't anything new; they were used to it. But it didn't make them any happier.

"Happen we might find some more," said River That Forks.

"More what—bodies?"

The scout nodded. "They prob'ly got more than one . . . and that woman was near dead when they killed her. Starved."

That one puzzled Captain Conway. Why in the world wouldn't they feed them?

"Right, let's get it moving," he growled. "Mr. Smiley, have your men pick up the pace. I want this bunch, Gatling or no Gatling."

fourteen _____

Mulberry, Jimson, and Evinrude were on their way to town again. That they'd received passes so soon after goofing up the previous time indicated two things: that life in and around the post was unusually quiet, and that they'd learned their lessons the previous time. And they had.

Mulberry, especially. The events that had transpired were burned forever into his brain.

The night they got back from town, Sergeant Cohen had come out to greet them personally. He was not in a good frame of mind. Jimson, tired and lightheaded, complained that the first sergeant was keeping them from barracks and bed. Whereupon Cohen made Jimson push a bullet from the gate to the barracks with his *nose*, with Mulberry and Evinrude keeping the cursing Trash company. Then they'd had to go to the stables and clean and groom damn near every horse in the place. Took them half the night, or what was left of it.

The next morning, when report was over, Cohen called Dobbs, Malone, Jimson, Evinrude, and Mulberry "front and center."

Cohen then made the five men assume raised push-up positions, weight supported by hands and feet, arms and legs fully extended. Mulberry had never been very good at push-ups.

Cohen then walked the line of miscreants and placed a small, round object on the ground directly beneath each of their heads. He paused in front of Evinrude to say, "I'm sorry about this, Private. Malone and Dobbs, I expected them to goof up yesterday, *fightin'* in town, and last night, gettin' in late. I already had plans for them. And Jimson, I knew he'd goof up too, but you, Private, and *Mulberry* . . . must say I'm disappointed." After which speech he placed Evinrude's little round object on the ground below his head.

Mulberry thought they looked like marbles. He wondered if they were going to have to pick them up with their mouths. Or eyelids.

"You will now touch them stones squarely and firmly with your heads, *without* lowering your bodies."

Mulberry dipped his head, as did the four others. He found that he most easily touched the stone "squarely and firmly" with the top of his brow, right about at his hairline. That wasn't so hard, except his arms were beginning to shake.

"Ah, Mulberry, I see that your arms are weakening. I have a cure for that. You, and the rest of you, will maintain your present positions exactly, *except* . . . except that you may rest one arm by placing it behind your back."

Malone, Dobbs, Jimson, and Evinrude did so. Mulberry didn't.

"Mulberry!"

Mulberry cried, "You said *may*, Sergeant."

"You *will* place one arm behind your back."

Mulberry did so. The pain, on top of the splitting headache, was excruciating. He sagged, and then he flopped.

"Mulberry. Assume the position."

Ed glanced at the rest. Red-faced, grimacing with the strain and pain but also bursting with stubborn pride—and fear—they were holding steady in their tripod stances. Mulberry planted his forehead on the stone and tried again.

And, after only about ten seconds, failed again.

"Mulberry!"

And so it went. His eyes smarted, got watery. Cohen announced that the other four men would remain in position until Mulberry—"I will have no goddamn weaklings!"—assumed the position and held it.

"For crying out loud, Mulberry," gasped Jimson and Malone, and Dobbs cursed low and steady. But Evinrude never made a peep, just squeezed his eyes tighter and tighter and drew back his lips, baring clenched teeth.

Lieutenant Price had gone back to the officers' mess, but

Lieutenant Kincaid had stayed to watch. And the set of his face betrayed no sympathy. Discipline was discipline. But Mulberry was simply a physically weak person. Four-eyes Bradshaw wouldn't do any better, didn't Sergeant Cohen realize that?

Yes, Cohen did realize that. But it wasn't an impossible demand he was making, and a man could do what he set his mind to do, including Mulberry. Cohen wasn't about to back off. Mulberry was going to learn a lesson about himself that day or . . .

The men shouted at Mulberry, ridiculing him, demeaning his ancestry, relatives, sexual bias. Cohen let them yell.

Mulberry shook all over, tears streamed down his face.

Kincaid stepped to Cohen's side and whispered, "Perhaps you could let the others quit."

Cohen's head snapped around, barking, "No!"

Kincaid blinked and Cohen's voice lowered, but not enough; his mouth was only a couple of inches from Kincaid's still-quivering ear. "Sorry, sir. Can't. He's not just gonna do it for himself but, more important too, for *them*."

He was right, decided Matt, but he still thought of it as "Cohen's Sun Dance," the Indians' Sun Dance being a religious ceremony involving excruciating self-torture that, among other things, tested a warrior's ability to withstand pain.

The yelling from the sidelines had abated. Cohen stepped to the head of Mulberry, who was prone once more. "Again," grated Cohen, "or your buddies are gonna wear them stones in their heads for life."

Mulberry's swimming vision sought out his friends. They were silent now, suffering but silent and unbending.

He remembered the Drovers Rest, the fight. . . . They'd fought for him, he knew that . . . but *please.* . . .

He got the stone under his head and slowly raised, stretching his legs out behind.

The *pain* . . . he *couldn't.* . . . But he fought the pain now, concentrated on it, even willed it to increase. . . .

"Steady," said Sergeant Cohen.

He *grabbed* the pain, clutched it, caressed it, loved it. . . . *"Steady."*

Tears streamed down his face and fell to the dirt. His shaking legs moved to maintain balance.

"Hang in there." A voice that wasn't Cohen's.

126

And then he saw no more, thought no more, cried no more; everything was black....

A voice from afar. "Get up.... You can get up."

He saw blurred feet by his head. "For Chrissakes, Mulberry, get the hell up." That was Jim's voice. Evinrude.

"And—Good God!—he was *still* in the one-handed push-up position, head down and driving the stone deeper into the ground.

He fell over on his side and lay panting until some of the pain seeped away, then he stood up shakily.

Faces came into focus. Ev, Trash, Malone, beyond them Sergeant Cohen ... and beyond him Lieutenant Kincaid.

Mulberry took a long while getting steady ... and then took two steps toward Cohen, finishing the move with a wild, round-house right.

Cohen easily avoided the punch and then, face impassive, he stepped forward and hammered Mulberry once, breaking Ed's nose and dropping him in the dirt as still as a corpse.

"Get him inside," said Cohen. And then he said, his voice low but audible to all, "Dismissed."

Evinrude picked Mulberry up and carried him off. Ed didn't remember being carried, but he sure remembered the rest. His friends probably remembered it, too. After all, they all had small, round bruises on their foreheads to remind them.

But Ed had a broken nose besides. Trash said it looked more manly. Ed wondered what Pamela would think.

Matt Kincaid sat in his office, trying to find something to think about and watching a squadron of flies circle and buzz. He thought, Maybe sometime in the life of one of those flies he lit on an Indian. Now he's planning to light on me. Wonder if that's supposed to mean anything?

He raised his eyes heavenward. "Lord, you've got to make things a whole lot clearer than that."

"What's that, sir?" called Cohen, from the next room.

"Nothing, Sergeant." Cohen. God of Outpost Nine. He heard the telegraph clacking. What now? Probably another IG inspection, as if there were nothing better to do. Jesus, what did it matter how neatly they were winning the West, as long as they won it? Highly commissioned nitpickers, that's what they were....

"Message, sir." Bradshaw stood there staring at him.

Matt took the paper and read it. Then he got to his feet and walked into the next room, his face grim. Cohen looked up.

"Patrol from Fetterman. Went out before they got word of hostiles. Didn't worry 'cause they were platoon-size." Matt's mouth creased into a bitter smile as he shook his head. "Just found them. Cut to ribbons, every last mother's son."

The telegraph was clacking again. More? Damnation!

"They figure it was a big war party, maybe Racing Elk."

"Bad," said Cohen. "Real bad. They use the Gatling?"

"No mention." Bradshaw handed him another sheet. "This one's from Captain Conway. They've got them."

"They're fighting?"

"No. Picked up sign, though. They're on their tail. Maybe forty braves. And the Sioux've got white women."

Cohen frowned. "Where the hell from?"

"Who knows?"

"It's funny, sir, thinking of the Gatling. Did you know Evinrude and his bunch rode with that gun crew coming West, into Cheyenne?"

"That's right, they did. Think I'll have a word with them. Still can't understand why that gun crew took off by themselves."

"Not to mention how Racing Elk knew the Gatling was being shipped."

"That too. Maybe an accident, but I'd sure like to know. By the way, how'd the men survive your Sun Dance?"

Cohen grinned. "Headaches, that's all."

"Are the men respecting Mulberry now?"

"Nope. Aw hell, Lieutenant, you'd think they might, but they saw him cryin' and floppin' around and . . . he made it, that's for sure, but he didn't cover himself with no glory. He's *still* different, y'know. Someone left a doll on his bed. A boy doll. They think maybe he's you know, *funny*."

"All men aren't the same, Sergeant."

"All *men* aren't, yeah. I know that." He scratched his head. "Still can't figure out where they found a *doll*."

Matt Kincaid propped one buttock on the corner of Cohen's desk. "What do you think of Indians, Sergeant? Do you think of them as men, real men, no question one way or the other?"

"Gawd, yessir. If they ain't nothin' else, they're men."

"Aha. Well, did you know the Sioux have men that dress

128

and act like women, that do bead and quillwork like women, and that those men often become powerful medicine men?"

"You don't mean it, sir," breathed Cohen.

"Close your mouth, Sergeant, there're too many flies around. Now, these men are called *winkte*. That's a Sioux word; what it means exactly I don't know."

Cohen wasn't about to guess. He didn't even want to hear any more. "Even Indians," he groaned. "Damnation."

"Who can you trust, right? Anyway, the *winkte* are recognized as *wakan*, that's Sioux for 'holy,' and even some of the bravest warriors sleep with a *winkte*—"

"Jesus!"

"Oh, it's kind of mixed. On one hand the *winkte* are greatly respected, but on the other they're sometimes shunned. Avoided. Seems the Indians aren't any more comfortable with men like that than we are. *But*—and this is important—nobody questions it, nobody says or thinks a *winkte's* doing wrong."

"How come?"

"You see, most Sioux men are what they are because a dream has told them to be that thing. When they're young they wait for this dream, and when it comes, that's what they've got to do, or be. 'Course, sometimes they don't like the dream and they wait for another, better one. But if it doesn't come they're stuck with the original. Now, these *winkte* are that way because their dreams told them to be like that, and believe me, no Sioux argues with a dream. To them, dreams reveal the real truth, are realer than real."

Cohen thought about that for a while, reviewing some recent dreams of his own, then finally said, "Yeah?"

"Yeah. And this I know for a fact—or almost a fact. One of Crazy Horse's childhood friends was a boy named Pretty One—"

Cohen made a face.

"That's right. He grew up to be a *winkte*, but Crazy Horse—and you know what kind of man *he* is—he never tried to change Pretty One or anything like that. Teased him, maybe, or maybe wasn't such a close friend anymore, but it had come from a *dream*. And even Sitting Bull can't argue with a dream."

Cohen's eyes narrowed. "How come you know so much about this, sir? Not that I—"

Matt held up a hand, laughing. "No big secret. Met an officer once, think his name was Collins. He grew up out here.

His father commanded Fort Laramie. This Collins, he knew Mr. Lo and liked them and studied them. He even knew Crazy Horse then, when Crazy Horse was young. He told me all this stuff."

Cohen's face assumed an extremely grim cast. "Are you telling me, sir, that Mulberry might be a . . . *winkte* . . . that he might have powerful medicine . . . and that I should have someone like Malone—ain't no warrior fiercer than Malone—that I should have Malone *sleep* with him?"

Kincaid nearly fell off Cohen's desk, laughing.

"If so, sir," continued Cohen, "*you're* going to have to be the one to tell him." And he got up, grinning, and headed for the booze stash. This called for a drink. "Bradshaw. Take a walk."

Bradshaw left and they drank. "But I think I'd better have a word with the boys about that gun crew," said Matt. "Where are they?"

"Sorry, sir. Town. Wish I'd known."

"That's okay. I'll catch them there. I guess you'll have to be in charge here."

Who the hell else? "Right, sir. I haven't seen much of Mr. Price, neither. An' good huntin'."

fifteen ———————————————

"Mulberry! Jimson!"

The two men stopped short. They'd come out of the Drovers Rest and were hoofing smartly down the boardwalk.

Kincaid dismounted and climbed up onto the wooden walk. Mulberry's hand made a vague pass at his cap.

Kincaid ignored the gesture. "Where's Evinrude?"

"Aw, he's back at the Drovers, sir," said Jimson, "Yakkin' with some dude. Me'n Mulberry, well, he's lookin' fer this pertickler gal an' I'm jes' lookin' fer anything that *moves*."

Mulberry? Looking for a woman? Cohen would be positively ecstatic. "Give me a few minutes. To talk."

"We're your'n, Lieutenant."

"Let's go in here."

"Here?" It was a hole. A saloon, yes, but darker than sin. They could hardly make out the bar. "How're you gonna see what yer drinkin', sir?"

"Out here it all tastes rotten, Jimson."

They entered, sat at a table, and called for drinks. "I want to hear about that gun crew you rode out here with."

Mulberry and Jimson exchanged looks, and then the drinks arrived. Jimson sipped. "Rotten," he said, grinning, "real rotten." And then he and Mulberry told Matt all about the ride and the gun, omitting the episode of the cows and the cowboys.

"But I don't understand why they just took off and left without waiting for the escort."

Jimson was busy shrugging when he froze, his blood running ice cold. He distinctly heard Mulberry calmly saying, "You'd probably better know, sir, that that was because we'd killed a man coming West. Or I should say men."

"Och, sir, what a load. He's crazy!"

But Matt's mind was working like lightning. He had the missing piece. Or pieces. "Now, you said *we*, so that means you three...but it had to be connected with the gun crew, with the Gatling....Damn! You were firing the Gatling out the door, you had to be—"

Incredible, thought Mulberry. Guessed it all, just like that. Mulberry gazed through the gloom at Matt with something approaching idolatry. He was ready to confess anything.

"Something came along, a couple of cowboys, you couldn't stop in time...or thought it might be fun to test it on—"

"Almost," interrupted Mulberry, a trifle disappointed. "But we weren't *that* cold-blooded. I was handling the gun—"

"You were *not*," cried Jimson, enraged. "*I* was. You was scared to touch it."

"What do you mean? I was the one that knew all about Gatlings."

"Sure, you *know* all about them, from *books*. Sir, I was the bucko firin' that gun, an' blowin' the hell outta that poor sod 'n' his horse what was settin' out there with his cows. But it was an *accident*."

"The other wasn't," asserted Mulberry, a bit put out.

Jimson glowered. "Go ahead, bigmouth."

Mulberry told how the second cowboy had been shot down.

"Mulberry," said Jimson, "he tried to tell the lieutenant they was *road agents*, dumb cluck." And Trash dove back into his drink.

"I don't think that would have made much difference, sir," said Mulberry. "That lieutenant was very green...and excitable."

Now the gloom inside the saloon seemed really abysmal. "And now he's very dead," Kincaid said, wondering what the hell he was going to *do*.

Jimson should probably be hanged. But who would pay for the second cowboy? And the gun crew, they let Jimson fire the goddamned gun, and they were dead. Did that pay for everything? It was a knotty problem. And, Matt realized, it was his problem alone because if the killings had already been investigated, then yes, the gun crew *had* cleared the books with their deaths. There'd be no more questions asked.

"When we got to Cheyenne," Mulberry resumed, and then he went on to describe what happened there. ". . . And then this man happened by and offered to guide them north and—"

"What? They had a guide with them?"

"Yeah," said Jimson. "Guess he got killed, too. Looked like the bastard could handle himself, though. And Mulberry, when you talked them into leavin', I thought you was worryin' about *me*. Some pal . . ."

Kincaid was trying to remember the body count. And even if it didn't match, they might have missed one, or the guide might have gotten away. "Describe him."

They did, and Matt said, "You didn't hear a name, did you?"

Jimson said, "No, sir," and Mulberry said, "Yes. I take notes, write things down. It had a good sound."

"Where are your notes?"

"At the post. I dropped them in the tub on KP. But the name I remember. Creed Scarborough. It has a ring to it."

Creed. Possibly a breed. A renegade white working with Mr. Lo? Possible. Hell, Windy was one step away from that himself. Matt decided to look into it further. "Okay, boys, go find yourself some gals. I'll take care of the bill here."

They left, and Kincaid found that Mulberry hadn't touched his drink. Why'd he order the damn thing, then? Matt tossed it off, shuddering.

Evinrude was getting a little drunk again. And his friend, Ben Crowley, wasn't helping. Or rather, he *was* helping. To get drunk.

Crowley didn't drink much himself. He was too involved with getting Evinrude loose and sucking the story from him, *and* too involved with feeling like a rat. Evinrude's tale of unrelieved disasters was incredible. And if Crowley had been in Jim's shoes, he probably would have killed that drunken logger, too. But he *hadn't* been in his shoes. Ben's shoes were the shoes of the law, and he was going to have to send Jim back to stand trial. And Ben was going to have to send a written statement to that trial, was going to have to repeat what Jim had told him, that Jim had been a little drunk when he'd killed the logger. Ben hated doing that, which was why he was feeling like a rat. But, he'd felt like a rat at other times, other places; it was the job.

"That's it," said Ben. "My ear's about to drop off."

Evinrude looked up, startled. "It's early."

"I've got things to do."

"But I've got to tell you. You're my friend."

Ben cringed. "What about those two other friends?"

"They wouldn't understand. *You* understand."

Ben groaned. "Come on, Jim, let it go for now."

"I gotta pee."

"So hop to it. There's the back door." He gave him a shove and sent him lumbering.

Crowley waited, his mind a turmoil, too much so to simply get up and leave. He waited. And waited. . . .

Either Evinrude had fallen down somewhere, he decided, or he was busy throwing up. Didn't seem *that* drunk, though.

Crowley let his gaze wander until it met the mean stare of one of the hardcases. Professional pride made Ben meet the stare and hold it.

"What the hell you starin' at, dude?"

Crowley was stunned. Well dressed he was, dude he wasn't. But he knew the routine. "Dude" wasn't much of an insult, but the way it was said, the nasty, sneering tone, that was supposed to get him to his feet. And before he could say anything, identify himself, there'd be hands streaking for guns.

Where was that other gunslick? . . . Damn! In back of him. They had him in a crossfire. Christ Almighty.

Ben searched his memory. Where had he crossed these two? Had they followed him here? They'd shown up soon after he had; maybe they had him mistaken for Deputy Marshal Long, that bad-ass working out of Denver. Long was good-looking and, as a rule, reasonably well dressed, too, but he had a mustache.

He read the eyes of the one he was facing. It was bad. He was sure he could beat *him*, but the other one. . . .

He wished he'd told someone who he was.

The room slowly stilled. Then he heard a voice, a heavy voice but kind of slurred. "Hey, Whitey, you still got that blunderbuss you keep hid? Well, haul it on out over here. . . ."

Crowley's eyes never left his man.

"See that man there, the ugly one—now don't everyone raise your hands—standin' in the tables? You watch him, Whitey. If he makes a move to shoot my friend in the back, blow his head off."

Evinrude slowly lumbered into Crowley's field of vision and up to the hardcase at the bar, whose face had lost its deadly certainty. Evinrude turned his head and grinned foolishly at Crowley—and then spun back with deceptive speed and buried his fist so deep in the hardcase's gut that his knuckles damn near came out the fellow's back.

Evinrude turned again to look at Crowley. He blinked, grinning again and spreading his hands. "Look at me. I went and threw up all over myself. Think I'll get on back to the post." He left.

Crowley stood up, looked at the other hardcase who was studying his boots and trying not to notice Whitey's shotgun, and then he, too, slowly left.

Outside, he looked around. Evinrude was gone. Moved awfully fast for a drunk. And also made things awfully difficult.

Mulberry had a hard time finding Pam. She'd moved from her room at the Drovers. He finally found her in a small restaurant that was pretty much deserted at that time of day.

"Where have you been, Ed?"

"I—"

"We've got unfinished business, sweetie. You already paid for it, and I want to thank you for that money you left. You didn't have t—What's that mark on your forehead? And your *nose*. No wonder you didn't show up."

"It's a bruise and it's broke. I'll tell you about 'em later. But first, why aren't you at the Drovers?"

"I found a better place. Next door. You see it?"

"Looked in, couldn't see anything. Awfully dark."

"Right. Dark as a mine. And you know who goes there? Miners, that's who. Suc*cess*ful, filthy rich miners, horny as all get-out. I got my ticket to Frisco already, and a bundle besides." She saw Mulberry's face fall down around his boots. She grabbed him and started dragging. "C'mon, we've got things to do."

A half-hour later she pulled the sheets up over her bareness, tucked her knees up under her chin, and said, "Now you don't

135

have to say you're sorry anymore."

Mulberry was grinning like an imbecile. "That was . . ."

"Better than playing with yourself?"

"Oh, infinitely better."

"That's a relief."

"How . . . how was I?"

Her eyes narrowed. "You don't really want to know."

"Yes I do."

"No," she insisted.

"Oh . . . something wasn't right, is that it?"

"Women need time, honey, time to . . . *build*."

"What in the world are you talking about?"

She told him, in non-Victorian terms, about a woman's needs.

"Ah . . . Aha . . . are you sure that's not a little . . . perverse?"

"Ed-ward!"

"Practice. I need practice. When can I practice?"

She stared at him, and then a smile broke. He was a refreshing, delightful child, certainly, but now also a sex maniac, of her very own invention. She lay back. "Anytime. Any old time at all. Just climb aboard."

An hour later, after climbing on and off an incredible number of times—

"Hey. Don't you ever *come*?" she gasped.

"Not anymore, Pam. It's called *discipline*."

He decided to broach a certain subject.

"Pam . . . there's something I have to ask you . . . ask you to do. . . . Now don't get me wrong, there's nothing, er, *personal* involved. Or not really. But it's a big favor. Please say yes. . . ."

Matt Kincaid sat at the rear of the Drovers Rest, quietly looking over and rejecting the miserable assortment of women. He'd witnessed the set-to involving Crowley, the hardcases, and Evinrude. And when Evinrude had blundered back in, he'd been set to play a hand, but then had been content to settle back and admire the way Jim defused the situation. Good man.

But he had recognized Crowley as the law—one developed a nose for that—and still wondered what the law and Evinrude had in common. They'd appeared pretty good buddies.

At the table next to Matt a crowd of young fellows—cowboys probably, what with ranchers beginning to move in—were drinking up a storm. Matt chuckled, recalling Crowley's expression when Jim 'fessed up to throwing up all over himself.

That hadn't needed any confession, not the way men were backing off.

A fellow at the table next to him suddenly stood up.

"Christ, not this way!" cried another man.

The first man turned, and Matt saw that he wasn't all that young, that he had a wicked scar from his left temple across his lip to his right jawbone, and that his face was screwed up something terrible. Then his mouth opened and spewed half-digested beer and rotgut all over Matt. Matt couldn't have been more startled had he been kicked in the face.

The next table burst into loud laughter until they found themselves staring down the wrong end of Matt's walnut-handled Scoff and pearl-handled Colt. Matt could endure anything save derision. He rarely had to handle it, and he'd never learned how. But fortunately his temper, though quick, wasn't unduly violent.

The men at the next table sobered fast, and then showed signs of anger.

"Don't do it, boys," snapped Whitey from the bar. "That's Kincaid."

"Who the hell's Kincaid?" snarled one. "He's just an effin' *sojer*." Made it sound like a disease.

"We'll etch it on yer tombstone, Merle," Whitey assured him. "*I found out who Kincaid was.*"

Matt stood, holstering both guns with slow but easy moves. Then he stood waiting, vomit trickling down his face, shirt, and trousers, and dripping to the floor. He made no move to wipe it off.

No one stood to face him.

He turned and walked out of the saloon. He didn't thank Whitey. It wasn't him that Whitey'd helped.

He walked quickly down the boardwalk to the barbershop. Hot Bath & Massage. It'd better be open.

It was. "I want a bath and all this washed and dried."

"Drying might take a while. Maybe while you're getting massaged."

Matt kind of doubted that he'd ask for that.

Jimson hadn't asked for it, either, but he was getting it. He'd found himself a woman, or the closest he could come. With only four bits in hand, a dime-screwing sounded just about right.

The gal was very large and muscular, judging by her forearms. She had yellow hair, the color of teeth that hadn't been brushed in a while. The hair was piled so high that it vanished above the light cast by three dim lamps in the Crazy Whore Saloon. The less said about her face, the better.

She had a chest bigger than that of the horse Trash rode in on. No telling how big her "thing" was. Hell, might find the missing Gatling somewhere in there. He giggled.

She—Irma was her name—took him by the scruff of the neck and marched him toward the darker rear of the saloon, and beyond, into a small room that was overwhelmed, and nearly filled, by a brass four-poster.

Trash had heard that Captain Conway had lost a four-poster, ordered, sent, but lost in transit, supposedly (and mysteriously) to Mr. Lo. Ha! Goddamn robbin' teamsters—Trash had never trusted them gorilla-bastards. They'd sell their maiden aunt's "gimme-some" for a shot of booze.

Irma told the awestruck Trash that an effin' dime didn't buy the goddamn night, and she proceeded to strip him. He grinned.

Then she stripped herself, and once the tight corsetry was off she seemed to swell, almost doubling in size.

She climbed on the bed, rolled onto her back, and pulled Jimson up onto her. He smiled gamely.

"Ain't you gonna *do* nothin'?" she demanded. "Hell, you ain't even ready."

True. He'd been distracted. "You jes' hang on there, mama."

"For what, Christmas?" She reached down and began to fondle Trash encouragingly. Trash had rubbed down horses' legs with a lighter touch. It was sheer self-preservation that brought him up to snuff.

"There you go," she crooned, sounding like a steamboat groaning against a pier. "I knew you could."

Trash figured he was getting just about a dime's worth.

"Well," she said crossly, "slip it in."

"Goddamn it, it *is* in."

She reached down. "So 'tis." A grin as yellow as her hair. Then she announced, "All right, you can come."

Hell, I ain't about ready to come, thought Trash. Seems like a dime don't buy nothin' these days.

He felt his testicles being gently stroked.

That was more like it, he thought, until he realized that both of her hands were on his shoulders. He looked around and saw two long-haired children seated at the foot of the bed. Not bad-looking, either, but then little girls never looked bad, not real bad, anyway. Theirs were the hands that were stroking his balls. He tried to raise a bit, but Irma held him fast. He grinned. "Cute . . . that one on the left kinda looks Injun—"

"You got it."

"Yeah? An' the other, she looks part nigger."

A pause. And then, "Mister," she grated, "I hope you've come . . . 'cause you have had it."

"Oh?"

"The nigger part I don't much cotton to myself, seein' the grief it's brought, but the way you talk, you just don't have no respect for a lady's feelings."

Was he hearing right?

"And that alone woulda been enough, but mister, she is a boy."

Trash tried to disengage, but the legs closed around him like a vise. So he said instead, "So what? What's to get excited about? One little mistake. Now lemme go!"

"Oscar! This here stupid galoot said you was a gurl." Oscar scowled fiercely. "Punish him!"

Jimson's eyes widened, then nearly popped from his head as Oscar reached out and really pinched his balls.

When Matt came out of his bath, his blues had not yet dried. "You kin wait or you kin borry a fancy set o' duds that'll fit," said the barber. "Feller died passin' through last week."

Matt accepted the clothes offer. They weren't bad; spiffy, gambler-type duds. But for an unusually large gambler. "What are these?" asked Matt, putting his fingers through a couple of holes. "Moths?"

"Yep. Wearin' lead jackets they was, too. That's where they went in and that's where they came out."

"Backshot?"

"Only way to shoot a gambler. They're sneaky."

Matt walked out, wearing the dead man's clothes, his army gunbelt strapped around his hips.

He entered a restaurant, and before he even sat down he ordered two steaks and fixin's. He hadn't eaten since morning.

There were just a few customers scattered around. It was a cheery little place, a breath of fresh air if one could ignore the stench of burning grease wafting from the kitchen. Matt could, and he found a table and sat.

He noticed a girl staring at him. He was used to being stared at by women, the boon of his rugged good looks. This girl was young, cute in a funny but nice way, and dressed damn near like a schoolmarm. Where the hell had *she* come from?

She stared, for sure, but every time he looked up she looked away.

The steaks came and he dug in.

Eats like he hasn't eaten for a long time, thought Pamela. Damn, I came in here to get away. First Ed, and *now* lookit.

She had some things to think about. Her Frisco ticket alone weighed heavy on her mind. And then sweet Ed and his crazy idea.

Jiminy, he just smiled at her.

And indeed Matt had smiled, between mouthfuls. But seeing her jump, he'd lowered his head and dug right back in.

Funny clothes, she thought. Dressed like a tinhorn, but smiles like brass and altogether looks like solid gold. His height when he'd walked in, the breadth of shoulder, that strong, solid face with the hint of mischief about the mouth and eyes . . . dear me. Paul, what'll I do? Your poor sinful sister's so weak. . . .

Matt finished and looked up. Caught her staring again. Her eyes jerked away, but then they came stealing back. The Lord loves soldiers tonight, Matt thought; she's sort of smiling.

He stood, stepped carefully around the table, and approached her. He smiled his warmest smile, reached up to tip the forage cap he'd forgotten wasn't there, and drawled, "Matt Kincaid, miss—" and there was that mischievous glint—"your humble servant."

"My, my, you Western boys sure are forward."

"No sense goin' backwards."

"You set right down and tell me all about yourself and this Wild West. Must be very exciting, working up the kind of appetite you just showed." "Oh, hell, she thought suddenly, why am I doing this? He's either going to guess, or find out. And if he don't, he probably won't even make a move. I can't win nohow.

She leaned forward and said, "Listen, before you get your tongue all tangled up being gentlemanly . . ." (I'm sorry, Ed Mulberry, I truly am, but you aren't exactly all a girl like me dreams about. You understand, don't you? A man like this don't often come along. I gotta. Forgive me?)

". . . I have to tell you that I am, ummm—" Pamela concentrated prettily—"what they call a . . . lemme see, what *do* they call me? A lady of easy virtue? And I'm gettin' hot just sittin' here lookin' at you."

Matt looked like he'd been poleaxed.

"Us forward *Eastern* girls, dontcha know."

"Like I said, no sense goin' backwards." He smiled as charmingly as he could manage.

"Nosirree, no sense at all. Got my ticket to Frisco, packed and ready to go." She frowned. "Maybe . . ."

"Maybe? Does it depend on me?"

Her frown deepened. She felt like saying, Hell, no—give a man a smile and he'll take all your teeth and work on down—but, brow smoothing and smile stretching to heaven and back, she said, "Why don't we just go and find out?"

They did. And the smile wasn't all that was heavenly.

Afterwards, lying contentedly in her bed, Matt took her hand in his.

"I can likely get back in tomorrow night," he said.

She looked at him quickly, and said, "Don't do it, not for me," and gave his hand a squeeze before dropping it.

"You're leaving?"

"It's not that. I didn't ask you for money and I don't intend to, but this is my *business*. If I ever . . . *stay* for a man, stay *with* him, have something *close*—" She was saying everything but "marry"— "if I ever do, it won't be because he's good in bed, but for other reasons."

"It's against my principles," said Matt, "but I just might be able to scrape up some money."

"I wouldn't take it. I wanted you because you're big and beautiful. I did it for fun, that's all, just sheer fun."

"We could have more fun."

She shook her head. "Fun don't last."

Matt nodded, got out of bed, and started donning his gambler's duds. His blues had to be dry by then.

He didn't like rejection, wasn't used to it, and, in this case, couldn't understand it at all, but he knew when to quit, when to cut his losses. He looked at her, smiling but beginning to notice her flaws.

"You're not married, I assume," she said.

"Nope."

"Must be tough out here, trying to keep a wife. But then,

havin' a wife's got its good side. I'm not boasting, but the gals I've seen around here ain't no bargains."

"No kidding."

"But they're outnumbered 'bout twenty to one, so they don't go beggin'...and the soldiers do. I've seen a lot of them around town, they must have it real rough. Any of them married?"

"Nope." He was having trouble remembering that he wasn't a soldier to her. "Or hardly any. You'll find officers married, and some noncoms, but the privates? Even if they are married, they can't afford to keep wives."

"Can't they live on post?"

"Sure, but the army doesn't feed wives and kids. The private does, and thirteen dollars a month doesn't go far."

"Any soldiers ever try to get married after they get out here?"

"Never. And if they try, there's not an officer worth his salt out here that'd give permission, not out here with *these* women." He didn't mean to insult, but didn't apologize. "'Course, that probably accounts for a lot of desertions."

"What happens then?"

"If it happens under fire, and they're caught, they hang. *Not* under fire, then they just waste a whole lot of time getting disciplined. Years, maybe. It's not worth it."

"Jail?"

"Happens."

"They hangin' now? They under fire, Indians and all?"

He smiled. "Don't rightly know. They're not catching any."

"But if they did catch one?"

"Then we'd find out, wouldn't we?"

She looked a trifle upset.

"But if you're thinking you're going to save someone from desertion, thinking you're going to nail one of those prize bulls, *don't*. They're spoken for, believe me. By the government. Besides, if *I'm* not good enough..."

She smiled suddenly and spoke sweetly. "Why Matt, are you proposing?"

It'd been a long time since he'd tied a necktie—the barber had done it before—so he just fashioned a quick knot and got the hell out.

sixteen ⎯⎯⎯⎯⎯⎯

The wind blew south along the Bozeman, bringing cooler air down from Canada. Soft, puffy clouds scudded overhead, and high above them ghostly mares' tails fanned out.

"Rain soon," said River That Forks.

"How soon?" asked Captain Conway.

"Two, three days."

They'd catch them before that. They had to; they'd been riding like hell, and Indian ponies couldn't hold that speed. They could trot for days or zing it for a mile, but in between those two extremes, for sustained speed, an Indian pony couldn't match an army horse. And even if the damned hostiles were *all* mounted on army horses, as apparently some were, or big horses anyway, they surely weren't graining them as they should, and the horses were bound to weaken. And they were dragging a Gatling besides. There was no way they wouldn't catch those bastards.

"Captain!" The cry came from up ahead. Bad news. He was getting so he could tell from the sound of the voice.

Lieutenant Fletcher rode up. He was riding the point and flanking squads that day. Conway'd lost some faith in Fletcher. The man's heart wasn't in it. But Price would have been worse.

"Ambush, sir."

"What? Ahead?" Conway stood up in his stirrups.

"Not *now*, sir. One wagon. Man, woman, and a kid."

"Damn."

143

"There're so many holes in them and the wagon . . ."

"Gatling?"

"Could be, sir."

There were indeed a lot of bullet holes, but the patterns were wrong. It wasn't the work of a Gatling. Besides, a helpless family, why waste it on them?

"How long ago did it happen?" asked Conway of anyone that could say.

"Not too long," said River That Forks.

"But the woman's bloated already," objected Fletcher.

"*Bloated*?" repeated Smiley, barely able to keep the scorn hidden. "This isn't a *drowning*. She's *pregnant*."

"Oh, God," said Fletcher.

Conway wished the enlisted men weren't around to hear Fletcher. Apparently this erstwhile dull, reliable, and satisfied officer had finally reached his personal Rubicon. The long drive north, under pressure, had suddenly awakened Fletcher's sense of mortality, or his sense of *something*. Conway knew it happened suddenly in unambitious men, and he knew his men, especially his officers. Fletcher had been with him awhile and Conway'd been waiting for this moment. What was this "no promotion" garbage? He'd be better off ranching, or farming, or even storekeeping, his own boss. . . . Yes, that was what they told themselves one morning when it had just gotten to be too much. It was probably Fletcher's wife showing up that had tipped the scales. Conway should have foreseen it and brought Mr. Price instead, but it was too late now.

"Sir," said Smiley, getting his attention. "Could I be alone with these bodies?" He had a knife in his hand.

For a moment Conway struggled with the ethics, but then he nodded. He and Fletcher and everyone moved off, leaving Smiley to his grisly task.

Smiley soon returned. "Got lucky. There *was* a difference. Baby's not been dead as long. Which means we're not too far behind."

Conway, for the sake of speed, doubled the usual size of the burial detail. And the thing that impressed the diggers the most was the savagery that Mr. Lo had shown regarding the pregnant woman.

They moved out faster yet, slowing for hills and rises, but not much.

Two hours later another white woman was found. Knifed in the side like the first.

How many white women were there?

Racing Elk knelt in the wagon over Josie. He held a hunting knife in his hand. "This knife belongs to Sit-Down-Cross-legged. He is my kin. He would not kill the woman. But you would. You are tough but you are also soft. I do not kill you because the woman was useless and the wagon travels faster. But I know you now, know you more truly than before."

He turned her over, pulled her arms free, spread them, and lashed her wrists to the wagon. He stripped her clothes off and drew designs on her back with the tip of the knife. He entered her from the rear, then he left her like that. Josie thanked God she was still alive.

First Lieutenant Matt Kincaid appeared in the doorway of his office. "Where's Windy, Sarge?"

"Right here, Matt," said Windy, stepping in from the parade.

Matt blinked. "Why aren't you at the village? Weren't you about to get married?"

The remark did not deserve an answer. "Thought you'd want me, Matt. Things're too quiet, and the sarge told me you were gonna want me."

Matt nodded. Cohen, God of Outpost Nine. "Well, you're both wrong . . . partly. I just want to ask you a question. You ever heard of a breed named Creed Scarborough? Runs with Indians?"

Windy's eyes narrowed. "He's no breed." And that's all he said. But he knew something.

"What do you know?" demanded Matt. "He was supposed to guide that gun crew north. He may have run them right to Racing Elk."

"I'll think about it," said Windy, and then he was gone.

"'Spose he's gone off to pray on the matter?" wondered Sergeant Cohen.

"Where's Mr. Price, Sergeant? Have you seen him? Except for morning formations, I don't think I've laid eyes on that man in several days."

"I've seen him with Mrs. Fletcher a few times," said Cohen,

looking down at his desk. Then he said, "But he's not the only one that's been missing." The remark was aimed at Matt.

"*You're* the one that's been giving everyone passes," said Matt, grinning.

"Didn't give *you* one," grumbled Cohen. "But it's all right. The captain's got the hostiles running the other way."

There was a knock on the doorjamb and Mulberry entered.

"Private Mulberry requesting permission to see the commanding officer, Sergeant."

"Goddamnit, Mulberry, are you blind? I'm standing right here."

"Yessir," said Mulberry, not taking his eyes off Sergeant Cohen, who was himself glaring at Matt Kincaid.

"Hard as hell to run an army post," groused Cohen, "in an SOP manner when you're getting back-stabbed. Yeah, go on in, Mulberry. And it better be good, the lieutenant's in one of his moods."

Mulberry entered the adjutant's office, followed by Matt, and waited at attention until Matt got seated behind his desk. He then saluted and barked, "Private Mulberry with permission to speak to the commanding officer, sir." He wasn't sure how it was supposed to go, but he thought he'd touched all the bases.

Matt thought he had, too. He wasn't usually in this position. "At ease, Mulberry." He watched Ed for a few moments, then asked, "Is that what you call at *ease*, Mulberry? Re*lax*, goddamnit, it's *hot*."

"Told you he was in a mood," said Cohen from the other room.

"Sorry, sir," said Ed, unstiffening somewhat. "Didn't hear you."

"All right, Mulberry, what is it? Spit it out, damnit."

"My . . . in a few days . . . ummmmm . . . my wife is arriving, sir. . . ."

As footsteps clumped toward the door to his office, Kincaid said, "Your *what*?"

"Wife, sir. She's arriving in a few days. I'll have to move into the married enlisted quarters . . . sir."

So that was it, thought Matt as Sergeant Cohen, looming in the door, thundered. "You're not married. It's not in your file."

"Yessir . . . no, sir . . . I mean, yes, *Sarge*. I mean I didn't

146

want to be married and that's why I didn't tell the army I was . . . but I am . . . she found me. She telegraphed that she's coming."

"We got no messages."

"Well, *I* telegraphed first, from town, to let my family know where I was. I was waiting to hear from them, checking the telegraph office, and I received this message from her. . . . Gee whiz, Sarge, she didn't even ask my permission."

Matt Kincaid listened closely, waiting for Mulberry to stumble. The "gee whiz" part was good, though, he had to admit.

"You got proof, soldier?"

"Yes, Sarge." He whipped out the appropriate document.

Not bad at all, thought Matt. He knew there was a drunk in town who'd once done time for forgery and had worked in the prison printing shop; the man could perform wonders with simple plates and a little acid.

Cohen seemed to study the certificate forever. Finally he looked up at Mulberry, scowling heavily. "All right, Private, so you're married. I don't know how you think you're going to afford it, but—"

"Sergeant," Matt interrupted, "this man is in here reporting to *me*."

"Oh. Yes. Sorry, sir."

"That's quite all right, Sergeant. Mulberry, report to Sergeant Cohen. He'll get you straightened away."

Mulberry did so, and Cohen told him what to do. Mulberry floated out the door. And Cohen trudged back into Matt's office. "You know, sir," he said, "that certificate's pretty good. That old rummy's improvin'."

Matt smiled, appreciatively but not humorously. "Up at Fort Keogh this spring, they lost about a third of their men. Deserted. Winters here aren't quite that tough, but . . ."

Cohen wiped the sweat from his brow, wishing the lieutenant would get to the goddamned point.

"No sense making it tougher for a man than it's going to be anyway. I think Mulberry deserves a break."

"Bull," said Sergeant Cohen, "sir."

"He still gets ridden pretty hard."

"*I* know that. And I don't know as he don't deserve it. You're gettin' soft, Lieutenant."

Kincaid smiled. "I doubt it. But what made *you* let up?"

"He had the certificate, didn't he?"

Matt gave Cohen the fishy look he deserved.

"I figure I can make a man of him, sir, and to do that, I have to have him around. I can't have him desertin'—"

"Ah. You *do* buy that, after all."

"Or beaten to a pulp by the men first. . . . Hell, I'll even teach that creampuff how to shoot. I'll—"

"He can shoot."

"Sure, he can shoot. Can't *hit* nothin', though."

Kincaid said slowly, "Sergeant, anything you can see, he can hit."

Cohen gave that information a lot of thought. "Can he now? Tricky little pup, ain't he? Y'know, Maggie saw him just once and she liked him."

"Did she now?" said Matt.

A half-hour later Ben Cohen dropped in on his wife, Maggie. Ben Cohen, as his name implied, was Jewish, nonpracticing. Maggie was black-haired, blue-eyed, Irish Catholic, and also nonpracticing. They were made for each other. He was her hammer, she his soft side.

"That new recruit you noticed . . ."

While Maggie supplied the warmth and sympathy he lacked, or withheld, she also gave him shrewd insights. Little transpired on post that escaped her notice.

"Mulberry?" She was ready to defend him.

"He's bringing his wife West."

"He's not married."

"That's what I thought."

"And I am telling you now, Benjamin, he is not married."

Ben Cohen made a face. "Well, if you say so, but someone's arriving that he's calling a wife, so . . ."

"Don't you be worryin', Ben."

"Who's worryin'?"

"If she acts like a wife, then so she'll be treated."

"Benefit of the doubt, eh?"

"Always, my wee Bennie."

"Oh, holy Moses, don't start that again."

seventeen ‾‾‾‾‾‾‾‾‾‾

Racing Elk led his braves up a short, steep pitch in the Bozeman. Beyond the rise lay Montana. Not that they cared anything for state and territorial lines drawn in "Wah-shah-tung." It was just another rise in what had always been, and would remain, their land. Not the white man's, but *theirs*. They would drive the invader out.

He looked back. The army horses were laboring as they hauled the wagons up the steep incline. He was disgusted. The army horses were supposed to be strong. And they *were* strong, and fast; they'd made life unpleasant for him and his braves on more than one occasion. Only guile and better horsemanship had allowed them to escape. So why were the horses weakening now?

The wagons reached the crest and Racing Elk ordered them halted. The horses were blowing and needed rest. Racing Elk hoped that soon they might find another small, foolish detachment of soldiers and get more horses. "Let them stand and eat," he said.

Then he heard a distant cry, looked back down the trail, and saw a brave riding hard toward them. Red Wolf, the trailing lookout.

Red Wolf rode up. "Soldiers come fast."

"How many?"

Red Wolf flashed both hands three different times. Thirty. "And that many again."

Racing Elk knew the size and breakdown of an army company as well as any army commander. Two platoons. Too big for a mere scouting patrol.

"Coming how?"

"All over."

Spread. A combat spread. It was clear; they were after Racing Elk. He smiled. There would be a great fight. And a great victory. And horses. "Scouts?" he asked.

"I saw none."

Red Wolf had good eyes. It meant the scouts were not in front where they should be. It meant the white man was being careless. It meant the white man would pay for it.

They would have a group of ten leading, and groups of ten on each flank. Ambush would not be easy. They would have to be bunched.

He looked around. The trail to the north soon narrowed, trees and brush closing in. The rise on which he stood was more a ridge, extending bare and exposed about a rifle shot to both sides, then gathering trees and brush as it climbed even higher.

"How soon will they be here?"

Red Wolf leaped to the ground and thrust his knife into it at an angle. "Before the shadow reaches there," he said, pointing to a spot on the ground that was about a half-hour distant.

"There is time."

Captain Warner Conway heard the moans. The McClellan saddle was doing its usual damnedest, the horses riding easy but the riders hurting. Maybe there was a solution, maybe not. Warner Conway had tried riding bareback once, Indian-style, and had figured out why the Indians were usually so testy, especially when they were riding. Up against the rocklike ridge of a horse's spine, a man's tenderest parts didn't stand a chance. Windy had given him instructions, telling him that he had to sit on his knees. Sit on his knees? What the hell had the man been talking about? Windy had explained later about gripping with the knees and legs, but it had been too late. And Windy himself sat on his own comfortable saddle that was definitely not a McClellan. He and his patient, stringy cayuse had apparently made a pact; Windy could use his own saddle if Knobby, the horse, didn't have to run very fast. Windy was a good scout because he was bright, sharp-eyed, careful, and thorough, not because he was fast. And Captain Conway wished like hell that he'd come along.

Up ahead, Mangrove, a private from Louisiana, was riding lead for the point squad, hoping River or Bear was up ahead somewhere scouting, but he didn't know. All he did know was that he didn't want an arrow or bullet in his own tender body to be the signal that something was happening. Why the hell couldn't Murtha have ridden up front, damn gung-ho Yank? Probably because Fletcher wanted company, a boy from his home state. Vermont, was it? Well, hell, at least he wasn't having to bushwhack, like his buddies off to the side. He'd ridden there the day before. Damn branches nearly whipped him to death, half the time spent getting off and picking up his hat if it wasn't tied down good, and tying down tight hurt the neck. Couldn't win, no way.

Mangrove looked down and saw a drawn-out string of horse-droppings. They might not have interested him if there hadn't been a certain gleam to them, a luster. If that ain't fresh horse-shit, he said to himself, then this ol' boy don't know his horseshit, and this ol' boy *does* know.

He turned in his saddle and yelled back, "Fresh horseshit!"

Fletcher, farther back, traveling the same path and unaccompanied by Murtha, heard the yell but didn't know what to make of it. This was *all* horseshit as far as he was concerned. They were obviously after a big war party that had a Gatling for crying out loud, and they needed more men, reinforcements, but Conway wouldn't listen.

Fletcher didn't mind that. He would be out soon. Finished. Gone. Tapping sugar maples in the spring in Vermont. Raising a family. He did mind, however, the idea of dying before all that good living could happen. And it took an effort of will, or just good military training, to keep him from letting Mangrove get completely out of touch.

He rode over the horse turds now and didn't notice them, shining or not. Even though cretin Butler, off to the side, was now singing, "Yankee Doodle went to town, riding on a pony, stepped in horseshit all the way and called it macaroni."

Mangrove heard Butler, too. "Beast" Butler, they liked to call him. And Yankee horseshit just about summed it up.

He rounded a bend and saw the trail widening considerably up ahead, as it led up to a steep hill. Uh-oh, he thought, pausing. Now he really wondered what the scouts were up to.

River That Forks was back riding with Captain Conway

temporarily while, unbeknownst to anybody else, Son of Bear with Limp, having feasted on a dead rabbit he'd found, was crouched in a thicket suffering the consequences of mild food poisoning.

Mangrove was still pausing when Mr. Fletcher absent-mindedly almost rode right by him. "What are you *doing*, Mangrove?" Great Scott. He, Lieutenant Fletcher, was practically riding point himself. "Get on ahead."

"There's a hill there, sir."

"I can see that."

"Ain't been scouted, sir."

"And what makes you think that? We've got scouts and they're out there scouting. If we could see them, they wouldn't be scouting."

"Guess that's true, sir."

"So ride on out there."

And Mangrove did, but not with any particular enthusiasm. He rode carefully, trying to look at the crest of the ridge and the ground and the flanks all at the same time.

He saw more manure. And then, up ahead, at the foot of the hill, he saw something light-colored that seemed to move, and then he heard a moan that almost made him add his own dung to the horses'. He rode forward a trifle slower.

Oh, God, it was a woman. A gaunt, pale, miserable-looking woman. . . . And she was alive.

To hell with Mr. Lo. Mangrove rode forward at a gallop and was off his horse before it had stopped.

He cradled the woman in his arms. She was alive, but not for long. Her scalp was missing. "Hey!" he cried.

The squad heard him and pinched in. Fletcher inched forward.

"It's a woman," said Mangrove, "hurt bad." Which wasn't the half of it.

Sergeant Chubb, farther back and over on the far right flank with the Second Squad, had the word passed to him and he closed in with his men. As he approached, he saw Mangrove and the others huddled around something on the ground. Fletcher was still astride his horse to the rear, chewing on a knuckle.

Chubb and his squad were getting close, maybe too close, when they came across the second body. What the hell was this, wondered Chubb? Where were the scouts? He was a brave man, but his flesh crawled. "Richards! Ride like hell to the rear, and tell the captain to hold up, tell 'im we got bodies and a ridge. Now move it!"

Captain Conway saw Richards riding toward him, saw Richards' horse stumble and go down, saw Richards roll to his feet and keep right on coming at a dead run. His horse got up and trotted after him, catching up just as Richards arrived. "Captain! We got bodies, two of them, still alive. Chubb says— beg pardon, sir—*Sergeant* Chubb says to stay back here. There's a ridge—"

"Who found them?"

"Mangrove, sir, riding point, and Sergeant Chubb."

Conway's eyes snapped to River That Forks, flaring with menace. "Where's Bear?"

River That Forks had a damn good idea, but he didn't say, only cursed under his breath, turned his horse, and lit out up the trail.

He read the scene up forward with a glance and yelled, "Get down!" as he rode by and then hit the ground himself, scrambling up toward the crest of the ridge.

He topped the crest carefully, but saw nothing other than the trail narrowing quickly up ahead, with trees and brush slanting down and closing in, a good quarter-mile distant.

He saw where the wagons had stopped, and realized the significance of the mounds of recent droppings. The wagon tracks led north toward the gap.

There was something in the air, an almost tangible presence. He strained so hard to see that his eyeballs almost started sweating. He stopped breathing, the better to hear.

But hear what? A horse moving or passing wind? The rustling of beads? A cough? The sound of a bird where its species did not exist? But he heard none of those things. And the explosion of his breath broke the silence.

He turned and looked back down the hill and made the sign to advance. No one did, right away, but it meant that it was safe.

River That Forks turned back around again to face north. He knew he'd better not be mistaken.

He looked back down the hill behind him again. Captain Conway had come into sight and was waiting. River That Forks could see him looking left and right, scanning the terrain, speaking to Lieutenant Smiley at his side.

Then River That Forks saw Son of Bear with Limp emerge running from a small grove, leading his horse. Son of Bear looked up, saw him and waved.

The scout waved back and gestured for Son of Bear to come up to where the scout stood. Son of Bear mounted his horse and began to ride forward.

River That Forks again turned back toward the north and began to move cautiously toward the gap. That feeling was still with him.

Son of Bear with Limp rode to where the first body was lying. He saw that she was near death. He looked around, seeing about thirty men. Spread some, but still too bunched. He began to ride by and up the hill.

"Where are you going?"

He stopped and looked at the lieutenant and gestured up the hill.

"River Whatshisname is already up there," said Fletcher, hanging onto the saddle as his horse moved uneasily. "You stay here. I may need you."

What for, God only knew, because Lieutenant Fletcher didn't. His mind was a turmoil. He'd seen the dying woman, and though it was nothing new to him, he thought of his wife and tried to glimpse the future but, mind frozen, saw nothing. Normally a sound officer and able fighter, at that critical moment he was useless.

Sergeant Chubb, from a distance, heard the exchange with Son of Bear and then saw the lieutenant's hesitation. It puzzled Chubb until he realized what had happened. Simple panic. He'd seen it before, but with green officers on training exercises, not in the field with a veteran. Unexpected, it shocked Chubb. But then, "Damn it!" he roared, taking command. "Spread out and *stay* spread. There ain't nothin' we can do for these women and there are probably hostiles somewhere close by."

His words made the men's scalps crawl, and sent them scurrying, but it only brought a bemused smile to Fletcher's face. He turned a vacant look toward Chubb, who'd moved closer, and asked, "Where, Sergeant? Where are they?"

"I don't know, sir," snarled Chubb. "Anywhere. Up *there*."

"Up there?" Fletcher repeated, and turned his face up to look and to take the full impact of a .56-caliber lead slug sent screaming downhill from the barrel of a .56-52 Winchester-made Spencer repeater. Seven-shot, the Second Type or New

154

Model (NM). Mr. Lo generally preferred the First Type, but wasn't all that fussy.

Fletcher's campaign hat and a portion of the back of his head went flying, all his problems finally solved, his worries over.

Riflefire poured down from the brow of the hill. Racing Elk's men had ridden the quarter-mile from cover and were stretched prone along the ridge. The soldiers below tried to hide behind tiny bushes and clumps of grass. Then they hid behind the bodies of their dead comrades.

Captain Conway, back at the bend, stared at the firefight, seemingly aghast, seemingly—like Fletcher—frozen.

"Christ, sir," snapped Smiley, "we gotta *do* something."

"Do what?" Conway snapped right back. "Charge?"

"Ain't fightin' like Indians usually do," said Sergeant Breckenridge laconically. He'd come up from the rear moments before, and now his men were pounding up after him.

"How would *you* fight, Sergeant," sneered Smiley, nearly unhinged by the inaction, "if you had the high ground *and* a Gatling?"

"I don't see no Gatling, sir, and I ain't an Indian," growled Breckenridge right back. "But if I was, I'd charge. Hostiles *love* to goddamn charge, git close and cut. Shit, sir, *you* oughta know that."

Conway frowned. "How many guns you count up there?"

Smiley fairly steamed at the useless gun-count, but Breckenridge, after a few moments, said, "Fifteen, maybe twenty."

Conway nodded. "That's what I count. Mr. Smiley, take a squad and swing around to the right. Keep out of sight getting there. Hold the flank. If nothing happens, then move up and take the ridge." But something would happen, Conway was sure. If the war party was as large as they thought it was, there were hostiles unaccounted for. The slope down from the ridge was much easier on the right side. And Racing Elk had proved to be a somewhat better-than-average tactician. Combine that with Breckenridge's accurate observation concerning Mr. Lo's need to get close and cut. . . . Conway watched Smiley take a squad and begin to circle back around toward the right flank.

Conway then ordered another squad, under Breckenridge, to move forward and lay fire down on the ridge. Then he took the remaining squad and lit out west, intending to cut in toward the left flank.

Conway rode like a madman, scrambling his horse through

155

low trees and resistant, savage brush. His men rode just as hard. The sound of gunfire diminished slightly.

He and his ten men reached the base of the hill. He paused, looking up, and then he heard a new, more distant sound of firing. He smiled grimly. Mister Smiley'd got his action and probably had his hands full. "Let's go," he said.

One man leaped off his horse. Conway cursed at him, ordering him to remount, and then started punishing his own horse, urging it up the steep incline.

Horses went down, men were unseated. But horses got back up and men climbed back on and the uphill struggle continued.

Sergeant Chubb, stretched out behind the body of Private Mangrove—practically *under* it, actually—winced as he felt each bullet strike the corpse. Mangrove must weigh about a ton by now, he thought irreverently. He glanced to the rear. A squad was coming, firing, but just one. Where the hell were the rest?

Then he understood the firing off to the flank. Christ, hold them, whoever you are. We're dead if you don't.

He glanced to the rear again—hell, every time he raised his head to look the *other* way, he damn near got it shot off—and witnessed Lieutenant Fletcher's final ignominy.

At the last moment, Fletcher had thrust one foot deep into the stirrup, and when he'd been shot off, that foot had hooked and he'd lain on the ground with one leg raised, fastened to the horse.

The horse hadn't moved for a while, spooked motionless by the rolling thunder of gunfire, but then it had begun to dance about, heaving Fletcher's carcass this way and that. Finally the poor animal had taken off. And Chubb watched now as it ran, tumbling Fletcher along beside it, down near its pounding hooves.

Eight Moons, commanding the ridge, had seen Conway split his men, but then new fire from the advancing squad had kept him from standing up and taking a good look around. Racing Elk had gone down to flank and close with the soldiers. Eight Moons sensed danger, but could do nothing about it. Racing Elk would win, though. No white soldier could stop him. Racing Elk had medicine.

And Racing Elk needed all the medicine he could lay his hands on. He hadn't ridden into a trap—he'd moved too soon and dropped down the slope too fast for that—but he'd met Mr. Smiley and his squad head on.

Bullets flew wildly as men and horses milled and fired and wrestled. The soldiers were able to knock the saddleless braves off their horses with some ease, but once on the ground, even if wounded, Mr. Lo was a slippery moving target who could pull the white man out of *his* saddle and then lock with him unto death.

In the end, the forces dispersed as quickly as they'd joined. Four of the eleven soldiers remained standing, and one of them wasn't Mister Smiley.

Smiley had been shot in three different parts of his body while dispatching two of the hostiles. He'd then taken a war-axe chop to the head that took off an ear and sent him down. But, feeling his hair gripped and pulled, he'd twisted and shot the brave who was bending down over him.

He then lay back, still alive but critically wounded.

Racing Elk had lost his rifle but managed to survive, killing three in the process, as had Two Wolves. Racing Elk considered, for a moment, fighting the four remaining whites to the death, but for what? He wouldn't be able to charge afterwards. But they could still win the day from the ridge.

He ran back up the hill, appalled not by the losses of his own men but by the savagery with which the whites had met them; the officer had fought like a demon, like a true warrior. He felt fleeting sorrow that such courageous men, red and white, had to die, but also sensed honor at having met and battled such a foe, hand to hand. Stories would be told in the lodges.

A shot came from behind and Red Wolf groaned and fell.

Racing Elk climbed on.

It had turned into a standoff by the time Captain Conway gained the western crest of the ridge with his men. He looked through trees and across open ground beyond to the Sioux, stretched out in a line and lying prone, concentrating their fire on the soldiers below. Conway's lips spread in a mirthless grin. Now he knew what Custer and his men had looked like to Crazy Horse. And he knew that Crazy Horse must have felt the same rush of triumphant excitement that he was now feeling.

Damnit, thought Conway, he'd done it, a picture-perfect tactical maneuver. They'd better write about this one too, damnit.

"Handguns, men," he said, and then urged his mount forward through the trees, taking both pistols out himself, holding one and the reins in his left hand. He glanced back. The men were doing the same.

They came out of the trees and Conway kicked his horse into a full gallop and, very uncharacteristically, let out the damnedest whoop.

The soldiers rode in a line parallelling the rear of the Indians, under the fire coming from below. The Sioux, deafened by their own gunfire, didn't hear the charge coming until it was too late, and they were rapidly cut to ribbons.

Of the thirty braves, eight managed to get off shots and three soldiers fell from their saddles. Another five braves scrambled to their feet and were shot from below by riflemen who didn't know why they'd stood up, but weren't refusing gifts.

The soldiers on the ridge, having completed one pass, turned their horses and rode back a second time, pumping bullets into anything that even twitched. Only Conway didn't make the second pass. He watched, proud, but also sad. He, too, appreciated a game fighter, and these Indians, if nothing else, were game.

A shout of warning from somewhere below made him haul on the reins, turning his mount.

A mounted Indian, alone, was charging along the ridge directly at him. Conway had only an instant to realize that the enemy he was now facing was Racing Elk himself. It was evident in the warrior's intangible aura of authority, something about the way he sat his horse, the level gaze, the mutual recognition of one commander for another.

Conway's breath quickened, as did his pulse. His men were all the way down at the other end of the ridge, and there was no hope that they would help him. He experienced a flicker of surprise that, instead of fear, he felt a surge of exultation. He brought up the pistol in his right hand to fire. As he did so, a Winchester appeared in the Indian's hand. Strangely, neither man fired; it was as if each were trying to get close enough to touch the other.

Suddenly he realized what was happening. Racing Elk had medicine, right enough, and it was working against Conway. He pulled the trigger of his Scoff.

The hammer fell with a dull clink against a faulty cartridge.

No time! he realized as he pulled the hammer back and saw, at the same instant, Racing Elk's finger begin to tighten on the trigger of the Winchester.

There was a loud explosion. . . .

And the rifle flew from Racing Elk's hand as the Indian tumbled backward over his mount's rump, and lay sprawled unmoving on the ground as his riderless horse raced past Conway.

The captain looked around. There, standing beside him, unmounted, was Sergeant Chubb, his features lit by a shit-eating grin, his Scoff in his hand, his chest heaving. It was obvious that the sergeant had run all the way up the hill when he saw what was shaping up.

"That was Racing Elk," Conway told Chubb, as though he couldn't quite believe it himself.

"Yessir," Chubb said matter-of-factly. "I figgered as much. But you got him."

Conway blinked. "Chubb, what are you talking about? I froze, and you saved my life."

The grin was still on Chubb's face. "Beggin' your pardon, sir, but I seed the whole thing"—he looked slowly from side to side—"and nobody else did."

"Chubb, this could earn you a medal."

The grin still hadn't disappeared. "The way things have been going in this man's army, sir," Chubb said, "I'll likely be dead or retired before I see hide or hair of any medals. But I'll tell you, sir, a nice little three-day pass . . ."

Conway frowned severely. "Sergeant, you must know that blackmailing an officer is a heavy court-martial offense."

Chubb's expression became suitably grave, to match Conway's. "Yessir," he said, "I reckon so, sir."

"But we'll see . . ." the captain said, turning his horse and riding away.

"Thank you, sir," Chubb said, as the grin creased his features once more.

Naturally, they didn't find the Gatling. But that wasn't surprising, since it hadn't been used against them and they'd had about a half-hour to get used to the idea.

What they did find were wagons full of new Army repeaters, plus ammunition: valuables gathered during the southern raids and on the move north; the body of River That Forks, mutilated,

159

bristling with arrows and hanging by his heels from a tree farther up the trail; and four white women in the wagons. The two older women were mute with shock. Clara couldn't stop crying, and Josie refused to put any clothes on, marching among the men buck-naked. The men were sufficiently Victorian to be made uncomfortable. But since they were also *men*, and she was a good-looking, streamlined young woman who appeared not much the worse, physically, for her ordeal, lust and uneasiness tended to lock horns. But it was also abundantly clear that Josie was no longer playing with a full deck. She would in time recover but it wasn't going to happen overnight.

They also found thirty-nine Indian bodies, as well as the corpses of twenty-four United States Army soldiers, including Lieutenants Fletcher (found hanging from the stirrup and unrecognizable a mile distant) and Smiley, who'd died fifty feet up the hill where he'd crawled in pursuit of Racing Elk and Red Wolf. Smiley had died reluctantly but probably happily; he'd nailed Red Wolf as he was dying.

While the Indians received more or less mass burials, the soldiers were buried individually, their names carved on wooden grave markings; one wagon was reduced to a skeleton to supply the wood.

With those sorry tasks completed, the decimated force, with fully a third of their number wounded, prepared to ride back south.

Conway looked around for someone to whom he could give commands. He realized that Platoon Sergeants Chubb and Breckenridge were it. He chose Chubb.

"Grain the horses, Sergeant."

"Got some extras, sir," said Chubb. "'Bout forty of them, includin' the wagon horses."

"Ponies?"

"No, sir. U.S. Army, every last spankin' one of them."

"Grain them too. And pick a couple of your best riders to herd them."

"Beggin' your pardon, sir, we'll be runnin' short of grain, then. Mind if I send a couple down to Casper and have 'em meet us with a load of grain?"

"Do it. And let's get going." He looked around at all his weary and wounded. They were stumbling around or hanging from their saddles. If he'd had any officers left, he'd be hearing,

"The men are tired, sir, perhaps we'd better rest until morning."

God knew, he could use the rest too, thought Warner Conway. His entire body was reminding him how old he was. And the battle had left him mentally drained. He almost wished Smiley or Fletcher had survived, if only to talk him down off his horse.

"Riley, Fitzsimmons," bawled Chubb, startling the captain. "Grab some men and grain them extra horses. Then you two're gonna herd them home. Prescott, you and Yates ride for Casper and have 'em meet us with a wagonload of grain. And vittles for the men. The rest of you, grain yer horses, grub yourselves, and then mount up. You got twenty minutes."

"Aw Sarge," a man groaned, "when're we gonna rest?"

"When I goddamn well feel like it, soldier, an' not a step sooner."

Chubb turned, grinning, toward Captain Conway. "Ain't nothin' like kickin' a little ass to get the kinks out—Let's move it!!—ain't that right, sir?"

Conway nodded. Christ, now even his neck hurt.

"Sir, we better ride up front. Set a smart pace that way. Breck, bring up the rear. Keep it closed and don't let Riley and Fitz get lost. They got them tendencies."

"Sergeant," said Conway, "get Prescott before he leaves. I'll have a message for him to take." *If* he had the strength to write it.

Seventeen minutes later, mouths crammed with bread and jerky, they moved out.

161

eighteen

Captain Conway, Sergeant Chubb, and the remaining men of Easy Company's Second and Third Platoons rode well into the night, not curling up on the ground until they were halfway to the junction of the Bozeman and the North Platte wagon road.

With dawn came a savage reveille, blown by a hungover and mean McBride, who'd found a bottle in River That Forks' saddlebags and nicked it before Son of Bear with Limp could claim it. And then they were off again, heading for a rendezvous with the grain wagon and fresh vittles.

That same dawn signaled the start of a very hectic day at Outpost Nine.

Hardly had assembly ended than a quartet of buffalo hunters came knocking at the outpost gate. They were let in and made straight for the sutler's food. A few minutes later, Lieutenant Kincaid, Sergeant Cohen, and Lieutenant Price joined them.

"Rode all night to get here, Lieutenant," one of the hunters said. "Cut some sign and got a little nervous."

"Just a little," said another hunter, with a sick grin.

"What kind of sign?" asked Matt.

"Hostiles. Cheyenne, I reckon. Big party, headed west. Didn't know whether things was peaceable around here and figgered we'd better not wait to find out."

"Sure it was hostiles? Cheyenne?"

"It was them. I can read sign. Ponies weren't shod, for one thing, an' there were some other things. . . ."

"How long ago?"

"Recent. Which is why we didn't hang around."

Matt wondered why the Cheyenne would be headed west. Picking some more fights with the Ute? Shoshone? Paiute? But hell, that was a Cheyenne problem, not his.

"Big, huh?" asked Cohen.

"Yeah. Looked like they was figurin' on a long march . . . or else chasin' someone *real* close."

Matt smiled absently.

"Could I see that?"

Matt looked around. Mulberry had appeared, with Malone and Jimson. Mulberry was asking one of the hunters about his gun. Actually, he was *telling* the hunter about his gun. "Sharps, I see. Forty-five, one-twenty, five-fifty. Beecher's Bibles."

The hunter regarded Mulberry with tolerant amusement. Not so Jimson. "What the hell you talkin' about, Ed, with all them numbers?"

"Forty-five caliber," said Ed, "a one-twenty-grain powder charge, and the bullet weighs five hundred and fifty grains. 'Beecher's Bibles' because the load of Sharps rifles that Reverend Beecher sent to John Brown were boxed and labeled 'Bibles.'"

The hunter grinned. "This one ain't it, though. And that one you mentioned warn't the ones that ol' Brown got. They was Beecher's Bibles, all right, though. We shot them Rebs silly with 'em."

"What *is* this, then?"

"Still a Sharps, but *fifty* caliber. Hunnert an' *forty* grains powder. An' a *seven*-hunnert-grain cartridge. Buffalers've been gettin' scarcer, as y'might have noticed. Spook faster, gotta have somethin' that kin drop 'em from a longer range."

"Longer than what?"

"Longer'n six, seven, eight hunnert yards."

"A mile?"

"Happens. More, even. But you can't hit nothin' from that far."

Ed paused a moment, then asked quietly, "Could I borrow this?"

"What fer? The gun's bigger'n you, heavier anyway."

"I'd just like to try it."

Malone gave Ed a funny look. He'd heard how Mulberry had shot up everything *but* the target.

"No harm, I reckon," the hunter said, grinning. "Give it a try. But *you* buy the ammo, which ain't cheap. An' *you* bring the empties back with you so I can use them again. Them babies cost near twenty cents apiece."

And they were longer than his thumb, Ed realized. And a nice sack of ammunition would weigh forty pounds.

"And just make sure you point that thing *away* from the post," said Matt, as he went out the door.

Ed hauled the gun and ammo back to the barracks to make ready.

Matt hadn't been back in his office long when he heard a shout from outside: "Ambulance comin'!"

Matt hoped it wasn't hauling bodies. Most times it wasn't; rather, it was used like any other wagon, and preferred by the ladies because it rode easier. He stepped outside the orderly room, curious. They sure weren't expecting any corpses, but no one else, either.

The gate opened and the ambulance, a canvas-topped four-wheeler drawn by two well-cared-for bays, entered and swayed gently as it swung to make a circular movement around to stop in front of the orderly room.

Pamela Burke disembarked. She looked up at Matt Kincaid and Ben Cohen, both standing in the orderly room door, smiled and said, "Hello. I'm Mrs. Mulberry."

Ben Cohen was astonished; he'd expected a skinny, school-marmy type, but he was not half so astonished as Matt Kincaid.

"I believe my husband is expecting me. He is, isn't he?"

It wasn't until then that she recognized the uniformed Kincaid. Her eyes began to widen.

"Pamela!" came a cry from across the parade. "Dear!" And Private Mulberry came bounding across the parade, the very picture of joy.

Matt turned abruptly and walked back into the orderly room. Ben Cohen, surprised, watched him leave, then turned back to the juicy new arrival. Pam had turned to watch Mulberry approach. Boy, did she have news for him.

"Ahem," said Cohen, getting her attention. "How do, ma'am, I'm Sergeant Cohen, top kick hereabouts, and I'm mighty pleased to welcome you to Outpost Nine and Easy Company."

Pamela gazed at him narrowly. Burned once by a sneak

who was out of uniform, Kincaid, she was on her guard. Was this another past customer, and how many others could she expect to encounter? She never should have listened to Ed. "Thank you, Sergeant, you don't know how happy I am to be here."

Then Mulberry got there and she was in his arms.

"For God's sake," she whispered, "don't overdo it. I'm supposed to be your *wife*." And she wondered how she was going to tell Ed the good news about Kincaid.

Matt was sitting behind his desk, breaking pencils.

Cohen wandered into his office, shaking his head. "Now that's what I call a surprise," he said. "Cute little thing. Wonder where he found her, or where his *father* found her. He's rich, I think you mentioned, probably bought the gal and sent her West." He grinned, then frowned as he said, "Something wrong with you, sir?"

Crack . . . crack . . . crack. . . .

"Don't use up *all* the pencils, Lieutenant."

Crack . . .

"Bradshaw! Hide the pencils!"

Matt looked up at Cohen, a rare look of despair on his face. How could Mulberry have done such a stupid thing? He'll be the post laughingstock. "Have you got Mulberry on guard?"

"No. He's in his new quarters. Why should he be?"

"That's your usual trick with enlisted men that bring wives, isn't it?"

"Hell, sir, this is different. We talked about that, remember?"

"But the rest of the men don't know it's different."

Private Mulberry was in a bad mood crossing the parade. A man would think the sergeant would give him a break, on this of all days. Oddly enough, Mulberry had almost convinced himself that he truly did have a wife. And hell, he thought, when am I ever going to get to test that gun?

The other enlisted men watched him cross the parade with open amusement. "Sergeant gotcha, didn't he?"

Climbing into the wagon—a wood-gathering detail, not guard—the detail NCO, Corporal Wilson, explained, "I guess you'd call it a custom. Every time an enlisted man is dumb enough to bring a wife out here, the first thing that happens, before she's even had a chance to unpack, much less anything else, he's hauled off on some detail, the dirtier the better. And it goes on for a while. He'll likely have another surprise for you tonight."

What the hell, thought Mulberry, he didn't care, not really. It was just a bargain, a woman doing a friend a favor, that's all. Someday he'd make it right; he'd have some family money sooner or later, they couldn't deny him *that*. And it wasn't as if she had to *do* anything with him; she just couldn't do anything with anyone else.

"She's a mighty pretty woman," said Corporal Wilson.

"Especially you," said Mulberry.

"What?"

When the wagon arrived at a cottonwood-choked draw, they discovered that one of the horses had thrown a shoe.

"So what? We'll have it fixed when we get back," said Private Cameron, a beefy, mustachioed six-footer whose specialty was latrines, not wood-gathering.

"Hell," said Wilson, "horse might go lame, and that ain't necessary. I could fix it myself if I had the tools . . . and the shoe. Somebody could run back—"

"I'll go," said Mulberry.

"—an' look for the shoe on the way, an' if you don't find it, bring another. An' pliers an' a hammer an' nails—"

Mulberry was already moving before Wilson finished instructing.

Ed was back inside Outpost Nine within twenty minutes, told the smithy what was needed, and then slipped around, in the shade of the overhang that fronted the housing, to the married-enlisted quarters.

He opened the door without knocking and was dazzled by the sight of Pam, half naked on one side of the room . . . and appalled by the sight of Lieutenant Kincaid, sitting on the edge of a table, over on the other side.

Matt Kincaid had waited until Mulberry cleared the post before strolling over to the Mulberry quarters and knocking on the door.

Pamela had thrown the door open and immediately said, "You bastard."

Matt made a shushing gesture, finger to his lips, and pushed

166

his way inside. "Calm down. I can explain how you made that mistake."

"How *I* made that mistake?"

"I sure didn't." He still remembered how much fun it was. "You were the one dealing and selling. And you tricked Mulberry into doing this. It's not going to work, though. Mulberry may be a jerk, but he's too nice a kid—"

"I didn't trick him." She paused, consternation showing, as if she'd suddenly remembered something. But then her mouth tightened in resignation, and she resumed, "This was *his* idea. These men, *your* men, these he-man soldiers, they've been making life miserable for him. *I'm* not getting any money, just some promises, and I should be halfway to Frisco. Instead I had to ride all the way to Laramie, get a wagon there, *pay* for a ride to headquarters, and *then* ride all the way over here to wet-nurse a soldier, and you think that's *fun*? When you're not being paid? I'm only doing it because Ed *is* such a nice fellow, and," adding more quietly, "he reminds me of my brother."

"And he reminds *me* of a jerk!"

"*And* if you know what's good for *you*, Matt Kincaid," said Maggie Cohen, emerging from the bedroom as Pamela squeezed her eyes closed, "you'll be gettin' your nosy, interferin' self out of here and keeping your blatherin' mouth closed."

Matt stared. "What are *you* doing here?"

"Helping Mrs. Mulberry unpack and get settled. That's more than I can say for you."

"You *knew*?"

"No one told me until just now, if that's what you'd be meanin', but I knew young Ed wasn't married. I know married men, Matty."

Pam smiled, deciding Maggie could take care of Matt, and bounced off across the room, beginning to undress. Maggie watched her, and then her eyes tore into Matt.

Matt looked disgusted. "*I* didn't ask her to undress," he said, "though that may be the best thing she does—" He dodged a garment thrown by Maggie and perched himself on the edge of a table. "But I'm not through. I want to know how many other soldiers know you from town."

"None," flashed Pam. "I found some miners and I stuck

with them. *They* had *money*. Your soldiers, it's scandalous what the army pays them." Her dress came off and then her chemise. "I hope no one minds, and I know *you* don't, but it's awfully hot in this outfit."

"I've seen it before," muttered Matt, suddenly regretting his words as Maggie's eyes narrowed dangerously.

"Me too," said Maggie, her eyes still slits, "but I'm going to finish unpacking, and if you know what's good for you, Matt, you'll finish *your* business, because pretty soon herself will be along—"

"The captain's wife?"

"Her*self*. She's bathing just now, but soon..."

Kincaid nodded, then glanced sharply at Pamela. "Damnit, get yourself covered. And you're sure no one else knows you?"

"As sure as I can be. Oh, wait a minute. Ed's got two friends. *They* know me."

And that's when Private Ed Mulberry barged in.

Pamela looked at him crossly and Matt, for all his steely composure, was dismayed. This day sure wasn't working out right. "It's not what you're thinking, Private."

But Mulberry wasn't thinking. He was being horrified, and then enraged. She was *his*, damnit.

Pamela tried to throw her chemise on. "Ed..."

Mulberry grabbed for his gun. Matt drew automatically, clearing leather before Ed had even got a hand on the damn thing. But then Matt left his gun pointing down and waited grimly and patiently for Ed to get the Scoff cleared.

Mulberry finally got it raised and pointed at Matt. Matt stared at him, neither flinching nor blinking, nor making any move at all.

"Why don't you *do* something?" Ed said.

"'Cause I could already have killed you, son." He hoped Ed wasn't too blind with rage to understand. But he also hoped Ed didn't suddenly start *crying*, or something like that.

Ed's breathing subsided. But that only made the gun steadier.

"I met your wife in town," said Matt evenly, if coldly. "We went to bed. She was working and I was out of uniform and I didn't tell her I was a soldier. I know she's not your wife."

"The hell she isn't," Maggie said from the other room, and

Ed started and almost pulled the trigger. Matt finally flinched.

"Mulberry," said Matt, taking a deep breath, "you're sure one peculiar person, and I can't figure you, but I only came here to find out who else knows what this girl is—"

"*Was*," said Mulberry. "And no one knows. I was careful."

"No one," repeated Matt, disgusted. "*I* knew, goddamnit."

"Me too," came from the other room.

Mulberry suddenly exploded, "Who the hell *is* that in there?" And then his eyes popped as Maggie Cohen came out grinning. She gave Ed a big wink and said, "This post is turning out to be a lot of fun."

Matt waited to get Mulberry's attention.

"I'm going to let it go," he said finally, "only because to do anything different would make things even worse for you with the men, although you've already shown them you have balls."

"Matt Kincaid!"

"Quiet, Maggie. No one invited you."

"No one invited *you*, either."

"Damnit, Maggie, I'm running this post."

"Ha! Tell that to Ben." She glanced at Pam, who was now smiling, and then looked at Mulberry. "Edward, will you put that thing away?"

Mulberry discovered the gun in his hand and slid it back in its holster.

Matt stuck his away too, and started to walk past Mulberry, pausing only to say, "Private, after you finish collecting wood, you come see me. We're going back out on the range. If you're going to insist on hauling that hogleg of yours out every chance you get, you'd better learn how to do it right. And *fast*."

"And there's no better teacher, Edward," added Maggie.

Matt Kincaid left.

Mulberry eyed Pamela. "You will please keep yourself covered," he said evenly, wiping the smile from her face, "and I will speak to you later."

"Are you going to beat me?" she asked fearfully, eyes twinkling.

Ed, confused, only muttered, "If I don't shoot my foot off."

The door suddenly opened and Matt barged back in again. There was an evil smile on his face. "Just remembered something I'd better remind you about. The army doesn't support wives, you know." He was ostensibly addressing Mulberry. "You're going to have to feed and clothe her and all the rest out of your thirteen bucks."

"We'll manage," said Mulberry stubbornly.

Pamela's eyes widened. "Oh, now wait a minute. I'm not going to have to pay for this, am I? Ed? Am I?"

"You *said* you had a lot saved."

"*Ed!!*"

"I'm going to pay you back, I *told* you that."

Kincaid left, grinning broadly.

Evinrude and Jimson stood at attention and stared at a point about two feet above the head of Lieutenant Matt Kincaid.

Why the hell don't he "at ease" us, wondered Jimson.

Matt Kincaid got up, stepped around them, and shut the door to his office. Then he stood immediately behind them and spoke into their ears. "Mulberry's wife. Do you know her?"

"No, sir," they said, and Jimson added, "ain't had the privilege, sir, but a mighty fine-lookin' gal. Unnerstan' she just come out from Philly—"

"Hartford," corrected Evinrude.

"Try the Drovers Rest," hissed Kincaid.

"Oh, shit," said Jimson.

"Now tell me straight, does anybody else know?"

"No, sir," said Evinrude. "Or none that are saying or giving any sign."

"An' if them pinheads knew, they'd be sayin', sir, b'lieve me."

"For once, Private, I do. And you two had better make sure they remain ignorant."

"What's going to happen, sir?" asked Evinrude.

"Nothing. The man's married, that's all. And by God he's going to stay married, like it or not. The army does not look favorably upon divorce."

"Aye," said Jimson, "it's an evil practice."

A little later that morning, Kincaid took Mulberry out and tried to show him how to handle the Scoff. But after a while he decided Ed would never make a gunfighter. He could shoot well enough, damn well in fact, having sufficient concentration and willpower to achieve nearly absolute immobility, but he

170

just wasn't strong enough to whip the Scoff around with any speed or ease.

"Maybe you're saving your strength till later."

"I've got another detail, sir?"

"Nope."

Mulberry caught on. "Oh, no, it's not like that, sir. It's an agreement, sort of a contract, it doesn't call for, ummmm . . . it doesn't cover conjugal rights."

"No fine print?"

"No." He sighed. "It just isn't like that."

"Well, it had better be like that, contract or no, or that little thing will get up and leave."

Mulberry gave it a lot of thought. He was still giving it thought when Pam started dragging him toward the bed. "It's not even noon yet," he said. "I'm not sure this is right."

"Is that so?"

"And furthermore, this matter of *pleasing* you, a woman's need, according to you, to *build* something or other, I've checked around and that's a whole different slant on things . . . besides being rather exhausting."

"Do you want me to look elsewhere on post? I can make some extra money that way. Long as I'm paying for all this, I might as well—"

Mulberry fairly leaped on her.

nineteen ─────────────

When Matt Kincaid got back to the orderly room from noon grub, he found Lieutenant Price chewing nervously on a fingernail. The telegraph was making a lot of noise.

"Where's Bradshaw?"

Price waved out toward the parade, and Kincaid assumed he meant the latrine. "What's it saying?"

"I don't know. I don't know code."

Sure know how to pick your nose, thought Matt. "Maybe you'd better learn. Bradshaw might not live forever."

"Nor I," muttered Price.

"You might have to use it someday. Save your life with it."

There was a pause in the clacking, and Matt seized the opportunity to tap out a short message of his own, asking for a complete repeat upon demand.

Acknowledgement was given. And Price looked at him askance.

"Bradshaw's better at it, that's all," said Matt. "But how is it they were sending? They have to get a response first."

"I gave it," said Price. "I know *that* much. I thought Bradshaw would be right back. I'm going to have that man's ass!"

"The hell you are, mister. Where's Sergeant Cohen?"

"He stepped out."

"Where to?"

"I don't know."

A low boom sounded from afar.

"Good Lord," breathed Price. "What's that?"

172

"Private Mulberry, I expect," said Matt. "Or I *hope*. I saw him going out dragging a Sharps and a load of ammo." He smiled. Mulberry had had his hands full.

Bradshaw appeared, got the word, and manned the telegraph.

Some ten minutes later there was another distant boom. And, fifteen minutes after that, yet another.

"Takes his time between shots, doesn't he?" commented Price.

Matt thought perhaps Ed was actually trying it at the one-mile range. It would take a lot of time and luck to zero the weapon in at that distance—time, luck, something to rest the barrel on, and a goddamn steady hand.

Now four booms came in a row. Sounded like he'd gotten the hang of it. Matt wasn't very surprised.

The telegraph clacking went on, but a full page had already been covered. Matt took that page and started trying to decipher Bradshaw's scratches. He was silent while he read. Then the clacking stopped and he took the second sheet. He read that one through.

Bradshaw was slumped at the telegraph, head down, eyes unseeing.

"Sorry, Corporal. Mangrove was a buddy, wasn't he?"

Bradshaw looked up, his eyes wet behind the thick lenses. He nodded, then said, ' They *all* were."

Price, who'd been staring fixedly down into the empty coffee pot, as if to will a miracle, looked up and said, "Sounds like Mulberry's finished."

"*He* wasn't on the list," said Bradshaw.

"Eh?" Price noticed something was up. "What is it?" he asked brightly. "Bad news?"

"They caught up with Racing Elk," said Matt.

"That's *great*."

"Smiley's dead. Fletcher's dead. And more than twenty others."

"We *lost*?"

"We won," said Matt, which baffled Price. "Indians lost more, that's all. Sometimes winning's not all that easy, Mr. Price." He looked up coldly at the second lieutenant. "There's always *some* price to be paid."

Price, flinching at the unintentional pun, said, "Surely

there's more to the message than that. It looks like the start of a *novel*."

Matt handed him the sheets, saying, "There's more. No Gatling, for one. The captain was sure Mr. Lo was hauling the gun because of the wagon tracks, but it turned out they were only chasing a couple of wagons." Matt scratched his head. "How could they mistake a wagon for a Gatling?"

Ben Cohen walked in just then, and Bradshaw gave him the message verbally, almost verbatim. Cohen swore up one side of the orderly room and down the other.

"Sergeant, how much does a Gatling weigh, gun and rig?"

"I don't know."

"Who does? Supply? Sergeant Wilson?"

"Doubt it. Maybe . . . er, maybe Mulberry, sir."

"That'd figure," said Matt. "I'll see if he's home yet. He's been out firing that Sharps."

"*Mulberry*'s been shootin' that buffaler gun? Shit, he'll be laid up a week."

Matt nodded. "If the gun hasn't kicked him all the way back across the Mizzou. He can still answer some questions, though."

"Had your fun?" asked Pamela as Mulberry entered their quarters. She watched him stagger across the room and place the gun and the sack of shell casings in a corner. "What the hell's wrong with you?"

"I can hardly move. My shoulder's about to fall off. My lip . . . is it real puffy?"

"Yeah. Oh, my dear. Let me kiss it."

"Please. Desist."

"Aren't wives supposed to do that?"

Mulberry looked at her and his expression softened. "Pamela, dearest . . . sweetie . . . love of my—"

"Now wait a minute." Her eyes had narrowed. "What is this malarkey, this 'dearest,' 'sweetie' junk? What do you want?"

"Lend me some money?"

"What?!"

"I'll pay you back."

"When? By the time your father dies I'll be an old lady."

Mulberry's eyes flashed. "I'll *kill* him!" But then he resorted

174

once more to entreaty. "Oh, please, Pam . . ."

"If you keep slobbering . . . Look, a deal's a deal. A rotten one for me, but . . . anyway, no 'dearest,' no 'honey,' none of that stuff. Maybe some fun in bed, but I'm just here to help you for a little while, and then . . ."

Mulberry just stood there mutely pleading. God, he reminded her of Paul, that miserable beggar. "How much?" she asked.

He told her.

"What for?"

"That gun."

She stared. "Jesus wept." Then she sighed and started wondering where Maggie Cohen had hidden her little jewel box.

Matt caught Mulberry coming back out of his quarters. He eyed the gun Mulberry was dragging. "Mulberry."

Mulberry snapped to and rendered a salute. "But sir, if I'm carrying a rifle that's not army issue . . . should I have presented arms?"

Matt was caught with his mouth open. He thought about it. "I think I may have to check with Sergeant Cohen on that. Look, Mulberry. Do you know how much a Gatling weighs?"

"Which one, sir? There are any number of models. There is, for instance, the camel gun, and that's—"

"The one that was stolen."

"Round figures? Nine hundred pounds. And that's without the ammo."

"Single vehicle? Break it down."

"Gun about two hundred, on a two-wheel carriage that's about three-twenty, and the two-wheel limber for the ammo caisson's another three-eighty. And the ammo's extra. Figure two hundred pounds. Hope I've got that right."

"Dragged separately?"

"Connected, one behind the other."

"Carry on."

As it happened, they were both headed for the sutler's store, but the unencumbered Matt got there a lot faster.

"Buffalo man," said Matt to the former owner of the Sharps.

"Abe, if you don't mind."

"Abe. When you said those Cheyenne were figuring on a long march, or chasing someone, what did you mean?"

"They had vee-hickles."

175

"Wagons?"

"Warn't no choo-choo train."

"How many?"

"Just one, far as I could tell, but it rode real deep, musta been carryin' a heavy load. And them tracks was shod, come t'think of it."

"Exactly where'd you see them?"

Abe caught the urgency of the questions. "Somethin's up?" Matt made an impatient gesture. Abe squinted real hard. "Lemme see, we come across the tracks jes' a bit west of Medicine Bow, best I could figger, an' we'd gone maybe a coupla hours..."

"Thanks," said Matt. He ran back to the orderly room and checked the wall map. He drew a line straight west from the point where the gun crew was killed. It passed Medicine Bow about twenty miles to the north. Goddamnit, that had to be them.

Matt turned from the map to find Sergeant Cohen and Lieutenant Price staring at him. He turned half back to the map, pointed to a spot on the Sweetwater Plains, and said, "The Gatling's there, headed *west*."

"But... but *why*?"

"God only knows. Cheyennes dragging a medicine gun out there to shoot up the Utes or Shoshone; who can figure the way a hostile thinks? But think about it, what else is there? The east, northeast, north, northwest, the army's had it covered with a blanket. The south? Cheyenne's had scouts out; not a sign. Laramie hasn't reported anything. The only way we didn't cover was the west, because it just didn't figure." Then Matt explained the significance of the deep wagon tracks with shod horses in among the Cheyenne war party.

"What do you think we should do, sir?" asked Cohen, his face carefully expressionless.

"You know damned well what, you faker. We've got three choices. Wire headquarters, and they'll send out some big troop that won't be us because we don't have enough men. Or wait for Captain Conway to get back to mount a chase, but he'll be tired, because if I know him, he's pushing hard to get back here. And by then the Cheyenne will be even farther away. Or I can take a squad myself right now and go get those beggars."

"Doesn't seem like we have all that much choice," growled

Sergeant Cohen. "Not if Easy Company's going to get any credit out of all this. Who'll you take, Matt?"

Matt grinned. It had been real tough convincing Sergeant Cohen. "Miller's squad. Malone's worth two or three in a fight. And see if you can find Windy. Price, you'll be in charge till the captain gets here, but"—stepping close and speaking confidentially—"if there's any problem, I'd advise you to ask Sergeant Cohen's advice and then follow it."

"Wouldn't think of doing anything else."

"Okay, Sarge, let's get it going."

twenty

Matt Kincaid and his men rode in two columns, Matt and Windy leading the way. Corporal Miller came next with Private Weatherby. Then Dobbs and Malone, Parker and Medwick, Felson and Carter, and, bringing up the rear, Holzer and Rottweiler. Rottweiler, pure German but third-generation American, had as much trouble understanding Holzer as anyone else. While Holzer had come to America looking for a homestead, a farm, Rottweiler had joined the army to escape a farm in Pennsylvania.

Holzer looked down at the ground they were crossing. "Diss iss not goot zoil," he said.

"Hey Wolfie," said Rottweiler, "this is great *zoil*. . . . Can't grow a goddamn thing but grass."

The column slid down across the territory on a southwesterly course. Matt figured they'd cut sign sooner or later. Which they did, a few miles west of the North Fork of the Platte River. Windy dismounted and walked along a ways by himself so he could get a clear count. He came back.

"Didn't that buffalo-stink say a big war party?"

"Yeah."

"Wrong. Ten or twelve at the most. And bigger ponies than usual."

"The gun?"

"They got it, almost certain. You were right. Looks like wagon tracks but the wheels don't follow each other like a wagon." He turned his head away and spat, then looked back

178

at Matt. "Don't figure River That Forks should have made that mistake."

"He's dead."

"That one neither."

They rode on, following the tracks.

The sign led them steadily west, angling south ever so slightly toward the South Pass over the Rockies and the Continental Divide. It was approximately the same route as was followed by the Union Pacific line, some ten to fifteen miles to the south. Matt and Windy knew the towns they were bypassing, towns on the UP line: Summit, Separation, Fillmore, Creston, Latham. . . .

Above Latham there was a choice. The Overland Mail Route swung up from the south out of Bridger's Pass, crossed the UP line at Latham, and continued northwest a ways before swinging west, then back southwest to meet the UP line again at Church Buttes, some 110 miles farther west on the Green River Plateau. At the same time, after Latham, the UP line angled sharply southwest, a route it would follow until just beyond Bitter Creek, at which point it would curve back sharply north until it reached a point about due west of Latham. After that it resumed its previous course.

Matt and Windy figured the Cheyenne might follow the Overland and pick off some unwary travelers, or ride straight west to shortcut the loop south, but they didn't. They kept on shadowing the UP line.

"Doesn't make much sense, does it?" said Matt. He and Windy had been over the route before, by horseback or rail, and knew its peculiarities.

"Not unless they got business with the railroad or they don't know their way, which might make sense if they was just kids. You know, a bunch of Cheyenne youngsters out to make a name for themselves."

"Now *that* might make sense," agreed Matt.

But what didn't make sense was a halt near Bitter Creek. The sign told Windy they'd stopped the gun carriage and limber there, just outside of town, and hidden them in a heavily wooded draw, then several from the party had ridden toward town.

Indians in Bitter Creek? Of course, there *were* friendlies all over these western towns. And maybe they'd gone in for some supplies. If Creed Scarborough—they were guessing now—

but if Creed was along, he could fake it with a uniform. They must have kept all those uniforms. . . . But Creed with a bunch of Indian *kids*? There wasn't anything making sense.

The sign also indicated the riders had also returned from town and then they and the rest of the party had struck out due west, probably to pick up the UP line again at Black Buttes.

Matt and Windy rode into Bitter Creek to find out what they could. Which wasn't much. No one had seen any unfamiliar Indians the last few days or nights. Soldiers, sure, a couple of nights back, but that wasn't so unusual.

Matt and Windy rode back. Night had fallen. Matt told his men, "Don't know what they did there, but they wasted time. They went in at night—had to, not to be noticed—came back out, camped here, looks like. They've got a day and a half on us, but with them dragging that gun, we can catch them fast if we ride right on."

The men had caught some shut-eye while Matt was gone and Matt was keyed up enough not to need sleep. He'd once gone without for seventy-two hours, trailing, and then fought a battle fresh as a daisy. *Then* he'd slept nearly twenty-four hours straight through. As for Windy, Matt always suspected that Windy could sleep while riding, that he *did* sleep while riding, and that Windy's famous long silences on the trail were actually a sign of peaceful slumber. And so they rode.

By morning they were passing Church Buttes, and the Overland and UP line had joined once more. They kept to the Overland—it didn't make sense not to, for them *or* the Cheyenne—and soon passed Fort Bridger.

"Musta come through here at night," said Malone, speaking the obvious, since the fort was well within sight.

A couple of hours later they spotted wagons, horses, and men a good distance up the trail ahead of them.

"What do you think, Windy? You're sure about those tracks?"

"What tracks?"

"Good God, man, the *gun* tracks. Could they have picked up a wagon and dumped the gun in there, gotten tricky?"

"Coulda, I guess. Anyplace after Bitter Creek. I can't see in the dark, y'know. An' can't see nothin' on this here trail. Been kinda guessin', but hell, Matt, there ain't been nowhere else to go."

"It was light at Church Buttes—"

"An' I thought I saw them gittin' onto this here trail, but I didn't put my nose right down on 'em."

"Windy—"

"We had to ride, Matt. They ain't movin' fast, but they ain't creepin'."

"So they actually could have picked up a wagon at Bitter Creek, or anywhere after that. Or turned off and gone in a whole different direction."

"They didn't, if it's Creed we're after. I once took a squaw away from him, y'know that? He ain't never forgive me."

Matt stared at him. "What the hell does that have to do with anything? Do you *know* what Creed would be up to?"

Windy stared off into the distance.

Matt shook his head and heaved a deep sigh. "Those wagons ahead—could that be them?"

"Could be. Not Creed, but it could be *someone*. I'd go cautious."

They did, fanning out as they rode up behind the two-wagon outfit.

Matt rode up abreast of the rear wagon on the right side, his right hand holding his Scoff down out of sight. Five other men on his side and six on the other matched his tactic.

"I say, happy to see you boys," called the driver of the second wagon.

Matt grinned tightly and kept on riding until he was abreast of the lead wagon. His grin was tiring now, and the driver of the lead wagon, reading seriousness on his face, pulled his four horses to a stop. The driver eyed Matt and said, "No one told us to expect a bloomin' escort."

The voice was English, the face long, narrow, sandy-topped Anglo-Saxon. Britishers on their way to Salt Lake, Mormons recruited in England.

Mormons. In the back of Matt's mind he'd known there was something fishy about the Cheyenne riding deeper and deeper into Shoshone territory, not to mention Paiute and Ute territory. And also cradled in the back of his mind was knowledge of the time the Mormons posed as Indians and wiped out a wagon train bound for Frisco. The Mountain Meadows Massacre.

Matt tensed. Was the canvas top of the wagon suddenly going to lift and a Gatling start to spray death?

"Mind if I look in your wagons?" asked Matt, though the

tone of his voice made it a command rather than a request.

The driver turned in his seat and yelled, "All right, people, everybody out. We'll take a little break here. Tend to private duties, if you wish." He turned to Matt. "All yours, Lieutenant." His voice was not fruity with welcome, but neither was it surly; he'd heard of the Mountain Meadows Massacre, too.

Men and women poured out of the wagons, about fifteen, all English, of varied ages.

Inside the wagons there were personal items, food, and travel supplies, but no gun.

"Sorry," said Matt.

"I understand, mate."

"You're a bit crowded."

"Serving the Lord is not easy."

Matt nodded, then turned and shouted, "Mount up." And then he turned his horse and kicked him into a gallop on down the trail.

After about a quarter-mile he glanced back toward the Mormons, and almost fell off his horse. Rottweiler was in the process of dragging some person up onto his horse in front of him.

The squad topped a slight rise and the Mormons disappeared from view. Matt stopped his horse and swung it around and rose back to where Rottweiler waited with a funny expression and . . . a woman.

Matt stared. "Kidnapping, Rott—" he began. The sound of hoofbeats caught his ear and he twisted around to see Windy riding off ahead. Where the hell did he think *he* was going?

"She was standing there when we were pulling out, sir," said Rottweiler, bringing Matt's attention back around, "and she said 'please' and, well, I just did it without thinkin', I helped her."

"Very commendable," growled Matt, but then he looked at the girl and a little bit of him gave way inside. She was damned pretty. Golden hair cut sort of short, a good, trim figure despite the baggy work clothes. She'd obviously been out in the sun a lot, the hard Plains sun, and looked to be about twenty. He made himself sound gruffer than he felt, "What's the big idea, miss?"

"Jennifer, sir. Oh, please, sir, my mum and dad *made* me come, sent me here, they're still in England but we're poor and they wanted a good new life for me but I didn't want to leave but they made me because they knew better, and Mum, it nearly broke her heart but they thought they had to do it." A deep breath. "I just want to go home. Please, sir."

Were his men actually glaring at him? Softhearted, they were, decided Matt. "I'm sorry—"

"You can't take me back, you *can't*!"

"Miss Jennifer, you don't understand, we're not out here riding for fun, we're . . ." Those big brown eyes . . . "We'll take you as far as the next town. Evanston, I think. There we'll have to . . . well, we'll have to do *something*."

She grinned and suddenly launched herself from Rottweiler's saddle, throwing her arms around Matt's neck and drawing herself onto his saddle right behind him. Rottweiler looked a bit put out, but she flashed him a smile that made him feel better.

Matt rode back up to the head of the column, keeping his eyes straight ahead and feeling his face getting warm, and then the troop moved on.

Matt wondered where Windy had got to. He looked ahead. The trail apparently curled around the south side of a low peak.

"Sir!" cried a voice behind him. "Over there!"

Matt looked to his right, northwest. A rider was coming hard toward them; it was Windy, whipping the hell out of Knobby. Matt halted the column and waited.

Windy rode up. He opened his mouth to speak, saw the girl, and, for a moment, was speechless. Then he found his voice and said, "Had an idea, Matt. Like I said, I know Creed Scarborough. Not good, but I know him. Heard him talk once, know his thinkin'. He thinks big. Gun tracks leave the trail right up ahead there. I been lookin' for them. Go that way . . ." He pointed back the way he'd come. "UP line's just over there. There's a grade. Train slows . . . and right after it gets to the top, the track's all ripped up."

"All this to rob a *train*?" wondered Corporal Miller.

Matt frowned. "Train headed which way? From Frisco?" At Windy's nod, Matt went on, "From Frisco. Train would slow down natural coming *up* toward the Divide, roll along pretty fast otherwise. They might not want to wreck it, but . . . what would Indians . . . why would anyone go to all this trouble?" He shook his head, baffled. He turned it absent-mindedly and found himself staring into the big brown eyes of Jennifer, the golden skin, the tousled— "Gold! Goddamnit, those trains carry *gold*. Coins and bullion. There's a U.S. Mint in Frisco. They ship East on UP. But they don't ship every time. Someone would have to know when it's being shipped."

"Who would know, sir?"

"Well, the Treasury, of course . . . and the army, that'd be automatic, and there's at least a squad of soldiers with each shipment, sometimes more. It'd be hard to take a train like that."

"Not if it's stopped and there's a Gatling pouring hot lead at them," said Corporal Miller.

That's certainly true, thought Matt. "But how would they know that this train's carrying bullion?"

Matt realized the answer at the same time that Weatherby showed an unexpected flair for analysis. "Prob'ly from the same place they knew about the Gatling, sir. From someone in the army."

"Yes," said Matt. "Yes, that's got to be it . . . but here's the thing. I haven't been that worried about the Gatling because I figure that a Cheyenne's going to have a damned hard time firing it, and the way it fires, they'll burn up all their ammo once they get it going. It'll fire something like one or two thousand rounds a minute."

"Matt—" began Windy, but Rottweiler's voice cut in:

"You talked to Mulberry, sir?"

Oh, Christ. "No, I haven't talked to Mulberry."

"He knows all about the gun, sir, and that ain't the way it fires. You gotta keep shovin' magazines in, and that slows it up somethin' amazin', an', well, I guess it'd give anyone a chance to conserve ammo and sight real careful."

"What's a Gatling?" asked Jennifer in Matt's ear, her breath hot.

"All right, so they can fire it," said Matt, "*but*—and here's the biggest thing—*why*? These are Cheyenne. What the hell do they want to rob a train for? What do they want with gold?"

"Matt," said Windy, "I been guessin' a lot of the way, but—" He smiled. "—I don't figger no Cheyenne's gonna be firin' that Gatling."

Matt looked at him, then said quietly, "Yes, that's about the only explanation that makes good sense." And he lashed his mount into motion, almost leaving Jennifer behind.

They rode hard northwest, Windy taking the lead. Knobby ran real good for a lazy beast.

"There was a *choof-choof-choof* in the distance that they might have heard had their horses' hooves not been making so much noise.

As it was, they'd just come in sight of the tracks, emerging from a cleft in the brow of the hill, when they heard the hellish roar of the Gatling somewhere deep in the cleft.

Matt spun his horse, unceremoniously unseating Jennifer, and charged into and down the cut at the head of his men. He had no choice. If he took the time to circle up through the scrub trees, he'd arrive to find an engine dragging a string of bullet-riddled coffins.

"I sure can't hear them hostiles whoopin' none," cried Malone as he tried to run his horse up Corporal Miller's backside.

There was the train. And a glance told Matt which side the attack was coming from: the right side, where the pitch to the train was more gradual, giving the Gatling better access. Realizing that, Matt swung his horse right and drove up the gradual slope studded with scrub growth. His men were strung out behind him, loosening their Springfields.

Bullets dug into the ground around Matt—where the hell were they coming from, the train?—but they'd gotten close now, and he left his horse and hit the ground running. And then went flat as the bullets continued to rain down.

He searched for their source, and found it up the hill on the far side of the train. The attack was from *both* sides. "Up there!" shouted Matt.

Rottweiler and Holzer eyed the far hill and started pumping rounds back up with Germanic efficiency. Matt and the rest got up and ran forward in a crouch. They had to be careful. The way they were coming in, they could take a round from either source, friend or foe.

Suddenly a man rose up before them. A white man in a blue uniform—a soldier—his rifle at port.

"Crikey, mate," said Malone, "what the bloomin' hell's goin' on?"

"Been hit by Indians," said the soldier. "They're all over the place. You go on, I'll watch the rear."

"Drop it," ordered Matt, and then he read the look in the man's eyes. The "soldier" died of a bullet from Matt's Scoff before his Winchester had come level.

"Jesus," breathed Malone.

Matt stepped over the body and then dropped and wriggled

185

forward. His men also dropped and squirmed forward on his flanks. They came to a dropoff and looked over the edge.

What the hell? wondered Malone. Those were *soldiers* right below them, no more than thirty feet away, firing down at the train. Some fire was being returned from the train, but it was light, at best.

Matt saw a number of blue-clad bodies lying about the ground outside the train. They'd been suckered out by the bogus soldiers and blown away. It must be passengers returning the fire, passengers and whatever soldiers were left.

Matt saw that the Gatling, set up down to his left, was concentrating on the first baggage car. The door and the area around it was a sieve. The door was ajar, locks blown away. There'd been soldiers inside. Whether they were still alive—

A bullet hitting close and throwing stone splinters into his face brought his attention back to the task at hand.

He didn't like shooting men in the back, but he wasn't about to stand up and start yelling to get their attention. He held up one hand to the other men, pointed his Scoff down, and squeezed off a round. It wrecked the elbow of the gent lying closest.

The man screamed and rolled over, but then drew a Colt and started throwing lead back up at them. His comrades caught on and they, too, rolled over and started slinging lead up the hill.

It was too easy, thought Matt, sending a bullet into the chest of the man with the shattered elbow, but he'd given them as square a break as he could.

And his men gave the rest of the Gatling crew the same chance, with the same result.

The man cranking the Gatling saw what was going on, realized the gun wouldn't swivel around enough to fire on Matt and his men, and took off running. Gunfire came from the train and he staggered. More gunfire, and he wobbled drunkenly downhill and finally pitched onto the tracks.

And it was over. Except for continued fire from the train.

"Hold your fire!" yelled Matt. "We're army!"

"So was them, you bastard," came the reply.

"No!" shouted Matt. "They were—" He looked down at the corpses of the white men. They'd all been white, as Windy, in his half-assed way, had told him right there at the end. But he couldn't yell down that they'd just been *dressed* as soldiers.

Those poor bastards in the train knew *that*. "Who's the officer in charge down there?"

A pause, and then the reply came, "Wilkes. Captain Wilkes."

Wilkes. Well, what do you know? "Hey, Captain Wilkes!" Matt shouted. "Did or did not the class duty officer at the Point have you walking guard in your scivies the day after Bobbie Lee surrendered?"

Another pause. And then, "Who the hell's that up there?"

"Kincaid!" Matt yelled back.

"Kincaid?! Goddamnit, *you* had to walk it *with* me! Where are you? Come on down here."

Matt stood up and led his men down the hill.

Captain Wilkes waited at the bottom for him. Wilkes' left arm was hanging bloody and useless, but he was grinning from ear to ear. "So *that's* a Gatling. Lucky you arrived."

Matt stared at him. "How the hell did you get to be a captain?" He smiled and added, "Sir?"

Wilkes backed up, flinching, and said, "Good Lord, Matt, you don't have to 'sir' *me*."

Matt and Jeffrey Wilkes then relived old times as the captain had his wound dressed and bandaged, as Rottweiler and Holzer tramped off grumbling in search of the horses, as the dead were buried, as the remaining wounded were tended to, as the Gatling was loaded onto the train, as the tracks were repaired. . . .

A small figure approached along those tracks, delicately picking her way along.

"Miss Jennifer!" cried Malone. "We kinda forgot about you."

Matt said the same thing when she was shown in to where he and Wilkes were chatting.

"I thought quite as much," she replied coolly. "But you're not getting rid of me quite that easily."

Matt smiled at her. "How about a ride, then? You do like trains, don't you?"

"Oh, I *love* trains."

Matt divided his men up. He took Malone and Dobbs, telling Wilkes, "We'll wrassle this gun as far as Como," and sent the rest back with Corporal Miller.

"Me too?" asked Windy.

"We can do without him," said Corporal Miller.

"Oh, hell," said Matt. "Okay, come on along."

"You want your horses loaded on, sir?" asked Miller.

"Stick them in the baggage car, the second one, it's supposed to be empty. And leave an extra couple to haul the gun. And I'll stop off and wire Sergeant Cohen what's happening."

He watched them ride off. And felt the train jerk. And saw a disturbed look on Windy's face. "No Scarborough?" he asked.

"Nope. Musta been up on the hill, him an' another. They musta rode when Holz and Rotty started bangin' at them."

Matt cursed. "We should've chased them."

Windy shook his head. "Nope. They'd be long gone. But tell you what; they'll be headin' east, same as us. An' this is easier. . . . We'll find 'em, Matt, sooner or later. . . ."

twenty-one

First Sergeant Ben Cohen could have been excused for feeling edgy. Captain Conway still wasn't back and he was down to two squads, neither of them Easy Company's choicest. He hadn't heard from the captain and he hadn't heard from Matt. He felt cut off. Vulnerable.

A shout went up outside and he jumped. Then he ran to the orderly room door in time to see a group of rough-looking, well-armed men ride into the post. Probably buffalo hunters.

Cohen was certainly army through and through, and adamantly endorsed the proposition that the army took care of itself. But he was not a foolish man. Pride had led to more than one man getting his hair lifted. Thus, with the post dangerously undermanned, he'd discreetly let it be known, both at the sutler's and in town, that the post would welcome visitors for the next few days.

He hadn't said why—hell, the army was supposed to be protecting *them*—but folks knew the post detachment was busy chasing hostiles from one end of the state to the other, and they didn't make a big thing of Cohen's subtle request for reinforcements.

Nonetheless, Cohen didn't like it. To a certain degree, every man on post that was not uniformed was, if not his enemy, a complete stranger and likely to remain so. And probably for that reason he made no effort to speak to the new arrivals. Hell, he'd hear about them soon enough.

Not nearly soon enough, though. Otherwise he might have been able to prevent what happened.

Pamela strolled from the dining area back toward her quarters. On the way, she glanced over at the sutler's and remarked to herself on what a mangy crowd was there, hanging about.

And hunkered down among them was one of Pamela's town customers, Big Boy, who had screwed her while Mulberry lay hidden beneath the bed. Like most of his confederates, he had eyes that could count the hairs on a buffalo's chin at five hundred yards. And those eyes followed Pamela all the way back to her quarters.

"Pretty nice little hunka meat there, huh, Brazle?" said his companion.

"Ah know thet gal," growled Brazle.

"G'wan."

"Thet ain't no bull. 'Bout a week ago, ah practical' pitched a tent right 'tween thet li'l gal's legs."

"Yeah? Mebbe we kin git us some right heah."

"Mebbe."

"Don' figger th' army's gonna knock themselves out defendin' one of them, once they know."

"Nope, don' figger," said Brazle.

James Evinrude leaned closer to hear what his friend Crowley was saying.

"I was just asking, in light of what you've told me, all the circumstances, whether you'd ever given any thought to voluntarily going back East?"

Crowley sure had some funny ideas, thought Jim.

"If I were you," Crowley continued, "I'd figure sure they'll come looking for you sooner or later, and you're not exactly in hiding, are you? Just walked down and joined up."

"They said they wouldn't chase me."

"That's what they *said*, but people and times change. How do you know that town marshal's still a marshal, or still alive? Maybe there's a new one, hellbent on making a name for himself."

Evinrude smiled. "Ben, you've been out here too long. Mellanee, Maine, ain't exactly Dodge City. I *know* damn near everybody what lives there. And nobody's gonna be out to make a rep."

"It'd make a big difference, Jim, if you did go back and turn yourself in...or even turned yourself in at some U.S. marshal's office—there's one in Cheyenne, I think. You tell your story, and you'd probably get off with hardly anything."

"Ben, will you just shut up and drink. I know you'd like to help, but believe me, there's nothing to worry about."

Willis and Slab, the two hardcases, eyed Evinrude and Crowley from the far end of the Drovers Rest.

"I never seen no marshal cozyin' up like that to some dude he was gonna arrest," said Willis.

"Me neither," said Slab.

"Bet he ain't gonna take him back at all."

"Shoulda got him when we had the chance."

"That warn't no chance. You let 'em get the drop on us. Since then, that marshal ain't even *slept* with his eyes closed."

"Why don't we jes' *take* Evinrude?"

"'Cause the boss said there might be a bonus for the marshal. One less marshal's gotta be worth a bit of change."

"Shoulda took 'em both when we first got here. *You* wanted to be cute."

"Shut up, Slab. Jes' shut up an' keep yer goddamn eyes open."

The train was poking along. It was getting dark at the end of their second day of travel and the train was running well behind schedule. There'd been delays to remove the dead and wounded and bring the army manpower up to quota, to wait for all the shot-up cars to be replaced, to tend to shattered passenger relations.

Matt was tired as hell. He'd talked most of the previous night away with Wilkes, then found there weren't any bunks left, and had to grab what sleep he could in a coach. And it hadn't been much.

And the coming night wasn't going to be much different. He'd reserved himself a bunk, but they were due to reach Como sometime in the middle of the night. No rest for the weary.

Jennifer came walking along the aisle of his coach and the train lurched and tossed her into his lap. She caught herself at the last moment, but only by planting a hand deep into Matt's crotch. "Oh, God, I'm *sorry*," she said, blushing brightly.

"It's nothing," gasped Matt.

191

"I didn't *hurt* it, did I?"

"Hurt what?"

She tried to avert her head, but Matt saw the slight smile. Which was annoying, because she *had* hurt it. "We're going to have to figure out what we're going to do with you," he said.

She looked surprised. "I'm going with you."

Matt said emphatically, "You most certainly are not."

She looked hurt, then suddenly got up and left the coach.

Matt tried calling after her, but it was too late. Shouldn't have been so gruff, he decided, but weren't Mulberry and his trollop enough for any post at one time?

But damn, he did like Jennifer. She had those fresh ways, different words, a kind of innocence. Because she was English, he reckoned. If she only had a place she belonged, a home or a job or anything like that, he'd enjoy spending some time with her. No strings, no obligations, just that pretty hair, those big eyes...

He yawned and stretched. Might as well use that bunk while he could. He left the coach, looking for Windy.

He found him, and told the scout to wake him when the train was about to arrive at Como. Then he walked back to the sleeping coach. The bunks had been pulled down. He eyed the bunk. And felt his flesh crawling. He realized that it had not only been a long time since he'd washed completely, but almost as long since he'd changed clothes. His clothes were up in the second baggage car with his horse, in his bedroll.

He eyed the bunk, promised it he'd be right back, and made his way forward, passing Dobbs and Malone, asleep in the coach just before the baggage car.

He entered the car and looked for lanterns. The horses shuffled about. The next baggage car forward was where they had the Gatling, along with the gold coin and bullion, guarded by the reconstituted army contingent plus Wilkes, who was trying to shrug his wounds off. *Captain.* Jesus. And with those wounds, they'd probably make him a *major.* All he and Captain Conway ever got for wounds were whiskey, bandages, Dutch Rothausen's knife, and a bullet to bite on. It wasn't fair.

He lit a couple of kerosene lamps. His horse nudged him with its nose. He grabbed some grain from a sack, shoved part of it into his pocket, and gave the animal the rest.

Saddles and gear were heaped at the far end. Matt found

his roll and pulled out a fresh shirt and some clean underwear.

He gave his horse some more grain, then stripped off his uniform. When he'd got down to his trousers, he wondered about them. He didn't have spares, but maybe someone else did. Stretch, for instance. Stretch wouldn't mind. The trousers would be too long, but tucked into his boots . . .

Hair brushed his back, and he told his horse to cut it out.

The animal didn't quit, just switched him harder. Probably wanted more grain. "Damnit, Rosie, that tickles," he said, sweeping his arm backwards.

It hit something and there was a stifled yelp.

He turned. Jennifer was there, smiling sweetly and holding the end of Rosie's tail in her hand. "Well hel-lo-," she said. "Fancy meeting you here."

Matt eyed her. Somewhere she'd found clothes that clung to replace her baggy frock. His eyes moved over her. Some kind of soft flannel material. A shift, probably a nightgown or something like that.

"Hello, I said," she repeated, amused by his inspection.

"You had me blaming poor old Rosie."

She smiled, glancing at Rosie. Then her eyes narrowed and she stepped back a pace, bending slightly and looking under Rosie. The neck of her gown, none too tight to begin with, hung down and open, so that her breasts were exposed to his gaze.

Matt swallowed.

Rosie's remaining sex organ was beginning to extend, dropping toward the floor of the baggage car, as horses' members are wont to do at odd times.

Matt grinned and found his voice, saying, "He's gelded, that's why he's named Rosie."

"Oh, poor thing. But look at that. He *remembers*."

So did Matt.

Rosie twisted his head around and gave them an inscrutable look.

Jennifer reached a foot out and nudged the member.

Rosie's head came up alertly.

"Now cut that out, Jennifer," said Matt. "You'll only get him prancing around."

"But he's been *fixed*."

"As you said, gone but not forgotten. Now, if you'll excuse me . . ." He turned away, planning to whip on the undershirt and shirt. He heard scuffling behind him and Rosie kicked him in the calf. "Hey!!"

He turned to find Jennifer sitting astride Rosie. And in order to straddle him, her shift had been hiked far up her legs. Holy smokes, thought Matt.

"Get down off him," he ordered. "Come on, get on down."

"Help me," she said, extending her arms toward him.

He reached up, took her under the arms, and pulled her off. She slid down along him, clinging to him until her feet touched the floor. But then still she clung.

Matt couldn't bring himself to push her away.

She smiled and moved gently against him, her cheek against his bare chest. His eyes suddenly widened as her tongue emerged to touch a nipple.

Then her hand moved down his side, exploring. His breath came faster. Her hand moved on, finding its way to Matt's crotch. "Why, *Rosie*!" she cried delightedly, discovering a hard knob.

Matt sighed. "It happens."

"What'll we do about it?"

"Only one thing."

"Here?"

"It'd get kind of tight back in that bunk of mine."

"Mmmm," she agreed. Then she smiled. "Over there, with the saddles, there're blankets."

"So there are. Of course." He set about arranging a comfortable little corner. "Hope Rosie doesn't get jealous."

Jennifer's shift slid from her shoulders to the floor.

Perfect, thought Matt, as his eyes slipped from the smallish but firm and pink-tipped alabaster mounds, down to the golden, silken life-source, slightly amber now in the dim light. His mouth felt parched, and there was a tightness in his chest, to say nothing of elsewhere.

"Once you get through looking," said Jennifer softly, "you might undress yourself."

Was he mistaken, or did she show a trace of embarrassment? Like a fresh gust of innocence. Odd in one so bold.

But then she added, seeming to put the lie to those speculations, "Looking's not only fun for men, you know."

Unbelievable, thought Matt, and quite invigorating. He stripped, exposing his hard, muscled body, its surface marred only by scars, most of them small, but one large one beneath

194

the ribcage, on his side. She ran a gentle finger along it.

And the finger dropped down over his abdomen. . . .

A long time later, his head fell down and nestled into the join of her neck and shoulder. His senses reveled in the sweet, musky fragrance, and he fell into a deep, deep sleep. . . .

Captain Wilkes, passing through, had to step over them, smiling down at Matt and the girl. Jennifer opened her eyes and smiled suddenly.

What vitality, thought Wilkes. Quicksilver, like a child. He nodded toward the lamps. "Should I get them?"

"Please," she answered.

He did so, plunging the car into darkness.

Rosie stretched his head down and smelled the blankets, smelled her and Matt. She spoke to Rosie softly . . .

Sometime during the night she thought she heard "Como" called, a distant sound. The train stopped, but then moved on. . . .

Private James Evinrude got back from town early and checked in. Sergeant Cohen was still in the orderly room, trying to work miracles with his duty roster.

"Back early for a change, huh, Private?"

Evinrude couldn't think of an appropriate reply.

"You run through all the girls? Or are you still talkin' up a storm with that deputy? He still around?"

Evinrude went cold. "What deputy?"

"Lieutenant Kincaid told me. You been powwowin' with a U.S. deputy marshal. Even pulled his fat outta the fire one time. Matt thinks his handle's Crowley, Ben Crowley. He's got a rep. That him? Ain't supposed to be a secret, is it?"

Evinrude stood there stupidly, stunned. Cohen went back to his work without noticing. Evinrude finally stumbled out of the orderly room and onto the parade.

He stood for a long time in the middle of the parade, staring at the heavens. What demonic power was at work? He understood Crowley now, and why he'd seemed so persistently solicitous. Crowley had come to get him. He'd prefer to talk Evinrude back East, but if that didn't work, he'd take him back any way he could.

How could he have been so stupid, so blind? He'd never been the kind of man to have friends clustering about, anxious to talk for days on end, and he still wasn't. He'd been so lonely, though, so full of self-pity, so . . . afraid.

He'd thought he was beyond despair, caring nothing for what might happen to him—whatever happened, happened—but that had been just a shield to ward off fear. Fear of the unknown.

And when Crowley had offered unexpected friendship, for no apparent reason other than camaradarie, he'd grabbed it.

And Crowley, he thought bleakly, had known exactly what he was doing.

"You know anything about stars, Jim?"

Evinrude blinked, lowering his gaze. Pamela stood there looking up at him. "Some say the future's writ in the stars," she went on. "You know what's writ there?"

He smiled sadly. "Nope. Sure wish I did, though."

Pamela passed on. It hadn't been her idea to play cards with the enlisted men, it had been Flora's. And it had gone on and on. Something to do for the poor dears, Flora had said. Pam had thought of something else the men might like better, but she *hadn't* said.

They'd played in the mess, and now Pam was heading for bed. She thought of poor Ed, stomping around up there on guard. She could see his shadow, a silhouette against the night sky. He'd said his shoulder hurt so he'd have a devil of a time carrying his rifle. But there he was, and she could see his rifle sticking up. He didn't seem to be as bad a soldier as everyone said.

"Hey, sweetie," growled a voice practically beside her. She spun, peering into the darkness.

"It's me, babe. Brazle. 'Member?"

Oh, God. That stinking monster. "What are *you* doing here?" she asked, appalled.

He laughed an ugly laugh. "Ah'm here blessin' mah good fortune. Didn't know there was gonna be any *ladies* here."

"There aren't," she snapped back.

"There sure ain't," he said, gurgling. She couldn't see his ugly, grimy grin, but she knew it was there. "An' ah figger there ain't nobody else here, 'sides me an' mah buddy, who knows about you—ain't that right? You got a real nice life here—an' a nice li'l business on the side. . . ."

Pamela couldn't think of anything to say, and Brazle rasped

on, "Now I figger you want to keep it thet way, so jes' me an' mah buddy, he's waitin' ovuh theyah in the shadders by th' stable. Whyn't we take a walk ovuh theyah?" He took hold of her arm.

But she pulled away and ran. His shout chased after her, and she ran faster.

Near her quarters was a ladder to the roof. She climbed it. She fled past one amazed guard, who fortunately recognized her, before she found Ed Mulberry.

He was delighted, then confused, and finally fearful, to find his "wife" in his arms. "You can't stay here, Pam," he told her urgently.

She clung to him harder. He hadn't realized he was so irresistible. And, damnit, he wasn't. "What's the matter?"

She dried her tears and said, "Do you remember that big ugly man that was on the bed while you were under it?"

Pam told him what had happened, what *was* happening.

"Well," he said lightly, and with an air of sophistication, "that *was* your life, you know, and will be again, according to you, as soon as you leave here. Which now may be a little sooner than you expected."

"Don't you *care*? I mean, this will be a disgrace for you, put you back in the barracks with those men that treat you badly. Don't you *care*? Don't you care about *me*? I've been doing this for *you*, Ed."

"I'll pay you, Pam, I'll pay you," he protested in a weak voice.

"Edward! I don't want to be paid. I just want—" What did she want? "What kind of man *are* you?"

What could he say? He didn't know what kind of man he was. He only knew that when she'd mentioned that big buffalo-stink, he'd felt scared, scared witless.

Oh hell, nothing was changed. He was still the coward he always was, even if he felt big, dragging that buffalo gun around. "I'm a coward, Pam, that's what I am." It was easier telling her that than having to show her. Safer too, he thought, recalling his one brief, mad moment of manly courage at the Drovers.

She clung to him, murmuring, "Maybe if I went down there . . . did what they want . . . they won't be staying forever. . . ."

Something inside Mulberry rebelled, but he couldn't bring

197

himself to say anything. He clung to her almost as tightly as she clung to him.

Then she pulled free. "I'd better go . . . do what I have to."

"Maybe it'd be better," he said reluctantly.

"I don't want to get you in trouble," she said, and then faded away into the darkness.

And Mulberry stood there in his own personal darkness for a long, long time.

Finally he could take no more. He walked down the guard post, passing the other guard, who said, "Oh, hell, Ed, it's gonna be your ass," and climbed down the ladder. He peered toward the dark corners of the parade, looking for a sign of movement.

He came to the door to his own quarters, and paused, listening.

Then he opened the door and silently entered. A lamp glowed. He crept to the bedroom door and peered into the darkness.

She was *there*. Lying there in bed, asleep. He started breathing normally again, and then he turned and crept away.

Pamela's eyes opened wide and she stared at the doorway where he'd stood.

twenty-two _____

Matt woke slowly. The train was stopped. He could see a crack of light by the edge of the baggage car door. That shouldn't be. With a sinking sensation he asked, "Is this Como?"

Jennifer blinked, nestling closer. "Hm?"

"Como. Where *are* we? How long did I sleep?"

"Como? I think I heard someone yell that, a long time ago."

"Christ!" Matt leaped to his feet. Jennifer watched, smiling, eyes half-closed, as Matt scrambled to the car door and peeked out. "Cooper's Lake!" he exploded. "It's goddamn Cooper's Lake."

He turned back to her. "Windy was supposed to..." But then he realized that Windy hadn't been able to find him.

"What will you do?" she asked.

"Do? Do? Go on to Laramie, I guess. That's about forty miles. There's an army detachment there, I can send a wire...." He smiled. "Well, hell, haven't been to Laramie for a while."

"Come on back here," she said as the train started moving.

He looked down as she threw the blanket off. He laughed. "Why not? And don't you get any ideas, Rosie."

"Don't talk to Rosie like that. Rosie's been a *dream*."

"Mmmmm," he moaned, sinking into her. "I'll bet."

Some time later, he rolled onto his side and, with a light finger, played with the curls on her forehead. "Now seriously, Jenny," he said softly, "what *are* you going to do? You know there's no room on a post for a woman, not for *my* woman, anyway. It's a hard life. There are only a few women who can take it. It's no life for a sweet thing like you."

"And I'd get in your way, wouldn't I?" she suggested, smiling. "Cramp your lovely style. Oh, Matty, dear, I don't want to catch you. You don't have to worry. I've *lots* of time."

She thought about it, her future, giggled some, and then turned, smiling, to face Matt. Matt thought she was taking it awfully well, better than most of his women.

"Oh," she crooned, "maybe I'll try to go back to England."

"I might be able to help," said Matt. "I've some money saved."

"Or maybe Denver. We came that way, you know, and I rather liked the place. The air was so fine for a city. I can probably find a family to live with, possibly an English family. I've heard there are quite a lot out here."

Matt nodded.

"Then perhaps I could finish school. That's very important for me, it would really open up an entire—"

"*College*? Do you mean to say your, uh, your mum and dad took you out of the *university* to send you out—"

"No, silly." Her laughter pealed. "Of course not."

Matt began to suspect the awful, awful truth. "Just how old *are* you?" he croaked. "And don't tell me 'young.' I want to know exactly."

Her face lit up with terrific amusement as she replied, "Fifteen."

The soldiers in the forward baggage car practically jumped out of their skins.

And Malone, sitting in the first passenger coach, turned to Stretch and said, "Hey, Dobbsy, did you just hear a yell?"

"Sure did," said Stretch. "Sounded like the time that horse kicked ol' Trouble Thompson in his jewels."

"No it didn't," argued Malone. "More like the time the boys picked up the privy and moved it with the sarge still inside."

"Yeah," said Stretch, "I remember that. I was there."

"You were the one that said to move it."

"How was I to know? He'd been in there near on an hour."

Matt rushed into the coach, stuffing his shirt into his trousers.

"Morning, sir," cried Malone, as Matt rushed by.

Windy, stretched out on a seat, his hat down over his eyes, tipped the brim up enough to see Matt. Then he let the brim fall back down, but stretched an arm out across the aisle to stop Matt. "No wonder I couldn't find you," he muttered from beneath the grimy hatbrim.

Matt snatched Windy's hat off. "You didn't look very damn hard."

"How was I to know you and the horses was—"

The far door opened and Jennifer entered, grinning, practically bubbling with merriment.

"Jesus!" breathed Matt. If she dared say anything...

"You know, Matt, in this light she do look kinda young, don't you think?"

"Of course I do. She's just a child."

Jennifer walked the length of the coach. She was carrying a kerchief. Matt's kerchief. She held it out. "You dropped this, Mr. Kincaid." Her face was very serious. "Or it fell off when that horse was acting up. I'd certainly like to thank you for getting up so early to teach me all about those horses. I would never have guessed there was so much to know about an animal that one usually regards as dumb and takes for granted...." Her voice was low and calm and adult, and Matt began to think she might pull it off. He, too, looked very serious, nodding gravely.

"That's quite all right," he said. "I was glad to. I'm inclined to think of you as the daughter I might have had, were I not devoted to the cause of the U.S. Army and—"

Just then, though, Jennifer's eyes fell on Windy, who was watching Matt, openmouthed. "Aren't you the one that stepped all around us last night?" she asked. "Where're all the rest..."

Windy snatched his hat back and pulled it down over his head. Dobbs and Malone sank immediately into deep comas. And Matt stared holes in the ceiling.

"Anyone seen Evinrude?" asked Corporal Wilson.

"Saw him riding out the gate," said Packer.

"But he's got guard."

"Maybe he didn't know. He was jawin' with one of them travelers what stopped by. Think he borrowed a rifle, one of them new Winchesters. Maybe he went outside to try it out."

"Who was he talkin' to?"

"Some feller that had a patch on his shirt. I remember them talkin' some about that."

Corporal Wilson went looking for the man, a man with a patch. He found one over at the sutler's, standing by a wagon. The man had a patch announcing the Maine Regulars.

"Was you and a big guy talkin' about that there patch?"

The man said, "Ayup. Him an' I was in the War together. Didn't know each other, but the same outfit."

"He borrow a rifle?"

"Ayup. Said he wanted to try it out. And if you can't trust the army, who can you trust, ain't that right?"

Right enough, but Wilson was beginning to entertain some doubts about Evinrude's trustworthiness.

Evinrude knew very well he was slated for guard duty, but didn't give a damn. He didn't give a damn about anything anymore. That marshal had *lied* to him, and was sweet-talking him right into a hangman's noose.

Well, he wasn't going to succeed. There were plenty of places in the West where he could hide. And this time they weren't going to know where to look for him.

But first there was a debt for Evinrude to collect. Coming after a man was one thing, but deceit was another.

He rode slowly, letting his anger build. Then, nearing town, he saw a familiar figure in the distance. Crowley, coming his way. Probably heading for the post to make his arrest. The timing couldn't have been much better.

Evinrude spun his horse around and rode back up the trail until he came to a place where it ran through a draw filled with cottonwoods. Sergeant Cohen had said this Crowley had a rep. Jim had never actually seen him draw, but he wasn't about to let Ben make good that rep.

Jim hid his horse among the cottonwoods and concealed himself up in the crook of a tree, and waited.

He had a good line of sight, and soon saw Crowley approach. Evinrude drew a bead, his sights sticking to Crowley's chest like glue.

The target got bigger . . . and bigger . . . and still Jim waited. He knew he couldn't miss, not at that range. Hell, he could've picked out a shirt button and hit it. But still he waited.

Then, suddenly, there was the sound of gunfire and Crowley

pitched forward out of the saddle to the ground.

Evinrude's eyes opened wide. What the hell?

Two riders came up the trail from town, the hardcases Slab and Willis. Evinrude didn't know their names, but he sure recognized them. "Those bastards," he breathed.

They dismounted and stood over Crowley.

Evinrude saw Crowley move, saw him roll slowly over and try to drag his gun out.

Then he saw that Crowley wasn't getting his gun out very fast. And the hardcases were drawing theirs again. Evinrude dropped out of the tree.

The noise of his drop brought the hardcases' eyes up. Slab smiled. "Wal, now, Willis, ain't this jes' about what the doctor ordered? This shore is our lucky day."

But the Winchester stock was snapping up into Evinrude's armpit and its barrel was rising.

The range was a trifle long for Colts. Slab missed and Evinrude didn't. Then Willis fired high as Evinrude dropped to his knees and fired dead on.

Evinrude walked slowly up to the tangle of bodies.

Crowley focused glazed eyes on him. "Thought it might be you . . . thought I saw you before . . . they been puzzlin' me . . . guess you were the one they were really after . . . weren't taking no chances . . . I was . . ." He fell quiet. Evinrude just stared down at him. Then Crowley spoke again, his voice weakening. "You lucked out, Jim. I was coming to take you in. . . . Sorry. I'm a deputy. Was going to have to send you back to Maine. . . . Had to . . . it's my job. Tried to talk you into going back . . . would have made it easier. But this way . . . you're a lucky man, Jim . . . but next time go far away . . . hide good . . . they'll be coming. . . ."

Crowley fell back, unconscious, and James Evinrude turned away and walked heavily back toward where he'd left his horse.

The new guard had been posted. Mulberry was grabbing some needed sleep and Sergeant Cohen was waiting for Evinrude, fire in his eye.

Pamela closed the door quietly. Edward hadn't said a word since getting off guard, and now he was sleeping. She couldn't stand just waiting around for him to wake up. Maybe she'd go comfort Lieutenant Fletcher's wife, poor woman. Or go see

Maggie. Perhaps Maggie'd have some advice; she debated telling her what had happened. At any rate, she stepped on out onto the parade.

Ed Mulberry heard her leave and sat up. Thank God she was gone. The silence had been hard to maintain, but even harder to break. He bowed his head before the impossibility of everything, and that's when he heard the ruckus start up.

Pamela had been walking toward the Cohen quarters when she saw the big buffalo-stink, Brazle, angling to cut her off. She increased her pace but didn't make it. Brazle swung alongside of her and said, "Now you c'mon, gal, and settle down t' business. Me an' mah buddy, we waited fer you las' night an' we ain't waitin' no longer. We're headin' back fer them stables, an' you better show up soon with them creamy white tits an' thet rosy—"

Pamela stopped, pivoted, and swung, her fist catching Brazle square on the side of his head.

It didn't hurt him one little bit, but it sure enraged him. "You *bitch*!" he roared, getting the entire post's attention.

Mulberry raised his head; guards looked down from the walls; Cohen looked up from his desk; Lieutenant Price's pencil dug into and ruined the paper he was writing on; several soldiers not on detail came out of the sutler's along with a few civilians; Maggie Cohen's hand on Carol Fletcher's shoulder suddenly gripped hard; Trash Jimson, across the parade, digging yet another goddamned latrine, looked up, saw, and dropped the spade. He leaped from the latrine and started sprinting.

"*You gawdamned bitch*," said Brazle at the same deafening level. "Yo're nothin' but a gawdamned *whoor*. Ah fucked yo' silly in town, an' bah God ah'm gonna git me some more heah an' now. Ah got the *money* and maybe ah'll *pay* yuh, but bah God, *fust* ah'm gonna git satisfaction—oof!"

The 'oof!' was caused by Trash ramming into him, full speed.

Pamela fell back, stunned.

Brazle righted himself and turned, grunting. Jimson closed in swinging and was punishing the big man when Brazle's buddy took him from behind. And together the two buffalo men began to make short work of Jimson. Just then, Ed Mulberry came flying in on top of the whole mess.

"Oh, sweet Jesus," cried Pamela.

That was when Sergeant Cohen, enraged by the sight of

civilians not only provoking a fight on post, but winning it, dealt himself a hand.

Mulberry was giving it his best, trying to punch Brazle's sidekick, trying to knee, trying to scratch, even trying to bite, but not succeeding and only dissolving into a bloody mess. Cohen pried the two men apart, took Brazle's friend by the scalp, weathered a couple of blows to the side of the head, and drove his fist into and through the man's mouth. The fellow dropped, moaning, spitting some teeth and threatening to choke on the rest.

Then Cohen turned, wrapped an arm around Brazle's thick neck from behind, and proceeded to squeeze it several sizes smaller. Brazle clawed at the arm. Jimson, regaining his wits, saw a monstrous midriff in front of him and began whailing away. Brazle would have started yelling if he'd been able to get any sound out at all.

Finally, Sergeant Cohen realized he was holding up a dead weight, and let it drop. Jimson jumped back nervously, then realized that Brazle wasn't moving. "Aw, Sarge," he complained, "I was jes' gettin' warmed up."

They all stood around then, in various stages of quiet hysteria or exhaustion, while the two buffalo men picked up the pieces and put them back together again.

Pamela stood back, silent, afraid, watching Mulberry list slightly to port. She wanted to go to him, to thank him, to thank Trash, but she couldn't. She was finished there, she knew that. Nothing could ever be the same.

Brazle and his pal staggered across the parade toward the sutlers, toward their friends and their mounts. They were moving more steadily, recovering fast, a tough breed.

They mounted their horses and turned them toward the gate. Two other men, part of their crew, rode with them.

"Corporal!" yelled Sergeant Cohen. "Open that gate fast and get those bastards out of here."

Pamela mumbled to Maggie, who was standing close, "Maybe I'd better go pack. I'll have to leave."

Maggie Cohen fastened an iron grip on her arm. "You stand right there. You're not going anywhere."

"Please, Maggie," implored Pamela.

Ed Mulberry, hearing her voice, turned his head toward her. Their eyes met.

There was a yell from the gate. The corporal there, Wilson,

had been clubbed to the ground. The gate was wide open. The two buffalo men were down on the ground, their horses being held by their friends. Trash saw the sun flashing on the Sharps rifles in the hunters' hands. He grabbed for his gun, but it was lying two hundred yards away, on the ground by the latrine pit.

The buffalo guns boomed and two heavy, fifty-caliber slugs slammed into Trash. He was dead before he hit the ground.

Cohen had his gun out, but it was too far for the Scoff. Still, he fired till it was empty. And gunfire came from the guards overhead, once they'd shaken off their shock. The two other members of the buffalo crew, the men holding the horses, suddenly pitched from their saddles. And Brazle's pal did a quick spin one way, then the other, and crumpled and sprawled on his face.

Pamela saw the other Sharps, Brazle's, adjust to draw a bead on Mulberry. Apparently, Brazle had lost track of Cohen, but considering the amount of gunsmoke in the air, that was understandable, and Mulberry happened to be standing exposed, presenting a dandy target.

"Ed!" shrieked Pam, and leaped toward him. Mulberry turned toward the voice, a smile automatically appearing on his face.

She threw herself on him, and took the bullet.

She sagged against him. "Pam!" he moaned.

Then Maggie had Pam and was pulling her to the ground, stretching her out. Flora was dashing toward them, angling across the parade, skirts high.

Ed Mulberry's vision swam around to the gate and finally focused.

He saw Brazle, bullets kicking up the ground all around him, leaping onto a horse. The horse sagged momentarily, under the terrific weight, but then dashed on out the gate, Brazle leaning forward over its neck. He drove the horse in a twisting run away from the post, to the east. Gunfire followed him, but no bullets touched him.

Mulberry frowned. Something was trying to surface, some thought, some ancient impulse.

Then, suddenly, his skinny frame was jerking this way and that. He looked to be in the final stages of St. Vitus' Dance, but he was really looking for a weapon, a horse, an answer, something to *do*.

"You'll never run 'im down," snapped Cohen, smelling the elemental bloodlust. Then he remembered something Kincaid had said. And something else he'd heard. "You got the Sharps?" he roared, and Mulberry nodded. "Get it. Meet you over at the gate."

Ed Mulberry sprinted for his quarters. A group was mounting up to pursue Brazle as Mulberry came back out, running for the gate, trying to shove a load into the Sharps as he ran, a bag of ammo hanging from his shoulder.

He clambered up onto the roof beside the gate, with Cohen at his heels. Cohen had his field glasses.

Ed looked off into the distance.

Brazle had been riding like hell and hadn't let up, but his horse was no racehorse and he was no flyweight, and he'd been dodging this way and that and down into gullies and back up, and he wasn't all that far away.

"Five, six hundred?" croaked Mulberry. He was out of breath and his throat was dry.

"More like seven," said Cohen. He peered through his glasses. "Shoot short, if anything. We'll walk it right up to the bastard."

Ed smiled thinly. "You'll never see it," he said calmly, getting his breath back. "Not in that brush."

"Well, shoot anyway. Just shoot."

Ed set some bullets out and slowly got himself and the Sharps down into a solid position.

"Shoot!"

"Gotta wait until he gets into my range."

Cohen looked at him, astonished.

Ed started squeezing them off. Fire, reload. Fire, reload. He hoped he wouldn't hit the horse. He'd hate doing that.

"I can't see where they're goin'!" cried Cohen, exasperated.

Ed paused to rub his trigger finger on the wall before him, rubbing it raw, raising blood. A buffalo hunter had told him about that trick. Made the finger real sensitive. It'd better work, he thought.

Captain Conway was riding at the head of the column, Sergeant Chubb by his side.

"What the hell's that, sir? That's the fourth one now." Chubb was referring to a distant boom.

Now they topped a slight rise, and the post, which they'd

207

seen before as something like a mirage, was now much clearer, only about a mile away.

"That firing's coming from the post, sir." Chubb was squinting hard.

A horse and rider were angling across some distance in front of them, riding east.

"Chubb," snapped Conway, "send someone and get that man."

Chubb gave orders and two men peeled off from the column and drove their horses to intercept. The rider saw them coming and started throwing shots at them. They pulled their Scoffs, but before they could use them, the rider arched his back, slowly lifted from the saddle, and then dove over the head of the running horse.

Captain Conway stared, incredulous.

"Whoever's doin' the shootin'," said Chubb, "we shoulda had him with us. That was near a mile shot."

Back at the post, a cheer went up. Cohen dropped the glasses and turned, grinning and saying, "Practically right in the old man's lap." But Mulberry wasn't there.

He was running across the parade once more, still carrying his Sharps and ammo. He paused to look down at the body of his friend, Trash Jimson, and then cried, "Where's Pam?"

"Just calm down, Ed, calm down." Corporal Wilson had laid an easy hand on him. "The captain's lady had her taken to her quarters—"

"Where? *Whose* quarters?"

"Th' captain's quarters. Dutch was gonna work on her—"

"Dutch? Sergeant Rothausen?" And then he fairly shrieked. "The *cook*?!"

Wilson nodded briskly. "Yeah. He cuts good. But we discover that this fellow ridin' through, fellow from Maine, Evinrude's pal, he's a *doctor*. He's in with her now."

"Is she . . . ?"

"Don't know. Sorry. But you know what a forty-five slug can do."

Mulberry thought about it. "It was probably fifty-caliber, as a matter of fact . . . damnit."

"You see where she was hit?"

Ed blinked. "In my arms. Right in—"

"I mean whereabouts on *her*—" He paused abruptly, looking

208

off toward the front gate. "Well, glory be, look what the cat drug in. Here's ol' Evinrude."

True. Evinrude was slowly riding his horse across the parade, trying to figure out what all the excitement was about. But whatever it was, he felt able to regard it with a certain measure of detachment. It didn't mean anything to him anymore. His life was now truly over.

His horse balked at stepping over a body.

Evinrude looked down and recognized Trash.

Trash's life was over too.

Evinrude didn't feel quite so detached, after all.

twenty-three ─────────

Matt stood at the saloon bar, nursing a drink.

They'd pulled into Laramie with the afternoon half gone. Matt had gone straight to the army office and wired his position and status to HQ.

They'd wired back for him to proceed to Outpost Nine, taking the Gatling with him. They'd send a troop to pick it up and take it on to its eventual destination. In the meantime, the men at the post could play with it. HQ didn't say "play," of course, rather "familiarize," but they meant "play."

Windy, standing on his left side, nudged him. "Matt. We hit pay dirt. They jes' come in. Sittin' over in th' dark end of th' room." Windy was hunched over the bar, staring deep into his drink.

Matt turned, leaned back against the bar, and laughed, as if responding to a joke. His eyes were fixed on the door. Then he slowly let his gaze slide back to the rear of the saloon, toward the gloom.

A three-man group came into the corner of his field of vision. None were looking his way. He looked straight at them.

He saw two men in buckskins and a third in an army uniform.

"Scarborough?"

"Yep." Windy remained bellied up to the bar. "Thought he might head this way, head here. That's why I didn't wake you last night.'

Matt had known Windy could be devious, but he was sur-

210

prised all the same. "And the source of all their good information was that effing corporal who's with them?"

"Headquarters. I seed him there, Matt. Jes' a clerk, but he hears everything."

Matt turned back to the bar, started to finish his drink, but then decided against it. He turned slowly, casually, and began to move with the economy and grace of the born predator.

His glide took him down the bar, and Windy shadowed him. Then Matt began to slant toward the trio at the rear table as Windy kept on sliding along the bar.

Windy slowly raised his rifle until the butt was nestling in his armpit. The gun was still pointed down, but could come up in a split-second. Windy was slow with a handgun, but greased lightning with his Winchester.

Matt neared the table. And the three men seemed unaware of his stealthy approach, of the imminent danger, despite the hush that had slowly enveloped the room.

But Matt knew better. He'd seen a twitch in the corner of Scarborough's eye and a giveaway roll of the eyeball, just a subtle change in the eyelid's surface. Scarborough knew *someone* was there, someone posing a threat, Matt would bet his life on it. Which was exactly what he *was* betting.

He couldn't see Scarborough doing it, but he figured the man was slipping his Colt free on his far side—he was seated sideways to Matt—if he hadn't already. Scarborough was the type.

Matt stopped and waited.

The corporal faced Matt across the table. The third man sat facing Scarborough, which also put him sideways to Matt, except that he was probably right-handed and his gun side was exposed. No sneaky move there.

Matt thought the corporal was probably unaware of his presence; his head was bowed slightly as he stared at the tabletop, mumbling something. But the other two had to be aware. They wouldn't have lived so long without that extra sense.

Finally Matt got impatient. "Scarborough," he called.

Neither Scarborough nor his buddy blinked an eye or changed their positions by an inch. The corporal, though, looked up quickly, first surprised, then horrified.

"Who're you?" asked Scarborough calmly, looking straight ahead at his buddy.

"Kincaid," said Matt. "Army. Been chasin' you."

"Aaaahh," breathed Scarborough easily, his position unchanging. He smiled thinly.

"I'm here too, Creed," said Windy quietly, though it cut through the hush so clearly that it sounded like a yell.

Scarborough's thin smile turned cruel as his head slowly turned toward Matt. "Shoulda known Windy'd have somethin' to do with that mess back there. I *thought* it was you, Windy, I seen below, creepin' up on my men. Shoulda killed you. Woulda, too, 'cept Murphy here started shootin'. I'll jes' have to kill you now. Kill you both." The thin smile held. "How come you boys didn't go chasin' Racin' Elk up t' Canada?"

"Chased him till we killed him."

That surprised Scarborough and he glanced at the corporal, spitting out, "Belkin—"

"Don't get mad at him, Creed. He did his job. You just didn't do yours. But you're both gonna pay."

Creed eyed him again. "Who'd you say you were, soldier boy?"

"Kincaid. Matt Kincaid."

Ah. It finally rung a bell. A loud bell. Maybe he'd better hurry up and shoot the bastard. Creed was holding his Colt by his leg. A split-second to swing it up and around, and goodbye, Mr. Kincaid. Then he'd take care of that nosy, squaw-robbing bastard, Mandalian. . . .

Unfortunately for his plans, Corporal Belkin lost control just then and grabbed his Scoff and started to raise it.

Matt, figuring the corporal for the weak link, the jumpy one, saw Belkin's eyes give it away and reached for his gun at the same time.

Scarborough and Murphy, concentrating on Matt, didn't see Belkin's move, just Matt's, and all Scarborough could think was the unthinkable. . . . *He's drawin' first. He ain't supposed to do that.* And then Scarborough tried to drag his Colt, suddenly heavy, around to bear.

Time seemed, for him, to slow to a crawl. His gun was nosing up over his leg, all right, but like molasses, and he watched, fascinated, as Matt's gun first blew a hole in Belkin and then searched for him. And found him.

Creed swore he could see Matt's knuckle whitening, see the bullet actually leaving the barrel, feel it. . . . But of course it all happened in a flash, and was over.

Murphy, though, left to last, did manage to get a shot off. Two, in fact.

Matt reacted to the first with a sudden, spinning move that took him full-circle and clear of the follow-up shot. Then, having already brought his walnut-handled Scoff clear to join the Colt that was in his other fist, and finding it conveniently pointing in the right direction, he sent a heavy slug plowing into Murphy's gut, doubling him over. A final shot straightened Murphy back up and sent him sprawling among chairs and tables.

Matt walked back to the bar, reclaimed his unfinished drink, and tossed it down.

Then he slid to the floor.

Blood began to spread in a pool.

Matt woke up some time later. A smiling, elderly man in a tailcoat was bending over him.

"You got the luck of a gambler, son. A *good* gambler," the man said in a warm voice.

Matt blinked.

"Bullet hit a rib, cracked it, kinda slid through, actually *bounced* off your lung—wasn't goin' too fast by then, I reckon—and then took up residence riiiiiight theerrrrre . . . I can see it now. . . .

"Hang on now, might be a little sensitive. . . ." The doc paused to smile down at him reassuringly. "Maybe you can hang onto your wife's hand."

The words sank in slowly . . . and fell all the way to the bottom, still making no sense. He felt pressure on his leg.

He raised his head a trace, looked down his sheet-covered body, and saw Jennifer.

Wife?! What the hell did the doc take him for?

"There now," said the sawbones. "Take it easy. Groanin' won't help. Miz Kincaid, grab his hand, will you? Hold on."

Jennifer reached under the cover and grabbed, but didn't grab his hand.

His eyes widened and his breath came faster.

"More sensitive than I figgered, huh?" commented the doc.

Jennifer squeezed gently. Matt continued to make small noises.

twenty-four

A week later, Matt, Windy, Stretch, and Malone arrived back at Outpost Nine. The others were mounted, while Matt drove the four-horse gun-carriage rig. Two horses were standard, but the damned Gatling had caused enough trouble already, and if they had to outrun anything, they wanted to be ready.

By the time they arrived, the post had just about gotten back to normal. The various wounded were recovering and replacements, some thirty of them, had been requested.

When Matt entered the orderly room, Cohen jumped to his feet and snapped a sizzling salute, grinning broadly. It was the closest he could come to hugging Matt, who responded with a salute of his own, and an equally warm smile.

"Welcome back, sir," Cohen said fervently. "You're a sight for sore eyes, that's for damned sure."

Captain Conway emerged from his office and the two officers exchanged salutes. "Hello, Matt," Conway said. "How are the spareribs feeling?"

"Seem to be knitting up just fine, sir. Itches a trifle under the bandage, is all. Congratulations on winning the fight with Racing Elk."

"Thank you, Matt. I'm only sorry it cost us so dearly."

"Yessir, I know. I heard about it before we rode out."

"They're sending replacements," Conway said, adding grimly, "as if you can replace lives...." Then he brightened a bit.

"But you haven't heard it all. Sergeant Cohen had his own excitement right here on post."

Sergeant Cohen then gave it the full treatment.

When he'd finished, Matt asked about Pamela.

"Touch and go," Cohen replied. "Lucky we had a real live surgeon handy—"

"Dutch?!" Matt exclaimed, appalled.

"No, not Dutch. The real thing, sir. Passin' through. And Private Mulberry and Miss Pamela are going to do it up right an' get married."

"You're joking," said Matt.

"Unless Mulberry's father, Edward Mulberry the *Second*, can get here first." Cohen chortled.

Matt looked at Captain Conway.

"Normally," Conway acknowledged, "I wouldn't allow it, for reasons we're all familiar with, even though it would greatly distress Private Mulberry and leave him and the girl in a bind, but he's just not a field soldier, Matt. He came through under pressure this time, but many more such incidents, and we'd be packing him off in a box or straightjacket. So I'm getting him a transfer to some office somewhere, maybe the Bureau of Indian Affairs. He seems to have a taste for something like that. And we'll get him a stripe; he's sort of a hero and the army's not so cheap at that level. Who knows, maybe they'll be able to make a go of it."

"Sounds good," muttered Matt. "Sounds good. Everything back to normal. Sounds good. . . ."

"Sounds too good, don't it, sir?" said Cohen.

"I knew it. What's wrong, Sergeant?"

Sergeant Cohen sighed. "A real surprise. I got me a royal, ten-stripe, deadbeat goof-up I never expected. Evinrude."

"Evinrude?"

"Yep. First he skipped out on guard, and since then he's been like a dead man. He's been pullin' guard seven days straight since, and *doin'* it all right, but Matt, he jes' don't care."

"What happened?"

"Beats the hell outta me."

Evinrude was lying on a bunk in the guardhouse, staring at the slats of the bunk overhead.

The door opened, and Corporal Medford entered and said, "Evinrude. Get your dead ass to the orderly room, pronto."

Evinrude got to his feet slowly, and trudged out of the guardhouse and across the parade. A horse was tethered in front of the orderly room. He entered.

A circle of serious faces met him: Sergeant Cohen, Matt Kincaid, Captain Conway, even Mr. Price.

"Howdy, Jim," said a voice, and Evinrude turned toward it—toward Bradshaw and the telegraph corner.

Ben Crowley stood a little straighter than usual, but that was probably because, beneath his clothes, he was wrapped like a mummy, bandaged from hip to neck.

Evinrude looked at Crowley, and at the rest around the room, but he didn't say anything.

"Bradshaw," said Crowley, "take this message down. For relay to the U.S. marshal's office in Cheyenne, to be forwarded to appropriate legal authorities in New York City and Mellanee, Maine. Subject, colon—"

"I can't send a colon."

"Spell it, then. Subject, colon, James Evinrude, wanted for criminal activities in state of Maine. Subject Evinrude has been determined to be dead, killed while on active duty with the U.S. Army of the West. Body identified by Deputy U.S. Marshal Benjamin Crowley, and ID further sworn to by officers of E Company . . . and the rest of it, regiment and so on." He looked over at Captain Conway. "Do you think I should specify exactly where he fell?"

Matt said, "Fletcher's Rise might ring a bell back East."

Conway smiled. "Died at Fletcher's Rise at the hands of Racing Elk himself?"

"That might be too much," said Matt. "We'll just let it go as is, but we still have a problem. Who is *this* man, if Evinrude fell at Fletcher's Rise? Now, if one of the privates that fell there didn't have any kin . . ."

Evinrude's head was spinning.

"Enright didn't," offered Price who, if nothing else, knew the rosters. "Jeremy Enright."

Evinrude's eyes flashed. "Enright was *small*," he protested, "and ugly."

"He's big now," said Sergeant Cohen, "but still ugly. So you move it on out, *Enright*. You've still got some guard to pull."

Evinrude threw Crowley a look. Was it grateful? Probably. And Crowley threw it right back, with a smile. A man could

216

go by the book just so far when dealing with a "criminal" who had picked him up, thrown him over a horse, and rushed him back to town and a doc and saved his life. The book kindof went out the window right about then.

Crowley watched Evinrude cross the parade, his step getting jauntier with each stride. Suddenly Evinrude stopped and turned and yelled, "You ever drop by again, Ben, you look me up. Ask for *Enright*." The sun flashed off his big grin. "*I'm* buyin'."

Crowley waved, then said to Bradshaw, "Add something about personal effects, where to send or dispose of them. That'll add just the right touch." He looked up and around the group. "Will your men keep the secret?"

Cohen smiled at him. It wasn't really a pleasant smile. "My men *will* keep this secret, Marshal, or my name ain't Killer Cohen." His smile broadened into a grin. "They'll keep it if they know what's good for them, and especially if I tell 'em it's good for them."

Corporal of the Guard Medford suddenly appeared in the orderly room door.

"What is it, Corporal?" asked Cohen.

"Something funny's happened, Sarge. Evinrude's gone loony."

"Who?"

"Private Evinrude."

"*Who?*"

"*Evinrude*, Sarge. He says his name ain't Evinrude. Says it's—" He stopped, scanned the circle of faces, eyed Sergeant Cohen very closely, and then said experimentally, "Enright?"

SPECIAL PREVIEW

Here are the opening scenes
from

EASY COMPANY AND THE GREEN ARROWS

the next novel in Jove's exciting
new High Plains adventure series

EASY COMPANY

on sale now!

one

First Lieutenant Matt Kincaid stood atop the eastern wall of Outpost Number Nine and felt the first gentle kiss of the rising sun brush across his tanned, handsome face. Although there was yet a coolness lingering from the night's chill, he knew the day would turn warm, then hot with something nearing a sudden vengeance. But as he stood there, tall, muscular and every inch a military man in both posture and demeanor, the faded blue of his forage dress uniform contrasting with the dull brown of the cut-sod wall, his mind was not on the heat of the coming day. His eyes and his thoughts were locked on two mounted men, both wearing buckskins with fringed trimming and holding elbow-cradled rifles in constant readiness, who were nearing the outpost from the direction of the tipi ring several hundred yards toward the northeast.

Behind and below him, Kincaid could hear the sounds of a military unit coming to life. The men of Easy Company moved to their assigned details and morning chores with no more than the normal amount of grumbling and complaining about the vicissitudes of army life. They had long ago accepted the fact that outpost duty was, by nature, an admixture of boredom and the ultimate thrill of facing death in battle. As part of a mounted infantry regiment, Easy Company had been assigned the sometimes precarious task of guarding the vital communications link between the Little Big Horn and the South Pass over the Rockies, as well as maintaining a strong American military presence in the heart of Indian country.

Recognizing the rider to the right, Lieutenant Kincaid smiled and studied his chief scout, Windy Mandalian. Windy was easily the most independent yet reliable, deadly yet compassionate, total man of the Plains he had ever known. There was about Mandalian a certain uncanny ability to perceive the thinking of the red man in a manner that made him seem equally as much Indian as he was white. There was a prominent hook to his nose, and because of his dark features, high cheekbones, and narrow face, he was often mistaken by white travelers passing through the area for a Cheyenne, and to Matt's knowledge, Windy Mandalian had never once denied it or offered correction.

Kincaid had never seen Mandalian's companion before, and now, as the two riders were lost to his view when they entered the outpost, Kincaid turned away from the wall and descended the steps onto the packed earth of the parade. Mandalian toed his horse in Matt's direction and the second rider followed. They met by the flagstaff in the center of the square, and Mandalian pulled his horse in before leaning back with a comfortable slouch in his saddle.

"Mornin', Matt," Windy offered, chewing laconically on a cheekful of cut-plug.

"Good morning, Windy," Kincaid replied, while the slight smile returned again to his face. "Up and stirring about a little early this morning, aren't you?"

"Depends on what you're comparing it to," Windy said, nodding toward his companion. "Lieutenant Kincaid, meet Seth Daniels. Me and Seth trapped beaver together up in the Windy River country a few winters back. His word's as good as his shootin' eye, which, if I remember right enough, ain't been bested by many men."

Kincaid stepped forward and offered his hand, which the trapper leaned down to receive with power and enthusiasm.

"Pleased to meet you, Mr. Daniels," Matt said cordially, "and welcome to Outpost Nine. Whatever we have is at your disposal. Please make yourself comfortable. A friend of Windy's is a friend of ours."

Daniels smiled his appreciation as he said, "Thank you, Lieutenant. I won't be havin' much time to stay, but a cup of coffee sounds mighty good, then maybe we should talk, which is why I come by this way in the first place." Daniels grinned openly. "That and to see how ugly the squaws are that this old bastard is sleepin' with nowadays."

"And?" Windy asked with a mocking stare.

"Ugly. Downright sinful ugly."

"Seth, you don't know ugly from a horse's ass. Now let's go get that coffee and you can tell the lieutenant what you've got to say and not keep an important man waiting."

Daniels clapped Windy across the back with a hearty laugh, which Windy returned in equal measure as they stepped from their mounts and followed Kincaid to the officer's mess.

When they were seated with their coffee, the trapper asked, "Why don't you tell the lieutenant what I told you, Windy? I'll fill in whatever you leave out or what I forgot in the first place."

Mandalian nodded, then sipped his coffee as his eyes went to Kincaid's face. "Seth just came down from the north, through Arapaho country, and he says word got to him that some medicine man up there—what was his name, Seth? Gray Bear?"

Daniels nodded over the cup moving to his lips. "Yup. Gray Bear. Who the hell ever saw a gray bear?"

"I'm familiar with Gray Bear," Kincaid said. "He was a signatory to the treaty which put the Arapaho back on their ancestral hunting ground, and to my knowledge, he's a man of honor and integrity."

Windy frowned. "Let's hope so, Matt, but that ain't quite the way Seth heard it. Accordin' to what he heard from some stockmen in the area, this Gray Bear might be trying to stir his people up and maybe get 'em back on the warpath. They say he's been promising his tribe 'New green arrows, as far as the eye can see. Arrows from Great Turtle, who wants us to live in the ways of the Grandfather Times.' Now, I'm sure you're the last man who needs remindin' that the Arapaho paint green stripes on their war arrows and that the 'Grandfather Times' means before the white man took their land away."

Matt Kincaid swirled the coffee remaining in his cup and shook his head. "I can't understand it. The Arapaho have just settled down after the Custer fight, they were given back their old hunting grounds for that purpose, and the man from the Bureau of Indian Affairs assigned to them is fair and doing the best he can for them. Gray Bear knows that any Indian leader who reneges on the treaties can and will be arrested and very

223

likely executed. He is an old man. Why would he like to see more of his people die in a futile resumption of a war he cannot possibly win?"

"Beats me, Matt," Windy said, stretching his long legs beneath the table and hooking his hands behind his head. "But remember, if they rise again they will be on familiar ground in the foothills where they love to fight. And that reserve of theirs is pretty damned close to the approaches to the South Pass and both the rail and telegraph lines. Could be a real ball-buster if they decide to paint up again."

Kincaid turned to the trapper. "What do you make of it, Mr. Daniels? Did they seem about to go on the warpath when you were up there?"

"Well, as you might guess, Lieutenant, I make a pretty serious effort to stay away from as many Indians as I can on the open plains. Helps keep the hairline in one place. The only thing I'm tellin' you, or know for that matter, is what those stockmen told me. They seem to think the Arapaho are goin' to try and run them off their grazing land, which borders on the Arapaho reserve, and I can tell you for a fact that they are willin' to fight, if not spoilin' for one."

Matt sighed wearily. "So we've got the stockmen on one side, the Arapaho on the other, the Bureau of Indian Affairs in the middle, and nobody knowing for sure what the other person is talking about. I guess I'd better meet with Captain Conway and see if he wants us to take a patrol up there and check things out." He rose and extended his hand to the trapper. "Thank you for your concern and taking the time to come out of your way to inform us of this possible problem. I'll send a soldier to feed and water your horse and refit you with whatever provisions you might need. If you would care for breakfast, just tell the cook and you will be taken care of. Windy? I'd like to talk with you after I've seen the captain."

"I'll be around."

"Good. I think we will be riding north this morning."

Lieutenant Kincaid stepped from the mess and angled toward the orderly room. He glanced toward the sun and estimated the time to be nearly eight o'clock. As he stepped into the front office, he saw the first sergeant, Acting Master Sergeant Ben Cohen, already at his desk. Kincaid closed the door and Sergeant Cohen looked up from the duty roster spread before him. He was approximately forty years of age, big, beefy, and thick through the shoulders and chest. His hands were gnarled stumps with blunt fingers protruding; the evidence of much 'behind the barracks' discipline was revealed through scars, and twisted joints and knuckles.

"Good morning, sir," Cohen said, smiling easily with the gap between his front teeth showing as a narrow black line. "I guess when my shitlist gets longer than my regular list, I won't have any problem assigning details, will I?"

"Morning, Sergeant," Matt returned with a chuckle. "Who's the newest addition?"

"Private Radcliff. Guess he didn't salute Lieutenant Davis fast enough to please the good sir."

"Radcliff? First Platoon, Second Squad?"

"Yessir."

"The First is Davis' platoon, isn't it?"

"Yessir. It has been for nearly two days now. Ever since he arrived here in a cloud of dust and ridiculous assumptions about Indian fighting."

"Well, don't worry about finding any particularly nasty little jobs for Radcliff. I think he'll be going on patrol with me this morning, along with Lieutenant Davis, and maybe they both might learn something from the experience. Is Captain Conway in?"

"Yessir," Cohen responded, rising and moving toward the door to the commanding officer's office. "Excuse me, sir. Lieutenant Kincaid to see you."

"Send him in, Sarge."

"Thanks," Matt said, stepping around the sergeant. "Be prepared to have the First Platoon ready to move out within the hour, rationed and equipped for several days in the field."

"Yessir."

Matt stepped into the captain's office, and the CO looked up from the dispatch he was drafting to regimental headquarters. "Good morning, Matt. Have a seat there and let me just finish this damned little note asking why it is impossible for the men of this command to get paid on time. As you know, I write one of these per month, so I've pretty well got it down."

Matt eased into a chair before the captain's desk and watched silently while the older man finished his letter. Somewhere in his mid-forties, graying at the temples but still commanding a lean and hard physique, the captain should have been a major, particularly in light of the fact that he had served as a lieutenant colonel during the War, but he had been passed over again by the promotions board. He looked every bit the Virginian that he was, but as regular army he had fought for the North in the Union Army under General Grant. No matter what personal disappointments he had suffered, however, Captain Conway retained his Southern pride and dignity, and was army to the marrow of his bones.

"What can I do for you this morning, Matt?" Conway asked while he creased his letter into three folds and stuffed it into an envelope. The captain was not given to small talk, and he watched his adjutant closely as he sealed the envelope.

Kincaid shifted his long, lean frame in the chair and adjusted the hat perched upon a crossed knee. "Well, sir, we either have an Arapaho uprising on our hands, or just a bunch of people getting nervous over nothing. I'm not sure just which it is."

"Explain."

Matt told of his conversation with Seth Daniels, then said, "The Arapaho are damned difficult to understand, both in language and actions. Although he didn't come right out and say it, sir, I'm convinced that Windy thinks we should check this out. I'm afraid I agree with him."

Conway was silent for several moments before saying, "Yes, I don't think this is something we can just ignore. I can't understand Gray Bear calling for any uprising, though, and I'm not certain I believe it. He was against the Arapaho joining the Dakota Confederacy under Red Cloud in the first place, and he knows that any violation of the treaty he signed could be a hanging offense, with his own neck in the noose. I think you'd better take a platoon and head on up there. I heard you tell Sergeant Cohen to make the First Platoon ready for patrol. Any particular reason you chose that platoon?"

"Yes," Matt answered without hesitation. "I think Lieutenant Davis might well profit through tempering of all that textbook knowledge he has with a little practical experience in the field. And there are some things I would like to learn about Private Radcliff. He's got the makings of a good soldier, but his attitude is definitely shit-house."

"I agree, for what little I know of either of them. Have a good, safe patrol, Matt. Use your best judgment and I'll back you one hundred percent on the outcome."

"Thank you, sir," Matt responded, moving toward the door. "We shouldn't be gone more than a week."

226

"However long it takes, do the job right. And Matt?" Kincaid stopped and turned, framed in the doorway.

"Yes, sir?"

"You know how I feel about these Indians, whether Arapaho, Sioux, or Cheyenne. They are to be treated firmly but fairly. Don't look for trouble, but if anyone has a lesson coming, make it a good one. The ink is still wet on those treaties we signed, and I don't think now would be prudent time to demonstrate any weakness."

"I understand, sir, and agree completely." He paused and the two men looked at each other. "Tell me, Captain, just what in the hell are we doing, letting cattlemen graze their stock right up to the boundaries of the Arapaho reservation? That's kind of like locking a dog and a cat in the same closet, isn't it?"

Conway nodded in agreement. "You're right, Matt, it is. But we aren't the ones letting them, the Department of the Interior is. Over my objections and those of everyone else who knows his ass from a teakettle, they issued those grazing permits with no limitations other than the boundaries established in the treaty. I don't think many of those longhorns read the damned thing and they're bound to wander across from time to time. Check the permits of any ranchers you encounter, and make sure their papers are legal and up to date. That's about all we can do."

"And if they aren't?"

"Then tell them to legalize or move out."

"Fine, sir," Kincaid said, adjusting his campaign hat on his head. "See you when we get back."

"Have a good patrol, and be careful. I need your help around here."

"I will, sir. I just hope this thing isn't as big as it sounds like it could be."

"Me too, Matt. Let's try to put a lid on it before it gets out of hand."

"I'll do my best, sir," Kincaid said as he stepped out the door.

two

The Rockies loomed high and majestic to the north. Their upper reaches were yet capped with snow, and the sparkling white outlined against the deep blue sky seemed symbolic of purity and peace within the Brotherhood of Man. And the verdant foothills, rolling in a sea of grass that caressed the earth with gentle strokes on a lilting breeze, stretched before the platoon of mounted infantry working its way northward, with Matt Kincaid and Windy Mandalian at the head of a column of twos.

"Probably the most beautiful country in the world, wouldn't you say, Windy?" Matt asked, drawing in a deep breath and exhaling the pure air scented by the scattered groves of conifers they were now passing through.

"Yup," Windy grunted. "And the most unforgiving."

"I'm a little surprised to see the grass so plentiful at this elevation."

"Don't be, Matt. All we've seen is a few scattered herds of pronghorn and elk, not to mention some sign but no trace of buffalo. When there ain't nothin' left to eat the grass, it should do pretty well."

They were nearing the crest of a swale nestled in the foothills, and Windy heard it first, then Matt. The officer raised his hand sharply and the column came to a halt while the scout slipped from his horse and ran in a low crouch off to one side. The muffled pounding of hooves in the tall grass became clearer, possibly three horses, maybe four, followed by a distant rumble of several more horses. Before Matt could respond and form his platoon into a defensive unit, three straining ponies broke from a stand of timber, hooves driving at full speed and mouths twisted against woven-hair hackamores. Upon their backs were three young braves, crouched low against their horses' withers and molded as one with their animals. The green warpaint on their faces and encircling their upper arms and chests created an eerie deadliness about them which belied their youth. Intent upon their escape, the Indians were unaware of the platoon of soldiers cresting the ridge, even though they hesitated as they cleared the trees.

Their horses broke stride for no more than an instant before the lead brave wheeled his mount and plunged into the ravine, followed by the other two. Clumps of sod and grass flew from their horses' hooves.

Matt Kincaid held the pistol in his hand high above his head, as indication for the men behind him to hold their fire. Seasoned veterans that they were, they watched the retreating Indian mounts in silence and contained the desire for action.

Matt looked across at where Windy had taken up a position, some seventy-five yards away and crouched with his rifle resting against the trunk of a huge fir tree, and he acknowledged the scout's nod toward the sound of the pursuing horses.

"Lieutenant Kincaid?" an excited voice said from behind him. "Second Lieutenant Davis requests permission to take a squad of troopers and establish pursuit of the green-faced heathen."

Matt could not conceal the look of contempt crossing his face, and his words came out more sharply than expected. "Permission denied, Lieutenant! Now get back there and make certain your platoon is properly deployed in defendable positions."

"Yes, sir!" Davis snapped, the sound of his voice irritating Matt before the young lieutenant faded from his mind and his thoughts returned to the horses thundering toward them. He glanced once toward the platoon. Each man was lying prone on the lee side of the gentle ridge, Springfields aimed toward the opening in the trees while their mounts were held in the bottom of the swale by handlers. Davis moved upright among the troops, and Kincaid silently damned him. Then the first horse burst through the trees, a beautiful, rangy, foam-flecked roan with nostrils flared and neck arched against the reins. The rider, seated on a silver-studded saddle of the finest tooled leather, was leaning forward, intent on the hoofprints in the grass and oblivious to the soldiers above him. He was young, lean, and tall, and as he leaned forward, hunched close to the roan's neck, Matt noticed a handsome wildness about him.

The shot was like a crack of lightning, rolling across the draw on echoing thunder. The roan pitched forward, dead before it fell, and the cattleman catapulted over its neck to land in a sprawled heap, ten yards in front of where the horse fell in a forward somersault. The other riders behind him, now breaking into the opening, wheeled their rearing, plunging mounts and raced back to the safety of the thicket. The rider who had been thrown scrambled on hands and knees, pulling the pistol from his holster as he moved, and tumbled into a cut bank, firing a shot as he disappeared, which snapped over the heads of the troops along the ridge. A volley of shots came from the thicket, and Matt heard Davis give the order to fire. The Springfields exploded on command and a hail of lead ripped into the stand of timber.

Matt Kincaid was dumbfounded for a second. In an instant he realized that the young Arapaho braves, unaware of the presence of the army unit, had set up an ambush for the pursuing cattlemen, and, in their haste to count coup, had fired upon their pursuers too early. And with the shot fired by the fallen cattleman, Lieutenant Davis had given the order to return fire. Now, two friendlies were engaged in a fierce firefight while the instigators made a leisurely withdrawal.

"Hold your fire, men, goddamnit! Hold your fire!" Matt bellowed over the roar of muzzle blasts. "Davis! You bring that platoon under control or I'll have your ass for breakfast!"

Fire from the ridge ceased immediately, but the cattlemen below continued their steady barrage. "Hold your fire down there!" Matt raged again. "We're United States Army, Easy Company, First Platoon, Mounted Infantry!"

Matt heard a voice rise from behind the cut bank. "Hold your fire, Ernie! Tell the boys to be ready, but wait for my signal!" The voice turned toward the ridge. "Hey, you up there, soldier boy! Show yourself and I'll do the same!"

Matt stood from where he lay in the tall grass and stepped to the lip of the ridge. "Lieutenant Davis? Have your men keep their weapons at the ready, but no one is to fire unless I am fired upon or until I give the command. Is that understood?"

"Yes, sir."

Matt heard Davis instructing his platoon as he moved down the hill, but his interest was given to the young cattleman rising from behind the cut bank. He knew Windy Mandalian's Sharps was trained on the man's chest at that precise moment, and any sign of treachery would bring instant death. Matt judged the man to be around twenty-two years of age, and the long blond hair curling about his face in a careless tousle made him seem equally as pretty as he was handsome.

Ignoring Kincaid, the young rider retrieved his hat from the ground, dusted it against his leg, then knelt beside his horse for a moment before rising to face the tall, square-shouldered man in blue.

"You killed my best horse," he said, his tone flat and accusing.

"Sorry, friend. I didn't, nor did my men. The death of that horse saved your life."

The contempt in the cattleman's voice was matched by the curling sneer on his lips. "What do you mean by that, soldier boy? And besides, what are you doing, ambushing American citizens? I thought you were sent here to protect taxpaying settlers like myself, instead of trying to kill them."

Struggling to control the heat rising in his chest, Matt said in a low, clear voice, "You are not talking to a 'soldier boy.' You are addressing First Lieutenant Matt Kincaid, United States Army. You would do well to remember that, and to get your facts straight. Your horse was shot out from under you by the people you were trying to catch. If you *had* caught them, you would be dead now. You weren't ambushed. After you fired toward the ridge where my troops were positioned, one of my officers exercised poor judgment, for which I apologize, and ordered return fire. And, lastly, I am here to *protect* settlers like yourself, but we will need some help from you to accomplish that goal. Like not grazing your cattle on ground set aside by the Bureau of Indian Affairs as part of the rightful Arapaho reserve."

"I'm not grazing my cattle on their fucking land! I have a grazing permit from the Department of the Interior and Land Management, authorizing me to graze up to their boundaries."

"I would like to see those permits."

"Sure, but you'll have to come to the main ranch. My sister keeps them in a safe."

231

"Fine, we'll do that," Matt said, detecting a thaw in the young cattleman's hostile attitude. "Why were you in pursuit of those three braves, if I may ask?"

"Sure, you can ask. They killed a beef of mine and were draggin' it away when we caught 'em."

Matt watched the other man closely. "As I said, my name is Lieutenant Kincaid. What is yours?"

"Ramsey. David Ramsey."

"Mr. Ramsey," Matt said, nodding his head and waiting for an offered hand, which never came. He smiled easily and continued, "Let me ask you, Mr. Ramsey, how many cattle have you got on this particular stretch of range?"

"Around a thousand head. Why?"

"And of that thousand head being grazed so close to reservation ground, wouldn't it be difficult for you to make certain that none of your stock strayed across the boundary?"

Ramsey hesitated momentarily, locking eyes with Matt, then glancing away. "Yeah, it's tough."

"I figured as much. On which side of the boundary was your animal slain?"

"Can't tell for sure. Could have been shot on our side and drug across to theirs."

"Shall we see? Surely, in this deep grass, a trail would be left. I have a civilian scout with me who could determine instantly the circumstances."

"Aw, to hell with it," Ramsey said, stooping to remove the tack from the dead horse. "I don't give a shit whose side it was on. We'd seen where some other stock had crossed. Went over to get 'em and jumped them three feather-heads butchering another one. Pissed me off, so I went after 'em. No big deal. We'll square accounts later."

Matt signaled for Davis to assemble the platoon before speaking to Ramsey again. "You're wrong, I'm afraid, Mr. Ramsey. It *is* a big deal. Did you get a good look at those braves?"

"Mostly back and ass," Ramsey returned with a grunt as he dragged the cinch strap from beneath the horse.

"They were wearing warpaint, my friend," Matt said softly. "To me, that makes it a *very* big deal."